Fading Sapiens

Disclosure of extraterrestrials is forbidden for a reason,
and the real history of humanity
is a manufactured illusion.

Are Homo Sapiens merely a link
to a truly advanced future?

Joe Pelati

A special thanks to my wife, Leslie, and good friends Celeste and Charles, who helped make this book much better than the first draft.

Dedicated to all the fans of speculative fiction and classic science fiction who wish to explore greater philosophical and intellectual concepts rather than ferment in vacuous emotional dramas. I salute Isaac Asimov and Michael Crichton, whose books inspired my writings.

Chapter 1.

Forbidden for a reason

Are all scientists born with an obsessive-compulsive personality, or does science drive them to it? Regardless of the cause, high-achieving scientists will shun the world and bury themselves in their work when a significant accomplishment is imminent. Perhaps this is the reason no one thought it odd that Professor Arun Chandra has been working in his office late into the night every day for the last two months. He is well known to the global physics community and is one of the premier academics at this prestigious university. He thinks he is near the completion of the confirmatory mathematics that will blow away the current tenets of theoretical physics. It will also change society's understanding of the world and the universe. The existence of other dimensions and how to traverse them is at hand. Space-time concepts will seem like flat-earth conspiracies. The staggering magnitude of his new theories could easily explain his obsession, but there is an obvious mania in his efforts. He has lost weight, has dark bags under his eyes, and his personal hygiene has suffered. Simply put, he looks like a hot mess. It is as if an invisible taskmaster drives him to his physical and mental limits.

It is after midnight. The physics building is found in a relatively quiet part of campus near the chemistry, mathematics, and engineering buildings. Professor Chandra toils away in his office on the sixth and top floor. The custodial crew has been by already, as they start on the top floor of the uninteresting six-story building and work their way down through the night. The other professors and graduate students left some time ago; however, the professor will not be alone for long.

Two men in dark suits are in a van disguised as a university maintenance vehicle and are parked at the back of the adjacent building. They are observing the activities via a tiny camera they have discreetly placed in the hallway. Several days ago, they broke into the secure area of the physics building through a window at the back of the building, by the loading dock. After a couple of days of surveillance, they knew when the professor would be alone.

The inside of the van is dark, as a curtain hangs down behind the front seats to prevent anyone from looking inside. The back windows are also covered. The only light comes from the four video screens showing the live feed from their cameras implanted in the physics building. The two men sit and watch.

"J.T., it's go-time. That weirdo postdoc has finally gone home for the night. I was starting to think that he lived in the building," says Curt, the ops leader for this mission.

Without speaking another word, Curt reaches into a pack next to him and grabs two coveralls like those worn by campus maintenance workers. Both quickly put on the coveralls and fill the pockets with items that have been lying about by the video monitors, including two 9mm pistols. They don baseball caps and pull them down to just above their eyes. Quickly and quietly, they slip out of the van through the back door. The two casually stroll across the grassy area between the buildings and head straight to the loading dock window they previously broke through for their first access. Once in, they proceed to the back stairway. Stealthily, they ascend the stairway up to the sixth floor. After checking for anyone in the hallway, they quickly move to the door to Professor Chandra's office. J.T. and Curt burst into the office. Before Professor Chandra can look up from his computer monitor, Curt pulls his 9mm pistol from his pocket and points it straight at the professor.

"Sit down, be quiet, and make no quick movements, Professor Chandra."

The professor stares at the pistol, then sits back in his chair. "What do you want? I have a little money on me, it's all yours," whimpers a shocked and frightened professor.

Curt keeps the gun pointed at the professor and walks right up to his desk and smiles. "We don't want your money; we just have a question or two we need to ask you. Answer them honestly and completely and we will leave. Do you understand me?"

Professor Chandra nods and keeps his eyes focused on the pistol pointed at him. J.T. walks around the professor to stand directly behind him.

"Okay, professor, we know you are working on a new radical theory. We are curious about several details concerning your work. First of all, who gave you the idea?"

The professor looks insulted and shoots back, "No one gave me the idea. I developed these ideas myself and have been working on them entirely on my own. Most other colleagues are too attached to the current theories to even consider radical alternatives."

Curt raises his voice, "Come on, professor. You are good, but you are not Einstein. You must be working with others. Be honest with me." Curt waves the gun side to side with the last statement for emphasis.

"Seriously, it is my work. Now, I did get some help with a few small parts of the mathematics, but that is all."

"See, now you are being truthful, and I can believe you. Who are the others?"

"My old friend, Professor Isaac Feingold, helped me with a key problem I was having several weeks ago. Also, my new postdoc, Ulak Tazarachabayev, has helped me a couple of times lately. No one has yet seen the full theory and mathematics. It is all mine."

"Are you sure about that, professor? Are those two people the only ones? I will be terribly upset to learn otherwise. So, you can guarantee that no one has seen the entire theory and only those two people have helped you with only small pieces. Is that correct?"

The professor nods. "That is correct. Why do you care about this?"

Curt chuckles, "Let's just say that we make sure that things with potential military application do not fall into the wrong hands. That is what we need to know. Now, tell me if you have any copies of your work saved on any computer network or cloud. Also, is it saved at any unsecured location, like your home?"

Professor Chandra looks down, thinking about the question. He looks up after a moment. "No, my work is secure. It is saved only on my computer and backed up to this external hard drive. I do not keep important material like this in any unsecured location. I am not that foolish."

Curt smiles and lowers his gun. "That is very good to hear, professor. It is encouraging to know that you are wise enough to keep important, breakthrough information in limited, secure locations."

Curt looks at J.T. and nods. Immediately, J.T. pulls a blackjack from his pocket and smacks Professor Chandra on the side of his head. The professor slumps onto his desk.

"He seems awfully foolish to me," J.T. flippantly says to Curt.

Curt frowns, "Make sure he is breathing. I hope you didn't hit him too hard like you did the last time we did this thing. Hand me his computer and you take the hard drive. Then we can take the professor to the stairway."

They both stuff the electronic booty down the front of their coveralls. They come around the desk and lift the professor without disturbing anything on it. They quickly carry the unconscious professor to the same stairway they came up. With one big motion, they throw the professor over the railing and down the center of the stairwell. A hideous thud is all that is heard to confirm their mission has been successful.

Chapter 2.

Beware of gifts from strangers

Professor Isaac Feingold does not like to arrive at his office before 9 AM. He finds his relatively short drive from his home to the physics building annoying, especially when the traffic is heavy. His days of working long hours to prove himself and gain recognition are over. He has been tenured in his position for fifteen years and has had several prominent accomplishments that have made him well known to the global physics community. His short beard and bushy hair may be starting to turn gray, but he is immediately recognized and respected by his colleagues at all the big conferences around the world. He has as much grant money as he wants and easily supports a large research group for a theoretical physicist. His ego is as large as his opinions, but he is wise enough to keep his disruptive theories to himself until the time is right. Life will remain easy and money plentiful if he plays the game for the stodgy physics institutions.

Isaac feels different this morning. He wakes up nearly two hours earlier than usual, feeling tense and anxious. Consequently, he wakes his wife up so she can make him breakfast. He feels compelled to get to his office as soon as possible.

Isaac exits the elevator at the physics building and heads down to the end of the hallway toward his spacious corner office. It's a little past 7 AM, much earlier than his usual arrival. He can hear a few graduate students milling about, but he pays no attention. He is eager to get to his office for some reason. Arriving at his outer office where his secretary, Ms. Bouche, is located, he finds the door locked. Isaac grumbles as he digs in his pocket for his keys. Typically, Ms. Bouche has the door open, the lights on, and a pot of coffee made, but today he is much too early. As Isaac enters his office and sits down in his expensive and very comfortable desk chair, he still cannot relax or ease his restlessness today. He leaves his office to go down the hall to spread his anxiety.

As the professor walks down the hall, he sees that the lights are on in the fishbowl. The fishbowl is one of his group's areas consisting of a large room with a conference table in the middle and a far wall holding white boards covering it from end to end. This is where he holds his group meetings. Offices surround the open area of the fishbowl. There are four small offices for graduate students and two larger ones for the postgraduates. He finds Jesse, one of his senior grad students, sitting in his office reading journal articles on his computer. Jesse is sitting there in his ball cap and wrinkled T-shirt, as usual; Isaac isn't sure if he's been there all night.

Professor Isaac pokes his head into Jesse's office, "Jesse, I need you to go to Ms. Bouche's office and start a pot of coffee for me."

Jesse pauses, then slowly looks toward Isaac, "Of course, my liege, your wish is my command. I will leave this dreary paper on quantum gravity and proceed to the coffee maker."

Isaac shakes his head at this typical insolent Jesse response, "Don't be a smartass this morning, I am not up to it today." Isaac heads back to his office.

Professor Feingold sits at his desk waiting for Jesse to start a pot of coffee. He has not been able to alleviate his unease. His mobile phone in his pocket rings, startling him.

He answers reluctantly before any morning coffee, "Hello."

A voice with a heavy Russian-sounding accent comes from the phone, "Hello, I am Ulak Tazarachabayev. I am a postdoctoral fellow with your friend, Professor Arun Chandra. I have some very bad news. Professor Chandra is dead; he appears to have fallen down the back stairwell by his office. This happened last week. The police suppressed the news on this until their investigation was concluded; they confirm now that it was a suicide. He often talked about you, so I thought I should call you to tell you before you hear it elsewhere. I am sorry to bring you this news. It is a great shock for all of us here."

Isaac is stunned. He struggles to respond, "That's... That's... That is terrible. I am so sorry. I recently helped Arun with some difficult mathematics. He seemed so excited about that project. I am so shocked, I don't know what to say."

Ulak replies with his deep monotone, "Sometimes there is nothing to be said. It is a great loss for his family and the physics world. I think he was nearing an amazing breakthrough. I, too, helped him with two or three specific problems he was having with his theory."

"Agreed, it is such a senseless loss. I wish there were something I could do."

"Professor, there is something you can do. Allow me to join your group and continue Professor Chandra's work with you. I have all the records of his work on his new theory. I have my own funding, so I do not need any of your funds. All I need is a place in a group at a university and an accomplished professor like yourself; his work can then be brought to a successful conclusion. It would be a great tribute to Professor Chandra."

Isaac frowns, considering taking on extra work from a new project and a new postdoc. "That would be a lovely tribute to Arun, but I do not think it is possible at this time."

Ulak instantly responds, "Professor Feingold, you must reconsider. *You will reconsider and take me into your group. You will...*"

Isaac's mind goes blank. He sits there motionless for a minute. The sound of Ulak's voice breaks the trance.

"So, professor, you now agree to let me join your group and continue Professor Chandra's work with you, don't you?"

Isaac is still a bit dazed, but replies, "Yes Ulak, that is a marvelous idea. We need to continue Professor Chandra's work. I look forward to having you join the group and start working with me. How soon can you be here?"

"Thank you, Professor Feingold. It will be an honor. I will be there in a couple of weeks."

Professor Feingold hangs up and puts his phone back in his pocket. He leans back in his chair, wondering about this phone call. He feels a little odd and does not fully understand what just happened. Suddenly, for no apparent reason, his anxiety turns to excitement and anticipation. He dashes back down the hall to the fishbowl. Jesse is still the only person there. "Jesse, tell Ruth to clean out the spare postdoc office when she gets in. We will have a new postdoc arriving next week. ...and make me a pot of coffee."

Jesse looks up with a confused look, "I thought you said that you didn't want a bigger group. What the hell? You are about three papers behind right now. How will you catch up on writing these papers when you add more people and projects? Also, remember that you said I could start writing my thesis next year. What gives?"

"Jesse, don't argue with me. Professor Chandra just died. I am taking one of his postdocs."

"Oh man. I'm so sorry. That sucks. He was a good dude. I'll help Ruth clear the office."

"Thank you. I want everything ready for him. We are going to continue working on a new theory that Professor Chandra was developing. It could be very big. I am very excited about it." Isaac turns and walks away.

Jesse sits there pondering this news. He thought the professor was getting lazy and kicking back. Maybe this will reignite his motivation. If this new energy is real and helps Jesse finish his Ph.D., then he is all for it. Jesse is not fully convinced at this point and remains a bit puzzled.

Chapter 3.

A tranquil life can collapse suddenly, proving it was always an illusion.

"Noah, wake up. I need to see you in person as soon as possible. Come to my office now."

Noah wakes from a deep slumber and sits up in bed in his dark dormitory room, illuminated only by ambient light from the window. He checks his watch and sees it is 5:00 AM. He wonders if the message in his head was just a dream.

"No, it is not a dream. It is very important that you see me at once," repeats the request.

"OK, I will get cleaned up and be there soon." Noah sighs and gets out of bed. He picks up his phone to text his professor and groupmates that he will be arriving at the physics building late due to a therapist appointment. Then he heads straight to his bathroom to get ready.

After about ninety minutes, Noah stops at the large glass door leading to the spacious atrium of the office building he needs to enter. He frowns at his reflection in the glass. He always feels self-conscious when confronted with his image. Sure, he knows he should be grateful that he is tall with long, thick, blonde hair and blue eyes, but his head and eyes look oversized for his body. It does not help that he is incredibly thin, making his head seem all the larger. He is still in a foul mood because his therapist made him leave campus and drive to her new office. Long-distance communication is his preference, now that he is good at it.

"You look fine. Do not dawdle; get to my office, please."

He sighs, opens the door, and continues to the office. He knows she is waiting for him. She is always with him. She has comforted him, advised him, or just talked to him with their omnipresent telepathic connection since he was a child.

After a short elevator ride, he stops at the wooden door with "Dr. Viera Torghe, Therapist" on the prominent nameplate. Before he can reach for the doorknob, a message enters his mind, *"Please come in."*

He steps into a large, immaculately furnished office. A dark hardwood desk sits to the left, with an overstuffed leather chair directly in front. On the shelves behind the desk are miscellaneous relics and collectibles from around the world. It looks like a souvenir collection from a world cruise. The opposite side of the room has a handsome couch, matching chairs, and coffee table ensemble. A refreshment center with a small, fully stocked refrigerator and an elaborate coffee maker is centered on the back wall between the desk and the couch. There is no computer or any books anywhere to be seen.

Dr. Viera is standing in the middle of the office as Noah enters. Viera is stunningly beautiful. She is taller than Noah, with perfect proportions and the loveliest cream-colored skin. Her hair is a blazing white platinum shade that hangs down past her shoulders like a mane of sunlight. She has always been impeccably dressed; today she wears a long, textured blue skirt with a matching blazer. Noah greets her in the special way they have been doing it since he was tall enough to do it properly. They each put their right hand on the other's left shoulder, then touch their right temples together gently. She taught him this greeting and Noah only does this with Viera. She is very special to him and has been working with him since he was four years old. Only his mother has a greater bond with him.

Viera motions Noah toward the chair facing her desk. She gracefully sits in her desk chair and turns to Noah. "Thank you for making the journey from your school to my office. I want us to have a verbal exchange because I need to speak with you slowly and precisely. First, I would like to hear your thoughts on your first semester of postgraduate studies in physics. Specifically, I need to know how you think it is going with your research advisor and his group that you have joined. We have not met since your classes ended for the semester. I want to see if my perceptions match yours. Tell me what you are now thinking about the semester."

Noah smiles, "I can now say that I had a very good semester. As you well know, I was quite nervous and fearful at first. I had not lived away from home and my mother. Thankfully, you were always there with me, supporting and comforting me. I never felt alone. Also, the graduate student dormitory made it much easier for me. It is a safe, comfortable place, and all my meals are provided, including sack lunches that let me stay at the physics building all day. I have two good friends in the physics department, Jesse and Ruth. Jesse is an older graduate student. His funny quips have defused many tense situations that made me very uncomfortable. Ruth is a new grad student like me. She is so pleasant to be around and is always happy to see me. I enjoy helping her with the coursework."

"I am curious about what your physics colleagues think about you. Do you think that these people have accepted you? Are they developing normal feelings toward you? Are there any odd sensations that you detect?"

"I think that they treat me like anyone else. They have shown no unusual feelings toward me, aside from a mild intellectual jealousy, because graduate school has been so easy for me. Noah pauses while thinking of Ruth, then takes a deep breath to continue, "I won't turn nineteen years old for another couple of months, so everyone else is older and more experienced. Living independently comes much more easily to them. It certainly was terrifying at first. At the outset, each day was rough, but ultimately, I think it really gave me much more confidence; you already know that, of course. The graduate classes were disappointingly easy for me. Thank goodness I was allowed to start research projects with Professor Feingold; it had been getting quite boring until then. Overall, I get along very well with my professor and his group. I like several hypotheses he brings up from time to time. I hope to be allowed to explore some of them. He must spend much of his time on derivative, uninspiring projects to satisfy the grant money directors, but he does understand that modern physics theory needs radical advancements. I hope to collaborate with him on some of these concepts for my doctoral thesis. I find them very stimulating."

Viera interrupts, "Noah, it is good that you are well ensconced in your research group. Your special intellect is beyond reproach. You will soon surpass the knowledge and skills of your professor, if you have not done so already. You have always been vastly more intelligent than all those around you. You cannot envision the lower capabilities of the normal human, so the realization of any alternative existence is not possible for you. You have no idea how vastly different it is for others here on this planet. Mathematics, physics, and other fundamentals are hardwired into your brain. All you need to do is learn the nomenclature, and it all falls into place. Your reading comprehension and memory are exceedingly high compared to the general population. Yet you do not understand that you are quite unique in deeply fundamental ways. I know you have never considered why this is. I believe it has been a mistake to shelter you from your true self and allow you to miss the details of the world around you outside of academics."

"I never think about it. I have always considered my intelligence to be normal. It has always been this way for me; I thought that I was just lucky, if anything. I have wondered why everyone else in school takes so long to learn things. I really don't understand why people struggle as they do, but I have never considered the reasons for this. I had three degrees before I turned nineteen; I could have had several more. I wanted to start graduate school when I was thirteen, but my mother did not let me, you know. I suppose that I am fortunate she held me back, or living alone and starting graduate school may have been too much."

Viera stares at Noah and smiles. She senses anxiety growing in Noah's mind, and she sends calming thoughts to him. "Your superior intelligence is not normal and your telepathic ability even more so. Noah, you are oblivious to the fact that the humans surrounding you cannot do the things you do effortlessly. I have shielded you from a great many things to give you time to mature and adapt to this world. As I followed you through the last several months, the first time you lived away from your childhood home, you still have not realized just how different the people around you are from yourself. We may have blocked too much of your mentality and caused your failure to appreciate your situation. As a glaring example, you fail to recognize that humans do not read each other's thoughts like you and I do. They can only communicate verbally or physically. They live alone, trapped in their fleshy shells, while you and I are connected mentally at all times. I have been with you constantly from the first time we met when you were four years old. You have reached out to me in times of stress, and I have responded to you just as real as if I were standing next to you, even when I was physically miles away. A small fraction of people have very marginal psychic abilities, but in general, Homo Sapiens do not have this ability. We could have this conversation without a word being spoken. Think back. How many years have we conversed mentally? I have been waiting and hoping you would discover your true uniqueness on your own. Recent events and circumstances make it imperative that I begin to divulge a new reality to you."

Noah is perturbed by the notion that he is ignorant of major aspects of his life. "What do you mean? I do not understand what you are suggesting."

Viera gazes at Noah with a look of exasperation, "Noah, you have been shielded from reality for your entire life. Many things have been intentionally blocked, so those barriers may have kept you from deducing certain aspects of your surroundings. I am sorry to have to do it this way, but you will soon be swept up into profound conflicts and need to know the truth about this reality. Listen closely and consider your new reality logically; do not react emotionally. You can sense that I am not lying to you. First, you are incredibly unique, mentally, physically, and biochemically. Human minds are weaker and unable to interact mind-to-mind, psychically like us. You never realized that your ability is unusual; it may be the hubris of your superiority or due to some of the blocks that were placed upon you. Beyond reading the thoughts of people, you can put suggestions into people's minds. You did not realize you had made all your classmates at school like you. Even fellow students who never interacted with you thought highly of you and had good feelings for you because you willed them to think this way. You missed how other people were bullied and abused, whereas those same mean people liked you. It is because you wished them to like you. You redirected their thinking; it is second nature for you. You have that power over human beings."

Noah interrupts, "I don't have that effect on you. We exchange thoughts, but I do not think I have ever directed your thinking or your actions."

"That is true. We are essentially equals, so we have balanced mental and telepathic abilities. You can influence any human, but not me. You do not realize that you could reach out to any human on the street and tell them to give you all the money in their pocket and they would do it. You and I are different. Also, we maintain a telepathic connection so you have never really known what it is like to be alone. This connection fundamentally changes social order. You have no concept of the inherent loneliness of a typical human. You will soon connect with others like us. When I first came to you, recall how overwhelmed you were by your ability to sense the vast energy that was incapacitating you. I taught you how to push that to the side so you could focus your mind, then speak and function normally. Now I want you to look closely at that energy. You will find most of that energy emanates from the billions of humans on Earth; this energy is crude, gritty, and chaotic. If you look closely, you can find several intensely bright spots that are quite different. Soon, I will be introducing you to these special ones."

Noah sits motionless, flooded with new thoughts and feelings. He is embarrassed that he did not figure this out on his own. Moreover, he struggles to keep his anxiety under control. He fears examining his new realities, which seem to hold a terrifying, disturbing future. Viera is there in his mind, soothing and calming him more effectively than one of his mother's hugs.

Regaining composure, he asks, "Very well. What are you saying? What does this mean? You seem to be implying something? Am I a random psychic freak or something else?"

Viera looks at Noah reassuringly while transmitting comforting mental messages. "I will be direct, so please do not get distressed. You are in an exceptionally good situation and may contribute greatly to the future of this planet. Here it is. You are not a Homo Sapiens human. Your mother was abducted and fertilized artificially with extraterrestrial-modified DNA. You are a hominid of the genus Homo, but you are not in the Sapiens species. You are a hybrid."

Noah reads Viera's thoughts and knows she is not lying. She has taught him how to detect lies, to recognize the mental "odor" produced by a deceitful mind. Noah fires a rapid succession of psychic messages, "How can that be? Who are they? Why? What planet are they from?..."

Noah's pulse is racing and his breathing becomes shallow. He blacks out before Viera can respond with any extra psychic support. Noah collapses to the floor completely unconscious.

Chapter 4.

Darkness can be frightening;
breaking free into the light is worth any hardship.

Noah wakes lying on the sofa with no idea of how long he has been unconscious. He begins to recover his wits, aided by a powerful, calming sensation from an unknown source. He feels an intense and beautiful energy gently soothing his frayed nerves. He sits up and looks to Viera and asks, "How long have I been out?"

"You have been unconscious for just a moment. You should feel better. Do you?"

"Yes, I feel better for some reason. It is not every day that you find out you are not human but are an alien hybrid."

Viera nods sympathetically and says, "I am sorry to have shocked you in this way. I would have preferred to lead you to this knowledge more slowly. However, we need you to join us in an operation with tremendous consequences possible."

Noah feels his pulse increasing and asks, "Just what are you talking about? I don't understand."

Viera continues calmly, "There is a galactic organization of advanced civilized planets. Our galaxy is filled with intelligent beings, but Homo Sapiens have been denied knowledge of this. This galactic organization is a necessary union for mutual protection from one another. As civilizations produce high technical achievements that enable galactic travel, each also has the power to destroy entire planets. It is the burden and consequence of high technology. Long ago, horrendous wars were fought. Billions of living creatures and entire civilizations were destroyed. There was once another planet in the solar system, but it was destroyed to form the asteroid belt now present between Mars and Jupiter. The planet Mars had a thriving advanced civilization, but it too, was a casualty of those wars. The Galactic Confederation was formed to enforce peace and prevent unnecessary conflict. Aggressive violence is strictly prohibited, and offenders are swiftly punished or annihilated by the council members. The Earth is not sufficiently civilized and is intentionally not part of the confederation. It is, however, a quarantined protectorate. Homo Sapiens are developing higher technology but have not developed the cultural characteristics necessary for an advanced civilization. Homo Sapiens are too violent, too untrustworthy, and too barbaric to be allowed off-planet travel. With human discoveries of nuclear weapons and rocket-powered spacecraft, the Confederation was compelled to be more active. Nuclear wars have been and will be stopped to protect the planet from self-destruction; that is the easy part. More importantly, the evolution of Homo Sapiens into a civilized species is being directed. Noah, you may be the prototype for the next human race, Homo Galaxus."

"Homo Galaxus, that has an interesting ring to it. So, I am not a human. This is so weird. I am not sure what to think right now. Are you another Homo Galaxus, like me?"

"No, I am a second-generation hybrid from parents who were themselves hybrids. My alien heritage is from the Pleiades Union of Planets. Humans and Pleiadeans have many physical similarities. After my missions here, I have the option to live there."

"Why can't this Galactic Federation just make itself known and land spaceships at the major capitals, then explain things directly? Why wouldn't that be more efficient than all this secrecy and making hybrids?"

Viera shakes her head, "Definitely not. Such actions would not go well. Likely, the Earthen societies would collapse due to fear, sloth, or mania. It is also quite possible that humans would feign higher civilization to acquire advanced technology, ultimately leading to barbaric aggression and planet-wide destruction. The Earth is not the first planet to be at this transition. Secret treaties have been made with several of the leading countries of Earth. The treaties prohibit disclosure of extraterrestrials to the public. It would trigger harsh consequences, such as another global flood, to reset the world. There are clandestine government agencies that work to stop anybody from bringing true galactic disclosure. Their mission is vital to maintain order and prevent self-imposed cataclysm. However, you need to know that there are enclaves of extraterrestrial refugees called Dracons hidden in several locations on Earth. They would like to see a catastrophic reset of Earth so they can claim the planet for themselves. Other government agencies and government-related organizations oppose those who support the treaties and are aligned with the Dracons. They seek advanced alien technology for their own self-serving ends. They are a great danger to the continued existence of Homo Sapiens. There are many hybrids like you and me, observing, directing, and preventing catastrophes. If you do not keep this restricted information completely secret, the contaminated humans will suffer mortal consequences. If you prove that you can keep your composure and confidentiality with this information, I will tell you more about the galaxy. However, I can sense you need time to recover and process this information."

Noah cradles his head in his hands, trying to comfort himself from his reeling thoughts. The gravity of this new reality sinks in. His heart is beating rapidly again, and his breathing is constricted. Telepathically, he feels Viera and several powerful unknown entities surround him. They cover him in a warm, soothing ether of support. Soon, Noah begins to settle down and calm himself.

Noah drops his hands and sits up straight letting loose a deep sigh. Without speaking words, he says, "*This is all so shocking. It does explain many things. The world is so incredibly different from what I used to think. It is like a bizarre dream, but I can now sense that it is all too real. My head is still spinning. I can sense you are being truthful, but I need some time to digest all of this. What do I do now?*"

"*You were put here for a reason. The gifts bestowed upon you carry an obligation. You have a mission. You must help prevent human physicists from discovering higher levels of physical realities and high technology that would trigger action by the Galactic Confederation. Humans must not harness the immense power of advanced physics and the knowledge of alternative dimensions, anti-gravity, and faster-than-light space travel. Humans, with their primitive nature, cannot be trusted with such power; galactic peace would be threatened. Your professor has recently been identified as one who will be given forbidden work from Professor Arun Chandra; that material could burst the current physics paradigm. This event has surprised us, and it likely has unknown, nefarious origins. He must be watched and controlled. We need you to find out how this information was gathered and stop it from getting out. That is your primary mission. Failure could result in the planet-wide destruction of Homo Sapiens society. We call it a triggering event; it would cause us to unleash the catastrophic destruction of all of the Homo Sapiens.*"

A myriad of emotions are now boiling up and on the verge of eruption. His entire life has just been turned upside down. Viera reaches out with more reassuring thoughts for support, but it may not be enough at this point.

Noah responds fretfully, "A triggering event that causes our world to be destroyed, for real? All humans get destroyed over some new physics discoveries; that seems crazy."

"Noah, this has been a tremendous shock for you. I did not want to disclose this to you in this manner, but there are consequential situations developing that cannot be ignored. There is much more you need to know, but not now. Right now, I want you to lie down on the couch and relax your mind the best you can. I will put you in a healing trance as I first did when you were a child and suffering from the massive flood of psychic input. It should help you adjust to your new reality."

It takes significant help from her extraterrestrial supervisors for Viera to calm Noah and get him into a healing trance. She understands the trauma, but there was no other way. Once Noah's mind is calmed and open, she adds a secondary mission into his subconscious.

Additionally, I have another personal mission for you that may help you understand your true situation. I want you to spend more time observing human society; you have been too ignorant of the human social atmosphere surrounding you. I want you to become closer friends with your lab mates, Jesse and Ruth. Spend more time with them. Go out with them, talk with them to learn about their motivations and views of society. Go experience human existence to understand it and in turn, to understand yourself. I especially want you to spend extra time with Ruth. You need to learn of the feminine perspective from someone other than your mother to learn the full details of the male/female dichotomy.   If you can develop a deeper appreciation for human motivations, you will understand why the planet is quarantined and kept out of galactic society."

Chapter 5.

Maybe we can help

Noah's head swirls with thoughts and questions as he drives back to the graduate student dormitory. His comfortable world of delusion has been wiped away in an instant. Even with Viera's long-distance telepathic support, he is having difficulty focusing. The familiar walk from the graduate student dormitory to the physics building does help his mental state, but only slightly. He arrives at the fishbowl to find Jesse and Ruth in the vacant postdoc office. Curious, he walks over to them.

Jesse looks up from pulling folders out of a filing cabinet, "Hey look, our relief is here. Noah, it's about time you got here to help us with the shit work PIF stuck us with. The wonder boy can finish sorting and cleaning this mess."

PIF is the secret nickname for Professor Isaac Feingold, the name the group calls him behind his back.

Noah misses the sarcastic humor of the friendly digs from Jesse and sheepishly responds, "Oh, I am sorry. I had an appointment with my therapist. If I had known…"

Ruth interrupts, "Noah, do not take him seriously. Jesse got his Ph.D. in asshole-ology. Anyway, the PIF told Jesse this morning to tell me to clean out this office. What a sexist pig. Let the new postdoc clean out his own office. I am studying for a Ph.D. for heaven's sake." She takes a closer look at Noah and asks, "Are you all right? You look troubled."

Noah looks down and answers in a low voice, "My therapist gave me some disturbing news about… about my family and me. I am still processing it all."

Noah looks up to Ruth, who is now standing right in front of him. He sees her sympathetic expression and feels gentle comfort from it. She is small and thin like him. Her round face is accentuated by her prominent features, especially her large brown eyes. She has often said that her nose is too big, but Noah thinks it looks noble and gives her character. Her long brown hair is pulled up into a ponytail that whips around as she moves her head. Right now, he stares deeply into her brown eyes as he is caught between the conflicting feelings driving him to cry or smile.

Ruth hugs Noah tightly. Noah, unsure of himself, can only raise one hand to gently touch her back. It feels good in a new way, but triggers embarrassment. Noah has never hugged, kissed, or even dated a girl. Panic is building, but Viera's consciousness is there with him, calming him and telling him to continue this interaction.

Ruth pulls back and drags a chair over for Noah. She hops up on the desk to sit nearby. Leaning in, she says, "Noah, sit here and tell us what's going on. Maybe we can help you work through it."

"I can't share any details with you; however, I can say that Viera, my long-time therapist, dropped several really huge things on me. It is about me and just everything. I suppose I am still in shock. I have a lot to think about."

Jesse chimes in, "Noah, you've got to stop letting that therapist get into your head. They just want to keep you messed up so that they don't lose a customer. They just monetize their patients, not cure them, especially the female therapists. I'll tell you what, you need to start going out with me and my buddies. We can have some beers, then just bullshit each other about the world. That's the kind of therapy real men need. It's not good to have all these women tell you what to do. A real man doesn't need stupid advice from a bunch of androgynists. It causes your balls to jump back into your abdomen, never to drop again."

"Jesse, you are such an ignorant chauvinist. Noah needs real emotional support, not a night of beer swilling, dick jokes, and blatant misogyny," counters Ruth.

Jesse fires back, "Hey, don't put words in my mouth. I like you gals just fine. Equality, yeah. What I don't like is the way women love to swim around in their self-imposed sheep dip of emotions, with no desire to get out of their own messes. It's good for anti-depressant sales, but ruins people. If I tell a girl in a bad situation to get over it, move on, and leave the negative stuff behind, they call me a misogynistic jerk. I'm only trying to help the way real dudes deal with stuff. No one cares if a man feels bad or shit like that. We have to suck it up and move on, you know. It's called tough love, sweety. That's what real men do. The men who don't plow through problems, rot away in their parents' basement or some bullshit like that."

Ruth ignores Jesse and turns to Noah. "Don't listen to him. You need to work through these emotions to get past them. Ignoring them by drinking and talking like a jerk does not get to the root cause to provide real healing, and it will not help to make you the best version of yourself. I understand what it is like to go through horrible family problems. My parents divorced when I started junior high school. It was an ugly divorce, and it hurt me severely. Luckily, I had friends and relatives who supported me through it. Ultimately, it made me stronger. I decided to reject the negativity and work on myself by striving for successful achievements. I turned to my schoolwork and became the class valedictorian by the time I graduated high school. I could not have done it with alcohol and dirty, mean-spirited talk; it was all the caring people who gave me the necessary emotional support. Noah, tell me how you feel. I am here to help."

Noah does not know how to respond and is beginning to feel overwhelmed by a surge of embarrassment. Viera is still there with him and starts giving him lines, which he slowly repeats. "Ruth, I have just had my world turned upside down, like you when your parents divorced. The future is cloudy, filled with serious unknowns. I am trying to process it all, but it is difficult. Your kindness is a great comfort to me. I think I will need your help to work through my issues. I appreciate what you are doing for me."

Viera sends a strong command to Noah, "*Stand up and hug her.*"

Noah stands and turns to Ruth. He reaches out for her, and she slides off the desk and into his arms. They hold the embrace, both lost in the moment.

Jesse breaks the moment with slow, sarcastic clapping. "Oh, very good. Can we end this sappy therapy session and finish cleaning out this office? I am starting to get hungry and want to eat lunch soon. Noah, start cleaning out that file cabinet over there. Save anything pilfered from the library or other groups; pitch the rest. A little physical labor will heal your emotional boo-boos more than that touchy-feely crap."

Ruth pulls back and makes a face in response to Jesse's quips. "Don't listen to him. I am here for you any time you need to talk things through." With that, Ruth walks out of the room.

Jesse mockingly calls after her, "Thanks for all the help." He then walks up to Noah and whispers, "Dude, she likes you. You lucky bastard. Girls from divorced parents are usually wild in the sack. Anyhow, you do need to go out drinking with me and get away from this place so we can talk. You may be the "boy wonder," but you are super naïve. You can use my advice to keep women, therapists, and other assholes from wrapping you around their finger. Now let's clean out this stupid office so we can get back to our real work."

Noah is a little unsure about several things Jesse was saying. As Noah goes over to the file cabinet Jesse wants him to clean out, he gets another message from Viera, "*Very interesting. I think you will learn many lessons from Ruth and Jesse. They can serve as a valid proxy for certain human motivations and limitations. Explore these interactions.*"

Chapter 6.

Sometimes, happiness is not knowing

Noah's mother, Miriam, is a nurse for a small office of family physicians. She has worked here for nearly fifteen years, since restarting her career after Noah was born. Once Noah had worked past his early issues and started school, she was able to resume her professional career as a nurse. She now enjoys the calm, predictable job over the intense hospital job she had before Noah. Today is just another peaceful drive home after another day's work.

She is unaware that two men in a white van have been surveilling her home for several days. These two men, Curt and J.T., meticulously recorded Miriam's daily schedule. They also know her husband, Fred, is a long-haul trucker who is out on the road for the rest of the week. They have also monitored her phone calls and emails. Today, they are waiting for her return from work.

Miriam arrives home from work as usual. Her first action is to get out of her work shoes and into her thick-foamed recovery sandals; a marathon runner patient suggested these for her. This has been the best advice she has received for some time. Before she can relax further, the doorbell rings.

Miriam answers the door to find two tall men in dark suits standing in front of her. They are trim and fit. Their short hair and chiseled features add to their imposing look.

The man closest to her smiles and says, "Hello ma'am, we are agents from the federal government." He pulls a billfold from his suit jacket, flips it open to show a badge and ID card, then quickly returns it to his pocket. "We are conducting background checks and are looking for Miriam Baurer. Are you her?"

"Yes, I am. What is this all about?" asks Miriam with a mix of anxiety and curiosity.

"We are fulfilling required bureaucratic mandates, that is all. You have a son, Noah, who has started graduate school in physics. Is this correct?"

Miriam nods.

"Noah has joined the research group of Professor Isaac Feingold, who has several grants and projects with military connections. For that reason, we need to conduct background checks. May we come in, sit down, and ask you some questions?"

Miriam pauses, then invites the two agents inside. She directs them to a sofa in her living room, and she sits in an adjacent chair.

The lead agent, Curt, pulls out a small notepad from his pocket and begins asking questions. The interrogation starts with mundane questions about past residency, relatives' names with addresses, employers, and other simple background information. Then the intensity increases.

"Have you or your husband been arrested or convicted of any criminal activities?"

"No, however, we may have some speeding tickets if that counts."

"Have you or anyone in your family ever been a member of the Communist Party or provided any support to it or any derivative organizations?"

"No, never ever."

"Miriam, have there ever been any other geniuses, other than Noah, in your family or in that of your husband?"

"No, none that I am aware of. Noah is a special boy and always has been. We initially thought he had autism or something like that; he just got off to a slow start. He didn't start talking until he was four years old. He would go nearly catatonic in crowds and would only show how intelligent he was when he was alone with me. He potty-trained himself as soon as he had the physical strength and coordination. I thought he was reading books when he could first pick one up. Fred thought he was just mimicking my behavior, but I know he was really reading. I was proven correct after he started talking. Fortunately, a therapist came to us before Noah was talking and said she had worked with other cases like Noah's. She agreed with me that he was super intelligent and that she could get him talking. Her notion was that his brain was too active, and he would get overstimulated by crowds and too much activity. She said she could work with him to slow his brain and help him control it. She did just as she promised, and Noah took off. He could have graduated from high school at twelve, but I made him stay at home; he was always so slender and frail. I was worried about his physical and mental health. I wanted him to grow up and fill out. Also, it's not right to put a child in places with people so much older than he is. The emotional damage could be quite bad, even if the child is a genius. He read and studied on his own, then took online college courses. He could have earned ten or more degrees if he had wanted to. He only cared about physics. That is why he is where he is."

"Who was this therapist?"

"She is Dr. Viera Torghe. She is a great lady, I really like her."

Curt pauses and looks directly at Miriam, holding the stare for several seconds. "Miriam, have you ever had repeating episodes of bad dreams or severe sleep issues?"

Miriam is surprised by the question and takes a moment to recover. "No, I can't think of anything like that. No, wait a minute, there was a time when I was having problems like that, but that was a long time ago. Shortly after I got married, I was having a few issues like that. My doctor told me it was just caused by anxiety from becoming a wife for the first time and adjusting to living with a husband."

Curt continues, "Have you ever been hypnotized, therapeutic, or otherwise?"

"What does this have to do with any kind of a background check?" Miriam asks to push back.

"Ms. Baurer, enemies of our country have used psychological methods to influence people or to gather information. Often, the victims are tricked into inadvertent disclosures."

Miriam gathers her composure and responds calmly, "No, I have never been hypnotized, at least not knowingly, if you say people can be tricked."

"Very good. I have one final question for you. Please think back as far as you can, and don't be afraid to comment on any past event that may not seem exactly what I am asking you. Have you ever had a lost time event?"

Miriam looks puzzled, "Lost time event? I don't even know what you are talking about."

"For example, have you ever gone a walk, a drive, or an activity by yourself and been told by others that you have been missing for a much longer period of time than you thought? Perhaps you have gone for a drive and found yourself miles away from where you thought you were. Perhaps it was many hours later than your last recollection? Any events like this?"

Miriam looks down and rubs her forehead in deep concentration. She looks up and says, "There was this one time shortly after I got married. We didn't have much money but wanted to take a vacation, so we drove to Colorado to do some camping and hiking. Fred was an avid hunter and outdoorsman when he was younger. At one spot in the mountains, we hiked up to a beautiful lake for two nights of camping. I don't remember exactly where it was. On the second day, I took a pan down to the lake to get water to boil. It was only about 100 yards away. I remember getting to the lake and filling the pan with water. The next thing I remember was walking back toward camp to find Fred running down the trail behind me. He was very upset, asking where I had been. He said I'd been gone for hours, but I thought it was only minutes. I thought the whole incident was about Fred being overly protective, since it was his first time camping with a woman. I teased him about it for the rest of the trip. Do you think that could be a lost time thing? I don't recall anyone being within miles of us."

Curt looks at J.T. and gives him a slight nod. "It might be. Thank you, Ms. Baurer. You have been very helpful. Noah sounds like an outstanding person, and I think he will do great things for our country. I appreciate your cooperation."

Without any further comment, Curt and J.T. stand up and leave. Miriam is happy she has helped Noah. However, she is still thinking about the weird questions and feeling a little uneasy about the implications. She has not thought about that camping trip for a long time. Reaching back to that time has brought on seriously odd feelings. Her memories swim in a dense fog. She can only sense a dark anxiety but it is floating in her mind at the very edge of her consciousness as a hazy, amorphous sensation.

Chapter 7.

I want to help you

Noah continues to struggle throughout the day. He tries to read journal articles, only to have his mind drift back to the revelations from Viera. Every attempt to do any mathematical derivations ends with repeated loss of concentration. The only thing that keeps him going is the reassuring presence of Viera with occasional advice. He received a text message from his mother, but didn't feel like talking with her right now. His struggles finally get the best of him. He opens the door of his small office to find that everyone else has left. It is much later than he thought. He rushes back to his dorm.

Noah makes it to the cafeteria with just fifteen minutes left before it closes. He chooses a simple meal: a piece of grilled chicken and soup. He pairs the food with his favorite drink, chocolate milk. His dinner does help his mood, but neither does the visual distraction of the cleaning crew shutting down the cafeteria. After finishing his meal, Viera recommends that he go to bed early tonight. The extra rest will help.

Noah goes directly to his room. It is small but has been a comfortable, safe two-room space for him. It has everything a graduate student would need, and not much else. He has a bed, a desk, and a small table with two chairs in the main room. Also, there is a kitchen counter against the wall near the door, with a sink, microwave, and a small refrigerator. Noah turns on a small speaker by his bed to connect it to his phone, then selects the most soothing playlist he has. It's a collection of soft rock tunes his mother likes. As the music starts playing, Noah plops down on his bed.

After nearly half an hour of futility trying to soothe his mind, Noah is startled by a knock on his door. He gets up and opens the door to a surprise. Ruth is standing there with a sweet smile on her face.

"I didn't see you at dinner. I know you are having a rough day, so I wanted to stop by and check on you and see how you are doing. May I come in?"

"Yes, please. I was just lying down and listening to music."

Ruth enters the room and shuts the door behind her. She has been here before to get help with a few difficulties she was having in their classes. Her prior visits involved several hours sitting around his table with papers and books. Tonight is different.

She takes Noah's hand, "Let's sit down and talk." She continues to hold his hand and leads him over to his bed. She sits, pulling Noah down beside her.

"You still look upset and stressed. Do you feel any better than you did this afternoon?"

Noah has new curious feelings welling up. He has never held hands with a girl ever before. Her small, soft hand feels so nice. "I don't know. I tried but failed to get any work done today. I lost track of time and almost missed dinner. Eating something tonight did help me a little. I hope a good night of sound sleep will make me recover."

"Noah, can you tell me anything about your issues? Sometimes talking through things with a friend is very helpful. It is not healthy to keep things bottled up inside you. Your emotional health should not be ignored, trust me. You need to face your troubled feelings and let them run their course. Bad vibes should be treated like a case of the flu. You cure it by treating the symptoms while working to preserve your overall health. You can use your friends to help cure yourself by talking to them. True friends will support you and make things better. Am I your friend?"

"Yes, you are. I have never had any close friends; I have only had my therapist. I was always so much younger than my classmates as I jumped up multiple grade levels year after year. Also, I've never had to face distressing news like the news I received today. This kind of problem is new to me, so I've never been in a situation where I needed to talk things through. You must be much better at this sort of thing. I admit that I am struggling."

Ruth breaks the handhold and begins to gently rub Noah's back. "You poor thing. I think it is so sad you missed growing up without friends. You must have been very lonely. No wonder you are having a difficult time getting through a rough patch. That's part of growing up naturally. You must feel like an onion in a petunia patch."

"You have no idea. I don't know what is normal or what normal should be."

"Noah, now that we are friends, I want to help you. Promise me that you will come to me when you need someone to talk with when you are feeling down. Will you do that?"

Noah finds Ruth's touch to be pleasant and enjoyable; he also feels energized and stimulated somehow. He would like to hug her again. He looks into her large brown eyes and says, "I will do that. I appreciate what you are trying to do for me. I can see how a friend can make you feel better because you are making me feel better right now. I don't think I can talk about the details of my issues, but I will tell you that it involves me and my family. Plus, it changes most everything I was thinking about my future. It is not all bad, but it is certainly a major shock and quite frightening. Maybe I am just too sensitive and lack the resilience that normal people have. I know mathematics and physics; I don't know about this kind of thing."

Ruth raises her other hand and puts it on Noah's cheek. She smiles, "It will be all right. I can tell you are feeling better after our short talk. This is just what you need and have missed growing up." She then leans in and kisses Noah on the lips.

Noah feels a surge like nothing he has experienced before. He instinctively puts his arms around Ruth and feels even better.

Ruth and Noah embrace and continue kissing. After a long while, she pulls away and whispers into Noah's ear, "I should go. I hope you feel better. I feel wonderful, and I hope you feel it too."

Noah smiles and can only nod. Ruth stands up and walks to the door. After blowing him a long-distance kiss, she turns and leaves.

Noah sits on his bed, his head spinning for a new reason. He enjoyed kissing Ruth. It was exciting, and a completely different experience than any other he had ever experienced. He thought he could feel the blood rapidly flowing through his body. He reads Ruth's thoughts and knows she genuinely likes him. Thanks to Ruth, he is no longer obsessed with the thoughts of aliens, missions, or his own biological engineering. He wishes she was still here with him. However, he is apprehensive about the deeper thoughts of hers that he viewed. It involved nakedness and extreme intimacy.

"*Are you starting to understand the enigma and limitations of Homo Sapiens existence?*" asks Viera. "*I have been silent during your encounter so you could experience it on your own. You just had your second quintessential all-human experience; the first was your mother's pure love. You encountered hormonal surges triggered by mental hard wiring reacting to physical stimuli. This series of events produces a short-term pleasant, biological feeling. It is a short-term effect, very primitive and exclusively emotional. You are now beginning to experience several possible negative secondary effects. Uncertainty, distress, and unrelenting desires are coming for you now. I believe you will gain much insight into the human psyche, but it may be a hard lesson.*"

Noah, still riding the emotional high, responds, "*Ruth did make me feel much better. I found her very comforting. Her affection and her desire to help me are real.*"

"*Yes, they are. However, if you were fully human, you would not be able to read her thoughts. Soon, you would be distressed by the possibility that Ruth may have ulterior motives or was only using you for a one-time thrill. Imagine how you would feel if you did not know what Ruth was thinking. Feeling is not knowing. Homo Sapiens communication is limited; it only happens through physical contact and unverifiable dialogue. It does engage biological actions involving hormones and neural transmitters, which provide feedback to one's mental state and feelings. These effects are fleeting and primitive; ultimately, an advanced society cannot maintain itself this way. Emotions can overwhelm cognitive analysis and thinking. A psychic connection is far more intimate and honest. An advanced society must have truthful interactions that are driven by cognitive decisions, not fleeting hormonal responses. Cultures united by only emotions and feelings are doomed. Telepathic ability is critical for advanced relationships because all deceptions and deceitful actions are not possible."*

Noah is disappointed, *"Once again, I have been oblivious to this. Apparently, my advanced hybrid abilities, compared with Homo Sapiens, have made me ignorant. You were indeed correct to recognize that I do not truly understand human society, let alone any advanced one."*

Viera sends more soothing feelings to Noah and says, *"You should not feel bad. You are very young, and this is just part of your education. It is not built into you as mathematics is. Your experiences will also teach you many lessons. We will advance your education and knowledge at a more rapid pace now."*

Noah feels better, but feels stress building about Ruth. He admits, *"I am starting to get nervous thinking about how I should act when I see Ruth tomorrow. I have no idea how I should behave and no idea how I should act the next time we are alone together."*

"Do not worry. Tonight, while you sleep, we will implant proper guidance for you. With the aid of my supervisors, I will put you into a learning trance tonight. There will be a group of other beings who will begin interacting with you. You will feel their essence as you do with me, and you will begin to receive messages from them; they are fully extraterrestrial and have a high level of mentality and spirituality. I hope you can meet them in person soon. We will also implant more information about the Galactic Confederation. As I told you previously, ominous signs have appeared. We need to advance your training more rapidly than originally planned. For your human side, you will awaken with knowledge of human social protocols and intimate relations. Trust your new instincts, we will give you. Remain calm and let yourself absorb new information. Enjoy the restoration of a good night's sleep. You will have a new outlook in the morning and will also know more about the galaxy."

Chapter 8.

What did I just do?

The next morning, Noah arrives at the physics building feeling strong and confident. So much new information is now implanted in his mind. He better understands what he is and what his mission entails. He now knows amazing new things. He was shown glimpses of a massive galaxy out there, its advanced beings using almost unimaginable technologies; he hopes to join them one day soon. He also wants to help Homo Sapiens advance past their primitive state. His mother is good and worthy of protection; there are others like her who should be saved. He wants to save them from any horrible act that could have been prevented by events he could have stopped.

Noah reaches the fishbowl and sees Ruth in the office next to his. He walks straight to Ruth, who is sitting at her small desk, reading from her computer screen. She looks up and smiles. Noah feels her thoughts of happiness and holds his hand out to her like a smooth operator. Whatever instincts Viera implanted have given him confidence with plans of action. She puts her hand in his and he pulls her into a hug and whispers in her ear, "Thank you for making me feel better. I feel great today and can see the world with a completely new outlook. I really appreciate what you have done."

Ruth holds the hug longer than a purely casual hug. She pulls back, "Noah, I am so glad you feel better. I told you that talking with me was helping. I'm glad I could be there for you. I will always be there for you; come to me whenever you need an ear."

Noah reads her mind and knows she is intending to share much more than an ear. He now looks forward to it. "Thank you, Ruth. I will. We had better get to work right now."

"Agreed, I am trying to catch up with my journal readings. You know how PIF likes to pick on people in group meetings. You don't have this problem with him. Actually, I think he is afraid to take you on, and rightly so. I am not a genius like you, so I am fair game for his ego trips. Jesse is presenting today, and you know how things get with him and PIF. Since the last group meeting, what journal articles have come out that are likely to be discussed today?"

Noah smiles, "Do not worry, I'll send you a list." He squeezes her shoulder for reassurance, turns and heads off to his office next door. He feels positive thoughts from Viera and the new, mysterious others in his mind.

Professor Feingold holds a group meeting every two weeks. Years ago, it used to be weekly. It is more evidence for Jesse that PIF is getting lazy and starting to coast.

Jesse opens the meeting with a presentation based upon the recent draft of a paper he gave to Professor Feingold last month. Jesse is perturbed that PIF is just sitting on it, rather than reviewing and editing his article for publication. This is fuel for their contentious relationship. Professor Feingold starts nitpicking on trivialities in Jesse's calculations. Jesse is competent enough to fire back with counterarguments. The intensity of the exchange rapidly increases until it becomes personal.

Professor Feingold starts it, "Jesse, you are just an arrogant punk. You will never get an academic job with your smartass attitude."

Jesse fires back, "Don't want one. I don't want to end up like you, a lazy, brain-dead tenured professor who works on useless shit. Your projects are like all the other worthless physics research efforts out there. Tiny bits of data are overanalyzed with overcomplicated mathematics to try to prove string theory, dark matter, or quantum gravity. It's all a show. Big questions need bold theories, not this shit you guys pass off as cutting-edge research."

"You are just a brat. I must raise money to fund this group. Grant agencies want what they want. Why don't you go out on your own and solve the questions of the universe while you flip burgers for a living? You just don't get it. If you think this is a waste, there's the door."

"You forget I am funding myself already. The defense contractor consortium is funding me. I have several of those companies wanting to hire me for a hell of a lot more money than a professor. I interned with a couple of them when I was an undergraduate; they would have hired me then. I have security clearances, do you? I'll be working on real cutting-edge technology and not thinking about the useless projects I had to endure to get my Ph.D."

Ruth and the other group members had shut down in the face of this troubling conflict. They all just stared down at the table to avoid any eye contact. This ugly exchange is stressing out the entire group.

Noah gets a message from Viera, "*Do something.*" He looks toward the feuding pair and sends his command directly into their minds, "*Stop. Stop it now.*"

Professor Feingold and Jesse stop talking at once and their expressions go blank.

Noah continues with his newfound ability: "*Now apologize.*"

Jesse starts, "I am sorry, Professor. I got a little carried away."

"Yes, I am sorry as well. Science does involve passion, and debates can get overheated," Professor Feingold sheepishly says. "This would be a good place to end this meeting today. Before you go, I have an announcement. Soon, I will be adding a postdoc. My old friend, Professor Arun Chandra, has suddenly passed away. I am taking on his postdoc so that we can finish Arun's final project. It is quite a project, and it may just be the world-changing theory that Jesse wants to see. This new postdoc is Ulak T-something; he's from Siberia or somewhere in the middle of nowhere in central Asia. He and I will be working together, and it will not involve any extra work for the rest of the group. I am very excited about this. I'll give you more details later."

Jesse and Noah sit alone in the fishbowl. All the other group members scurry away and shut their doors after being traumatized by the angst of the group meeting. Jesse is turning off his computer after disconnecting from the projector and retracting the screen back into the ceiling.

Noah is trying to understand what he has just done. Viera and the others must have unlocked new skills besides implanting new knowledge. Upon Viera's prodding, it was so instinctive to send a direct command into a human's mind. It was even more surprising to see how quickly Jesse and PIF complied. These are two very headstrong men, yet he directed them easily. Homo Sapiens are completely defenseless without any psychic abilities of their own.

Jesse turns to Noah, "After that shit fest, I need a beer. Come on. Let's go."

"*Go with him and experience this new vector for yourself,*" advises Viera.

Chapter 9.

Buck's Bar and Grill

Noah is excited about going out to a bar with Jesse and thinks that it could be a real teachable moment like Viera is recommending. Jesse has an interesting outlook, so Noah readily agreed. After quickly stowing his computer in his office, Noah calls out to Jesse, "I am ready to go. I believe you have a lot to get off your chest, so I will help you decompress." He senses Viera's approval.

Jesse and Noah lock their office doors and quickly leave the building for Jesse's favorite watering hole. Jesse doesn't start talking until they get about 100 feet from the physics building. "You see what I have been telling you. Physics professors are holding back the field of advanced physics from progressing. They get us as excited graduate students ready to change the world, then they have us chase our tails in their logic games and overcomplicated mathematics. If anybody goes off their well-beaten path that is actually a deep rut, they boot you out of their club. Our discipline has been dead for nearly a century. I can't wait to get out of here."

"Yes, Jesse. I certainly understand your frustration. Perhaps the changes needed are so enormous that they would cause too much disruption. It seems a series of small steps is an easier way to make progress rather than a giant leap while taking slings and arrows from the establishment. The granting agencies are conservative for tangible reasons."

"Maybe or maybe not. The physics world is such a messed-up brick wall covered with shit. When you joined the group, I was really, really encouraged because you are a true brainiac, much smarter than all those stuffy bastards. I hope that you can overturn their rotten apple cart."

"Thanks. I am going to do all I can. I have just started. I am curious to know about this project PIF is going to finish for his old friend, Professor Chandra. It sounded big. Do you have any idea what it involves?"

"No idea. I met the guy a year or so ago at a conference. He had a small rebellious streak, but seemed more like someone who would just fall in line like the rest of them. I wonder what got into him. I would be surprised if it was something big, but who knows? People can snap. PIF sounds like he is going to keep the project for himself and this new postdoc dude. He usually passes on the hard work to us in his group, so maybe there is something there. He would want all the credit if he thought it was as big as it sounds. My guess is that he will get tired of hard work after a few days, then he will come to us for help."

"I hope you are right. Let me know if you hear anything. I am very curious about just what new theories the professor has received from Professor Chandra."

After a little further, Jesse stops walking, "Here we are. BBG, or to be more specific, Buck's Bar and Grill, is my favorite place to go to get away from physics.'

Jesse's favorite bar is a gritty old bar that looks like it has been around since WWII ended. It's long and narrow with a long wooden bar on one side and booths on the other. Small tables and mismatched chairs are squeezed into the middle, leaving little room to spare. The kitchen is located at the far back end. The dusty, dark walls are decorated with old beer and liquor signs, including old neon-lit ones. There are other odds and ends of nostalgia tacked up that once had stories, but now their stories are lost. The dust on them could probably be carbon-dated to pinpoint their origin. Jesse does appear to be correct about the place; it is certainly the opposite of the physics building.

The pair walks down the length of the bar, and Jesse directs them to empty stools at the far end. Noah can sense that Jesse has spent quite a bit of time here.

The bartender comes over and Jesse orders two beers, pointing at the patron down the bar with a long-neck brown bottle in front of him.

The bartender turns to Noah, "Let me see your ID."

Jesse winces, realizing that Noah was not yet 21. Noah calmly reaches for his wallet and pulls out his driver's license. He hands it to the bartender as Jesse starts to panic.

The bartender stares at the ID, then says, "OK, thanks. Two beers on the way."

Jesse whispers to Noah, "Dude, is that a fake ID?"

Noah shakes his head and shows it to Jesse.

"Hey, this is a real one and shows that you are not old enough. What the hell?"

Noah smiles and calmly says, "Look again."

Jesse looks at the ID one more time, "OK, so you are old enough..." He pauses and cocks his head in total confusion as Noah puts his ID back in his wallet. "Wait, what just happened? The first time I looked, you were too young. The second time, everything was good. I don't get it."

"I studied hypnotism. Plus, people seem to like me," says Noah with a jovial tone.

"Sure, why not. The boy wonder has all kinds of special powers. Speaking of that, what kind of hypnotism are you using on Ruth? I see what's going on. She has the hots for you. You're a lucky SOB. She's cute. What's going on with you two?"

"You are correct. She does like me, and I like her. I don't know what is going to happen. I have never had a girlfriend, as you might imagine. Everyone around me at school was five to ten years older than I was. She has been so nice to me and grateful for the help I gave her with the classwork."

"Man, you need to be careful. You can't trust modern women. She'll either dump you for the first tall, muscled-up bad boy she finds, or she'll charge you with some kind of harassment. Either way, it will end badly for you."

"Ruth would not do that."

"Don't fool yourself. Women are fickle. They blow hot and cold with their emotions. No matter how they feel today, it's guaranteed that it will take a 180-degree turn instantaneously. That's why the world is doomed. Women are unstable, and now they run everything. Look around; society is collapsing. Populations are declining, countries are going broke, and violence is everywhere. Dishonest people running the government and big banks are robbing us blind. It's just a matter of time."

The bartender drops two beers off just in time to stop Jesse's rant. Jesse takes a long drink of his beer and lets out a big sigh of relief. Noah takes a tiny sip of his beer. It tastes horrible. He hopes he can choke it down. He wonders if he could get a chocolate milk, but won't dare order one.

Jesse picks up his bottle of beer and looks at it, "God gave us beer to show us that he loves us. Amen. Is this your first beer?"

Noah nods, but the expression on his face tells Jesse everything.

"Don't worry Noah, it's an acquired taste. Keep drinking, it will get better," Jesse says with a wry grin.

Noah changes the subject, "So Jesse, you don't ever want to be a professor. Are you sure about the academic world?" He chokes down another sip of beer.

"Yep, sure as shit. I don't want any part of their inbred world. I interned every summer as an undergrad with high-tech defense companies. I got a security clearance by my sophomore year. That's where all the cutting-edge work is happening. I can't wait to finish up here and start up with those guys. I have only seen a little bit of what is going on there, but if you saw what I have, it would blow your mind. It's all super top secret, so no one on the outside knows anything. I still give a presentation every year to the consortium funding me. I give them an update on the current events in physics. It feels like a comedy routine to them. They have little use for physics professors. They are doing groundbreaking things for real that these stuffy, arrogant professors would say is impossible. That may help you understand why I get crossways with PIF."

"Well, that does make sense. So why go through all this to get your doctorate?"

Jesse chugs the rest of his first beer, burps loudly, then waves to the bartender for another. He then says, "Money and power. These defense companies are still corporations with HR policies. A Ph.D. is on a higher pay scale from the outset. Also, you get more rapid advancement up the chain of command if you want to go that way."

Noah senses Jesse is starting to relax. He probes for more information. "So, these defense companies have advanced technology because they ignore the physics community?"

"That is only part of the story." Jesse leans in and whispers, "I couldn't tell you even if I knew for sure, but I have overheard talk that they have been gathering technology from weird non-human sources. You know the military had to finally admit there are things in the sky they cannot explain. These unidentified things demonstrate a much higher level of technology. I am pretty sure that there has been spillover from them to us, but if you tell anybody I said that, I will deny it."

Jesse flashes a devious wink at Noah and asks, "Do you think there are extraterrestrials hanging out on the Earth?"

Noah suppresses a chuckle, "It would not surprise me at all." He chokes down another sip that doesn't taste quite as bad as the earlier sips.

Noah finishes his second beer as fast as his first. Jesse orders a third round and a greasy cheeseburger for each.

After just a short while outside of the shelter of his physics bubble, Noah is fascinated by the outside world. He can see why Viera wanted him to get more involved with the people around him; his growth will not progress unless he breaks free from his introverted lifestyle. He wonders what else he has missed.

Chapter 10.

Curt and J.T. arrive

Curt and J.T. sit in their newly rented apartment. Professor Chandra was the second professor they terminated, though the first for this particular mission. Ulak is the real target and source of conflict. They are following him from a great distance. They failed to hold up Ulak's student visa and desperately need a new plan. The assassination of the prior Russian professors he worked with only caused him to move on to Chandra, so it is not an effective option. Previously, they lost two assassins who tried to take out the being called Ulak. One was supposed to do it Mafia-style by walking up behind him to put a bullet in his head. That man dropped dead ten yards from Ulak. The next was a top sniper who tried to shoot him from a distance. Ulak somehow killed him as he put his rifle scope on him, or more worrisome, Ulak may have powerful associates watching over him.

"Curt, what's our new plan now that Ulak is on the way here to join up with the Feingold group? We cannot stop his arrival, and now we know that the elimination of the professor is only a delay. If snipers and hit men fail badly, what can we do now? Maybe it is time to consider using killer drones or missiles?"

Clearly frustrated, Curt strokes his chin and then responds, "I think we need to get electronic surveillance at the physics building again. I also think we should do the professor's home this time. Let's get eyes on the full situation. We cannot terminate Ulak ourselves; that is abundantly clear. The good guys are zero for two. I am not ready to start blowing up buildings. After the interview with his mother, I am fairly certain that the new genius in Feingold's group is a hybrid, but not necessarily like Ulak. We need to find out whose side he is on. It is too risky to confront him directly. We need an indirect approach. If he is on our side, we have a good chance of success. If he is on the other side, it spells doom for us all."

Chapter 11.

Ruth steps up

The cheeseburger sobered up Noah briefly, but after the third beer, he was drunk. Jesse sees Noah wobble around on the barstool and knows it is time for him to go home. He orders a car to take him back to the dorm. The car arrives in five minutes, and Jesse hopes Noah doesn't puke in the car on the way home, knowing that it is an extra charge for cleanup, and a big one too.

Noah staggers into the car. He really enjoyed his evening with Jesse. He met several other regulars who knew Jesse and had a few unusual conversations. They are certainly much different than the academic people he is used to. The movement of the car weaving through the traffic is starting to make Noah feel sick. He reaches out for help. Ruth, he must connect to Ruth.

He is able to focus his mind through the effects of the beers to connect with Ruth. He senses she is in her dorm room reading. *"Ruth, I need help. I am not feeling well. I am on my way back to the dorm and will be there soon. Please, help me."* He can sense the strong feelings she has for him and arouses those to get her help. He also stimulates her inherent nurturing urges. He feels a surge of emotion and sees her anxiety spike after his message is received.

Noah lets out a deep sigh as he leaves the car that has dropped him off at the front door of his dormitory. He weaves his way down the sidewalk and enters through the front door and into the large lobby. It is filled with chairs and couches as it is one of the socializing areas in the building. He sees someone pop up from one of the chairs and quickly heads towards him. It is Ruth.

Noah waves and gives a silly smile as she approaches, "Ruth, I am feeling a little poorly. I should not have stayed out so long."

Ruth stops right in front of Noah and grabs both of his arms, "Noah, I was so worried about you. I felt that you might be in trouble, so I came down to the lobby. You never returned to your room, and I didn't see you at dinner." She looks into his eyes and then gets a whiff of his breath. The goofy smile on Noah's face confirms it. With a furrowed brow, she howls, "Oh my gawd, you have been drinking. Jesse took you out and got you drunk. What a jerk he is. Let's get you to your room."

She grabs Noah by his arm and drags him towards the elevator. Ruth cannot steady Noah with one hand and must wrap her arm around his waist, pulling him tightly to her side. Noah puts his arm around her shoulder for further support. The pair clumsily make it to the elevator.

After the elevator door shuts, Ruth asks, "How many beers did you have? Your breath smells like you have had a keg. I was worried about Jesse's bad influence. Have you ever had alcohol before?"

Noah chuckles, then sighs loudly. "No, first time. It seems like beer has affected my motor control, that's all. I now see why people drink it; it is fun and relaxing. I didn't like the first one, but it got better with each bottle. I had a good time and met some interesting people. I didn't know exactly what they were always trying to tell me, though. Thanks for helping me. I'm sorry to bother you this way. I'm so sorry I made you worry."

"Noah, I am happy to help you. We have a real connection. I worried about you because I care about you. That's what couples do for one another. Do you understand what I am saying?"

"Yes, I like you very much. Thank you for caring." Noah misses the thinly veiled hint.

Then the elevator doors open, and they weave their way to Noah's room. They only bounce off the wall once. Noah struggles to get his key and open the door. The door flies open, and he stumbles forward, crashing into his table and chairs. He falls to the floor, flat on his face. As he struggles to turn over and sit up, he feels a warm liquid flowing down his face. A large gush of blood flows from his nose. Ruth gasps and quickly grabs a towel from the sink to hold it to his nose. She grabs his arm and pulls him up into a chair.

"Hold this towel to your nose, pinch it shut, and tilt your head back. You have a bloody nose."

Ruth rummages through the drawers and finds more towels. She soaks one in cold water, then swaps it out for the first towel. "Oh, Noah, you are a mess. Sit there until the bleeding stops. Let's hope you didn't break your nose. Does it hurt?"

Noah shakes his head while looking pathetic. She straightens up the table and chairs that Noah had crashed into. She then sits next to him in the other chair. Noah senses her growing attachment to him as she cares for him. He feels his emotional attachment to her is also growing.

Ruth dotes on Noah, checking every couple of minutes to see if his nose stops bleeding. After a second cold towel, his nose dries up. "Finally, I think you have stopped bleeding. That was a lot of blood. I bet you will have two black eyes tomorrow. You should be fine now. For a minute there, I thought you were going to need to go to the infirmary. Right now, you should hydrate and get cleaned up. Sit there and don't fall over anymore."

Ruth goes to the refrigerator and grabs two bottles of water. She strips off his bloodied shirt and pants. She empties his pockets, puts his possessions on the table, and throws the clothes into the sink to soak in cold water. She retrieves a washcloth and a towel from the bathroom. She carefully cleans the dried blood from his face and chest, then sits next to him. She steadies Noah with an arm around his shoulder as he drinks water.

Noah looks at her, "Thank you for helping me. Why are you being so nice to me?" He knows what she is thinking, but wants to hear what she actually says.

"Noah, I really like you, like you very much. You have helped me with classwork, and I have been trying to watch out for you. We have been good friends. We are becoming more than just friends. We need to spend more time together, share meals, and go on dates. Have you ever had a girlfriend before?"

Noah shakes his head, "No, never."

I keep forgetting you haven't had a normal childhood. I have had only a few dates myself and only one boyfriend, sort of. I had given up on men until I met you. I think we could be good for each other. Do you want to be my boyfriend?"

"Yes, you do. Explore this relationship to its fullest."

Noah didn't need the prompting. He smiles and says, "Yes, Ruth. I would really like that."

Ruth gives him a gentle hug and kisses him on the cheek. "Now, let's get you to bed. I will make sure you don't have a relapse tonight. Since you owe me for cleaning you up, tomorrow night you need to take me out for pizza, fancy wood oven-fired pizza."

Noah sensed the emotional attachment and desire for a relationship. He did not sense the plans and obligations from the logical part of her mind. He will need to be more attentive.

Ruth somehow drags Noah to his bed and rolls him onto his side so that he doesn't choke if his nose starts bleeding again. She then removes her shoes, pants, and shirt to climb into bed with him. She puts an arm around him and scoots up close.

Noah feels great comfort from Ruth's presence. He is also experiencing more as Ruth's near-naked body presses up against him. He feels stimulation, primitive urges, and an erection.

"Rest Noah, you have had quite a day. We can analyze all your experiences tomorrow. We will put you in a healing trance while you sleep tonight; you will feel fine tomorrow. You have learned many things about humans today. There are serious events heading our way; rest and recover now."

Chapter 12.

It consumes him

Professor Feingold sits at his desk in his home office staring at his computer screen. He is pouring through the work of his old friend, Arun Chandra. It is 2 AM, much past his usual bedtime; however, he cannot stop.

It has only been a short while since he received the hard drive copy of his old friend's last project. Upon accessing the collection of odd journal articles spanning multiple disciplines, incomplete mathematical derivations, and rough texts explaining conclusions, Professor Feingold is working essentially non-stop. This work clearly has paradigm-busting concepts. Conventional physics will be completely blown to pieces. Society will be changed forever as a new understanding of the universe and the reality of existence will be changed fundamentally.

His first reading of the work brought fear. The scope of the disruption to the long-held theories that defined his worldview is nearly too much to handle. A cold chill ran down his spine the first time he read his deceased colleague's full hypotheses, which suggested a complete revision of physics and reality. He understands how it all could have driven his friend to suicide. However, those disturbing initial thoughts were somehow swept away and replaced with an insatiable desire to finish the work.

Extraordinary claims demand extraordinary proof. He has been given the hypotheses and the beginnings of mathematical proof, but much more is needed to convince the physics world. Data from particle physics to astrophysics must be compiled and inserted into the new models with complete mathematics to prove these extraordinary claims about multidimensions, electromagnetism-produced portals, and the next generation of nuclear theory.

Professor Feingold is starting to make progress, but deep down, he hopes he has the ability to prove this to the world. He knows if he does, he will be bigger than Einstein. The multidimensional mathematics he needs seems staggering and too much for him, but somehow, he pushes himself forward. He hopes his new postdoc has the skills he lacks.

Professor Feingold is interrupted by his wife poking her head into his office.

"Isaac, it's past 2 AM. You need to go to bed; you can work on this stuff tomorrow. You hardly eat or sleep since you got that stupid thing from your friend. You look terrible. Come to bed and get some rest."

Professor Feingold looks up angrily and snaps back, "This project is too important for me to ignore. I am already making real progress. I will go to bed soon."

"I hope so. Don't get obsessed like your friend. Keep in mind that it killed him. Tell me you won't let it consume you."

"I told you I will go to bed soon. Now, let me finish this thing I am working on right now," says the professor curtly before turning back to his computer screen.

His wife scowls and heads back to bed.

Chapter 13.

Viera reports

Viera sits in the dim light of her office. She reviews all recent interactions with Noah because she must report the details of her efforts to the council. It has taken great effort to keep him calm after the extreme revelations she disclosed. She is encouraged that most of his angst stems from his need to know more about the true galaxy that has been kept from him and the people of Earth. She sensed no signs of emotional collapse that would be expected from most Homo Sapiens. This is further evidence that Homo Galaxus may be a sufficient improvement and worthy of an expanded future. She is pleased that the "Ruth initiative" is unaffected by the rushed disclosures.

Viera has been delaying the meeting requests from the council until she was satisfied that Noah was stable. Now that Noah is resting, it is time. She quickly leaves her office and goes to the top floor of the attached parking garage. She looks up and reaches out mentally. She senses a large, gleaming cylinder is suddenly hovering above her. A glowing cylinder of light surrounds her, swiftly lifting her into her familiar vessel.

She feels great comfort once back aboard her ship. Restoring her full psychic link with the vessel is soothing; it is an entity in its own right, and it welcomes Viera's contact. She commands the vessel to move out to a high Earth orbit. To further enhance her comfort, she walks down the long, gleaming hallway from the entryway foyer to her private quarters. She strips off her crude earth-made clothing to put on her tight-fitting bio-controlled jumpsuit; it is the most comfortable attire imaginable, manufactured by highly advanced technology many millennia beyond human achievement. She sits in a large high-back chair with full arm and leg supports. The chair has intricate metal-like mesh cushions that cradle Viera with a temperature-controlled softness. Now she is ready to engage the council.

Viera closes her eyes and reaches out to the council, and makes immediate contact.

"We have been anxious to communicate with you. We have been following Noah with you recently and agree with your conclusions concerning his status. We went deep into his psyche to find that he did not suspect his truly fundamental differences from the other humans. We may have blocked too much of his mentality, but that is irrelevant now. His Homo Galaxus disclosure was a terrible shock. It is too bad we must rush his full development, but several potential triggering events are pushing us to do so. We do not have enough hybrids in place to address all the emerging

triggering events. A new Dracon strategy must have begun. The Dracon ability to cloak themselves makes it imperative that we get our hybrids in place to detect and intervene as they can only be detected by direct contact at close distances. These events are quite troubling and definitely not fully controlled at this juncture."

"I understand completely. I feel we are losing control of human disclosures," affirms Viera.

"We must deliberate and decide our next steps with Noah. Time may be very short, as his professor may have mathematical proof of the hyper-dimensional universe. This material is surprising as it seemed to appear out of nowhere from a scientist we did not expect to be a problem. We believe the advanced mathematical derivations began in Russia and then reached Professor Chandra, a Western professor. That professor passed this on to Noah's professor just before supposedly taking his life. We discovered that our governmental allies killed him, and they believe there is a common link. They believe a postdoctoral student is transmitting this information. Upon closer investigation, we sense Dracon shielding in all of these people. That would explain why we did not see this sooner. Noah must get up close to this person to verify the Dracon connection. As best as we can discern from the minds of people surrounding the professor, the forbidden physics that he is on the verge of proving may include the ability for intergalactic travel, which is a definite triggering event. If Homo Sapiens have this ability, we will have no other option but to destroy Homo Sapiens civilization to keep their hostility and corruption from the galaxy. Noah is in a good position to discover the details and to stop this specific triggering event. It will be the best course of action versus an outside intervention by us, which would be severe and distasteful to many in the Confederation. Moreover, direct actions by the Earth Council could drive more support for the Dracons."

"Agreed, however, the council is blocking Noah's full telepathic abilities and access to galactic knowledge. He may need more of his powers to stop a motivated, Dracon-compromised human or perhaps another hybrid. He will also need basic galactic knowledge; otherwise, his drive to learn such things may become an obsession and a distraction from his missions. He may even bring on a triggering event himself due to frustration, which could lead to rebellious actions. Conversely, he is only on day two of his first disclosure. Too much, too fast, and too soon could be an issue for him. I have spent the entire day calming him. The alcohol consumption and Ruth's presence were fortunate distractions. The shock of full disclosure could cause mental and emotional instability."

Viera could only follow bits and pieces of the subsequent deliberation going on with the council. Even with her extraterrestrial composition, she lacks the intellect to keep up with the highly advanced and powerful council members. Their full pace of mentality is beyond her. Multiple images, ideas, and deliberations speed by like multiple movies playing simultaneously on the highest fast-forward setting.

"*Viera, we have decided. Noah will be granted 75% of his potential psychic abilities and will be implanted with an overview of galactic reality. You will need to fully explain the possible trigger events and consequences in more detail. He will have the higher levels of physics implanted, which are currently forbidden to humans, because he must stop any human who approaches such knowledge. To be effective, he must be able to recognize what he needs to stop. Tomorrow, you must help him understand his new knowledge and abilities. Are you prepared to assimilate our full details?*"

Viera opens her mind and receives the council's decisions. She also has a detailed list of orders and recommendations from them.

Chapter 14.

A step change

Noah awakens, surprised to find himself refreshed and energized. He senses a great change in himself. Ruth's nearly naked body is pressed against his with her arm draped across his chest. That sensation stirs feelings that bring a smile to his face.

As he opens his mind, he realizes he has new knowledge of the galaxy; it is as if dreams have become real. He feels like he has somehow become a totally different person overnight. He quickly reviews what was once unknown to him but has now been given to him overnight by Viera and others. Amazing planets with strange, highly intelligent beings flash through his mind. Extraordinary technologies, hyper-dimensional travel, and unbelievable glimpses of fantastic societies are seen. The Galactic Confederation looms over the Earth's future. He sees why humans are quarantined and why they are not civilized sufficiently for formal acknowledgement. He now knows with certainty that he really isn't one of them, a Homo Sapiens. However, he still has a great attachment to Homo Sapiens.

As he explores the newly implanted knowledge, it becomes clear to him that human ignorance is only exceeded by their arrogance. Ignorant, violent savages should never delude themselves into the belief that they are sophisticated and noble. He still loves his mother and does not want her harmed. He has a mission that could help avert a catastrophe on Earth; he will do whatever it takes to complete it. The consequences of a triggering event are horrifying, and he craves to learn more about triggering events. He remembers Viera told him that he must help prevent the Homo Sapiens species from gaining knowledge of higher physics. There must be more.

"Wake up Ruth and send her home to get ready for the day. I will give you further information. Be nice to her. I will give you further details for her also."

Noah rolls over and gently kisses Ruth on her cheek. She opens her eyes and smiles.

She kisses him on the lips and says, "Good morning. You look well, much better than I was expecting after last night. How do you feel?"

"I feel fantastic. I cannot thank you enough for caring for me last night. I overdid it a bit."

Ruth chuckles, "Now that I see you are okay, I can laugh about last night. You were really drunk. Jesse is just a filthy jerk. You need to keep him from dragging you down to his level."

Noah nods, "Yes, I need to be careful. However, I did learn a lot from going out last night. I never saw that side of life, you know, stuff outside of school and studying. I have been living such a sheltered life. Believe it or not, I have never been to a dance, gone on a date, or ever had a girlfriend. So tonight, I would like to start paying my debt to you. I recall you requested pizza. Will you go out for pizza with me?"

"Of course. That would be great. If you are nice, you might have your first girlfriend too."

Ruth kisses Noah again then hops out of bed. She hurriedly put on her clothes and heads for the door. She stops at the door, turns, and says, "Meet you down in the cafeteria in an hour?"

She smiles broadly as Noah nods in agreement.

Noah immediately reaches out after Ruth leaves. *"Viera, I think I am going to be in an odd situation tonight. I am not sure about human interactions of this type."*

"Relax and do not overthink it. Review the new implanted information and know that I will be available if you are having problems."

"I will do my best to stay calm and do my best."

Chapter 15.

Truth permanently changes presumed reality

Noah quickly cleans up and is ready to start the day. His mind is filled with incredible visions, and he wants to verify all of these amazing images and thoughts. He struggles to understand where it came from and if it is real. Viera reaches out to help him.

"Now that you are alone, you will find you have a great deal of new information to process. This is a gift from the Earth Council, a group of very advanced beings. I work for them, and they are working to civilize the Earth. You should be able to sense them, but their minds are far too advanced to follow their thoughts unless they intentionally slow them down for you. I am mostly human genetically, and that dulls my mentality so greatly that I cannot keep up with the full pace of their thoughts. It turns out that a certain level of Homo Sapiens DNA is needed to keep us hybrids looking human. We hybrids are essentially translators and diplomats for highly advanced extraterrestrials to human society. We have just enough mental power and psychic ability to allow rudimentary communication. You will see that our extraterrestrial directors will appear unlike any you have ever encountered. Reach out for them, they will stand out like a shining lighthouse in the turbulent sea of billions of simple humans."

Noah concentrates and reaches out. *"Yes, I think I see them. They are the sparkles in the drab light of humanity. If I try to focus on one of those sparkles, it is almost too much for me. I fear I cannot approach them too closely without being overcome. I am certain they noticed me and sent greetings. That was something else for sure. It felt like I was hit by a spotlight."*

"You can now start to appreciate the immensity of the galaxy filled with extraordinary beings. Humans are quite backwards in comparison. Yesterday, you asked why the extraterrestrials have not just landed at the White House and introduced themselves. You have just experienced your first contact, and it humbled you. I want to offer an analogy to illustrate how Homo Sapiens appear in relation to the galactic standard of an advanced, civilized being.

Consider humans and squirrels as an example. Humans are the most advanced creatures, as they now conceitedly believe. Humans are the greatest intelligence on Earth, especially when compared to squirrels living in the park. As the highly advanced humans drive their automobiles through the park and see the squirrels, what do they do? Humans do not stop, get out of their vehicles to establish communication with the park squirrels.

They pass on by with maybe a brief glance. Humans consider squirrels a lower form of life and are not motivated to develop relations with them. The squirrels may see the cars going by without any understanding of them or the humans in the cars, yet the squirrels consider themselves to be the masters of the park. The squirrels have their reality, but it is an illusion. Squirrels are subordinate to humans; humans see them as sub-creatures. Humans allow the squirrels to have their reality until they decide to impose their human intentions upon them. Some people might feed the squirrels from time to time or help keep the park lush and fertile to support the squirrels and other wildlife. Other humans may bulldoze the park to construct buildings and kill all of the squirrels. The squirrels exist only by the grace of the humans. Most humans are benevolent and moral; they support the existence of the park and the squirrels. On the galactic scale, humans are merely park squirrels in comparison to the extraordinary, advanced beings that travel through the galaxy."

Noah pauses as this idea sinks in, then admits, "*I get your point, there is no reason for extraterrestrials to try to make contact with humans, because humans are too primitive. There is no real reason to develop diplomatic relations.*"

"*That is correct; however, humans have now developed something that demands attention. Let me introduce the notion with an extension of the park squirrel analogy. Now, consider the scenario in which humans notice the squirrels are making firebombs. The firebombs could destroy the squirrels and burn the park into a charred wasteland. Also consider the consequences when humans notice squirrels starting to migrate outside the park with their firebombs. At that point, the humans would need to intervene. Humans developed nuclear weapons and a means to get them off the planet. Humans are now the galactic equivalent of park squirrels with firebombs. This is unacceptable.*"

Noah begins to get defensive and interrupts, "*So is that the moral of the story? The advanced beings of the galaxy view Homo Sapiens as lowly animals carrying firebombs. Humans do not realize that they are nothing more than irresponsible squirrels compared to the galactic civilizations. So, highly advanced extraterrestrials are threatened by humans with nuclear weapons?*"

Noah pauses while considering what he just said and the sobering conclusion of Viera's analogy. Of course, nuclear weapons in the hands of unpredictable beings should be problematic. The realization of this planet's extreme hubris and ignorance now becomes undeniable to Noah. Park squirrels with firebombs or humans with nuclear weapons would think that they are the kings of the world until the truly advanced beings easily wipe them out with their advanced technology. Would the squirrels realize their false arrogance and uncivilized nature before their deaths? Would humans? Probably not.

"*So are the triggering events you describe based upon this squirrels-with-firebombs and humans-with-nuclear bombs analogy?*"

"*Yes and no. The quarantine placed on humans to keep them from the rest of the galaxy is partially based on that concept. Homo Sapiens have developed dangerous high technology that is beyond their cultural and social achievements. Galactic Confederation interventions have prevented nuclear destruction of the Earth on more than one occasion. Triggering events that could disrupt the quarantine are the most critical items at this time. Secondarily, it is highly desirable for Homo Sapiens to evolve into a galactic-worthy civilization. Technological breakthroughs that threaten the quarantine or disclosures that could cause societal collapse must be prevented. That is your prime mission; you must help prevent humans from developing forbidden physics, a definite triggering event. The disclosure of extraterrestrial beings is also forbidden, but it is not your primary mission. Others are working in this area. Disclosure is not allowed because it has been observed that other developing planets have had their societal progress disrupted by such disclosure. Extraterrestrials and top-secret government organizations have worked for decades to prevent disclosure of the existence of extraterrestrial intelligent life. Homo Sapiens society would likely collapse upon disclosure, or sadly would need to be destroyed if galactic peace is threatened by irrational response to extraterrestrial existence. However, there are many who want the civilization of this planet to be by Earth-based-DNA beings; sadly, many others do not want it. There are both terrestrial and extraterrestrial forces working against us.*"

Noah furrows his brow as he considers her words, "*That certainly explains so much. It is logical and based upon sound reasoning from the vantage point of an advanced galactic union of peaceful civilizations. I also fully understand the threat coming from my professor. I am surprised that he has the intellect to prove the complicated mathematics of forbidden physics.*"

"*You are correct. He lacks sufficient ability, but he is most likely receiving help. His colleague, now dead, gave him the framework to prove an unauthorized breakthrough in physics. You need to distract or mislead him to stop his effort. You must figure out if he is getting help from others, especially if that help is from extraterrestrial sources. That would be a severe violation of galactic rules. There are rogue elements that could be clandestinely working to cause a triggering event. We suspect the new postdoctoral fellow joining your group is an agent for the Dracons. Be careful if you detect a telepathic influence. In the meantime, you need to explore your new implants of galactic knowledge. You will see the details of* the advanced physics forbidden to humans, so you know exactly what must be stopped."

"You mean that the Dracons are involved with my professor?"

"Yes, you are correct. You will receive the full story about the Dracons soon. I have more pressing things to discuss with you at this time."

Noah is led by Viera to quickly access the most critical aspects of this new knowledge. He is thoroughly amazed by it.

Viera senses his astonishment. "Yes, it will be quite a day of discovery for you to thoroughly go through this new knowledge. However, do not neglect the cultural part of your mission. We still want you to increase your interactions with your human friends. To aid you with both parts of your mission, you will find your telepathic abilities are much more potent. Your prior level was enough to influence humans mildly. You could make people like you; you can read their thoughts and emotions. You can direct humans to take simple actions like ignoring your real age shown on your driver's license. Yes, I saw what you did. You should now have much stronger and more dangerous powers. Slowly and carefully explore them; the consequences can be severe. You can now remove memories from humans, but if you go too far, you can completely wipe out all their memories, causing total amnesia. Likewise, you should be able to place strong commands into people's minds to force them to do things. You can tell people they are sleepy, and they will fall to the ground fully asleep. You can tell people they need to go home, and they will leave at once. That is the type of control you now have over humans. Be very careful because you can also kill people by stopping their breathing, constricting their heart into defibrillation, or other such biological interruptions. You need advanced training to master these new abilities, so be careful with your new powers. You will soon get advanced training. Do you understand?"

Noah finds this revelation quite shocking, yet he can fully sense these powers. "That is troubling. That means I am like a loaded gun with a hair trigger."

"That is true. As I have told you, great power requires greater responsibility. This may be enough for now. Reach out to me anytime if you have any issues. You now need to get ready to meet Ruth for breakfast. I want you to be good to her. Before you go, you need to know something about her that can be important going forward. Ruth was emotionally damaged by a past relationship when she was an undergraduate. She was a young, naïve sophomore who was preyed upon by an unscrupulous senior who was trying to engage in sexual congress with as many girls as possible before he graduated. He was tall and good-looking and knew how to trick girls into his bed. He would string them along until they became a problem. Ruth was one of his victims. She felt affirmation and prestige by being involved with a top-level man. She developed an unfounded emotional *connection. She did not realize that she was just being used for carnal pleasure and that there was no real relationship. She pushed for commitment, only to be unceremoniously dumped. This caused deep depression and emotional damage, which ruined her for future relationships. She set standards for future relationships based upon a top-level man; all other men became invisible to her. She grew bitter and gave up on men and romantic relationships. I went into her mind and helped heal her by dulling the memory of the incident and reducing the emotional damage. Otherwise, she had purged herself of any desire to engage in another relationship with a man. My therapy made it possible for you two to interact and become more than friends. You must be respectful and kind to Ruth. If you do, you will have a very good relationship. Keep in mind that Homo Sapiens lack the psychic connections that advanced beings have. They live alone, fully trapped inside their bodies. They try to truly connect through words and actions, but that is limited and frustrating. Without the psychic connection and its ability to detect lies, corruption is their constant disappointing reality. Do not trigger the collapse of the psychological repairs I have made. Do you understand?"*

Noah is somewhat confused because he has no experience with romantic relationships. *"I think I understand. I really like Ruth and enjoy spending time with her. I cannot begin to describe my feelings I have when we are kissing."*

"It sounds like you are on the right track. Keep exploring those feelings. Now go to her."

Chapter 16.

Confirmation

Noah makes it to the cafeteria for breakfast before Ruth arrives. He sits at an open long table, back towards the far windows. Ruth arrives with her tray and sits by his side, not across the table. They share pleasantries about how good each other looks, then switch to physics. Noah senses glowing feelings inside her. He dares not meddle with her thoughts, at least until he can understand his new abilities. He is not sure whether he can detect any of the emotional damage Viera mentioned and fears going deeper into her mind. He can sense the swirl of emotions and the delight of being paired with Noah. She reminds him of the pizza date he promised. After breakfast, Noah and Ruth walk together to the physics building. They arrive at the fishbowl looking very much like a romantic couple.

Upon hearing them walk into the fishbowl, Jesse sticks his head out of his tiny office and wryly says, "Oh my gawd, it's puppy love. Tell me it ain't so."

Ruth bristles, "Jesse, you can stuff your smartass comments. You got Noah drunk and sent him home alone, staggering. You are a filthy beast. It was a good thing that I was there to help. He fell and bloodied his nose, no thanks to you."

"Hey, I was just toughening him up. He needs to man up now that he is a big boy and living on his own. He needs to get out more to grow up. His momma ain't here, and he doesn't need you to mother him. Let the poor boy grow up, it's way past time."

"Oh, is that what you call your crude, perverted ways? You know what you need to do, you need to shove..."

Noah knows he must intervene. *"Ruth. Jesse. Stop this bickering and lose the anger. There is no ill intent. You two are friends. Apologize now."*

Both Ruth and Jesse freeze for an instant.

Jesse speaks first, "Hey Ruth. I'm sorry to upset you. I'll take better care of Noah next time."

Ruth responds calmly, "Jesse, sorry I got angry. I may have over-reacted."

Jesse smiles at her, "Friends?"

Ruth returns the smile, nods, and says cheerfully, "Friends."

Noah thinks to himself as they all head to their offices that Homo Sapiens do seem to let emotions overtake their thinking and actions far too easily. This is what Viera was trying to get me to understand.

Noah settles down in his office and starts up his computer to open a couple of journal articles to pretend to read. He is now thinking of his mission and just what Professor Feingold was doing. He reaches out and senses that PIF is already in his office down the hall at this early hour. That is very unusual; he is a middle-of-the-morning guy. His mental state is more troubling. He is clearly very agitated and manic. Again, this is not like him at all. Noah also senses an odd presence, like an unusual shadow engulfing the professor's psyche.

"Viera, what is going on with Professor Feingold? I have never sensed anything like it."

After a few moments, she responds, *"He is obviously under the influence of Dracon telepathy. We can be certain that its source is from those unfriendly to our cause. Be very careful and attentive. There may be adversaries nearby. Try to see what he is working on right now. Find out if he has forbidden physics in his current project. It may be difficult with the Dracon influence. I want you to go to his office and..."*

Noah waits until no one is in the fishbowl. He quickly heads toward the professor's office. He stops just outside the outer office and sends a strong command to his secretary: *"You must go to the grocery store right now and buy more coffee for the office."* In less than 60 seconds, out she goes with her purse in hand.

He enters the outer office and knocks on the professor's inner office door. "Professor, this is Noah. May I speak with you, please?"

"No, I'm busy. Go away and save your questions for the next group meeting," replies the professor in a rather terse manner.

Noah turns to Viera's advice. He concentrates on the professor's memories, searching through images. Since Noah's approach is an immediate memory, he can easily detect images of the last few minutes. Using some of his new abilities, he wipes the images away. He tries to install positive feelings but finds a dark resistance. Hoping for the best, he knocks again. "Professor, this is Noah. I need to speak with you?"

Noah gets the exact same response, "No, I'm busy. Go away and save your questions for the next group meeting."

Frustrated, Noah again reaches out to the professor's agitated mind and begins sending messages of exhaustion and sleep deprivation. Then he drops in a command to move to the couch in his office and take a nap. Noah keeps repeating the command until he hears the professor move from his desk. In less than a minute, Noah detects that Professor Feingold is in a deep sleep. Noah has no time to think about how handy these new powers are. He hustles into the office and shuts the door behind him. He sits at the desk and starts pouring through all the work, articles, data, and mathematics that the professor is working through. He recognizes key information and sees the mathematical progressions that are coalescing. The direction of this work is clear and undeniable; forbidden physics for Homo Sapiens is being developed. Space-time, electromagnetic fields, gravity, and the prohibited unknown realms are approaching a collision course and ultimate disclosure. Once these things are proven, there is no going back.

"Viera, do you see what I see?"

"Yes, this is what you are here to stop."

Chapter 17.

The Date

After his visit to Professor Feingold's office, Noah sits in his office looking at his computer screen. He is not working on his physics project, but he is really exploring his newfound abilities and astounding knowledge of the galaxy. He can only chuckle at the absurd notions that Homo Sapiens are alone in the universe and that they believe themselves to be the most advanced beings in all creation. He understands why extraterrestrials do not land and show themselves to the planet. The extreme Homo Sapiens arrogance in the belief that they are the pinnacle of existence is a dangerous folly. This prideful conviction is a global phenomenon, fully supported by potent emotions that perpetuate the denial. Perhaps without telepathic connections, Homo Sapiens fool themselves just as they tend to fool those around them. Modern human society is not prepared for the truth. There was a time when primitive man had the humility to coexist with the gods on Earth, but that situation eventually corrupted humanity. Certainly, the rapid destruction of their false beliefs and unchecked egotism would cause mass hysteria and societal collapse.

Ruth pops into Noah's office to disrupt his deep concentration, "Hey, are you going to sit there all night? Remember, you promised me a date tonight. I want pizza, good pizza, not the cheap stuff. Pack up your computer. I'll be back in five minutes, and we can walk back to the dorm."

Noah takes a moment to snap out of it, but recovers to look up and smile, "Of course. I have not forgotten. I'll be ready shortly."

In a couple of minutes, Ruth is back with her backpack slung over her shoulder. Noah is sitting, ready to go with his computer in his rucksack. However, he is beginning to realize that he may no longer need his clunky machine. He thinks he can now access more data telepathically than through his computer. He stands and walks over to her. Ruth wraps her arm around his arm, and they begin to leave.

Jesse, who had been listening to all of this, pokes his head from his office, "Hey, you kids have fun now. You two are so cute at this age. Make sure you are home before curfew." He laughs loudly.

Ruth turns her head back and says, "Oh, you're such a comedian. Just remember, jealousy is a stinky cologne. Have fun playing with your keyboard tonight."

Noah is fascinated and confused by the symphony of emotions roiling in Ruth. She is definitely feeling pride in making her relationship with Noah known. Noah's mutual feelings also bring her a certain joy from the affirmation. There are deeper sensations rising that are more primal. He begins to question if he is acting appropriately; he wonders if he is doing the right thing. Maybe he is now acting like an emotional Homo Sapiens. He knows cognition should come before emotion for himself and apparently all advanced beings. Then suddenly Viera ends his confusion.

"Noah, you are doing the right thing, so do not overanalyze. You need this interaction for your development. This is positive for both you and her. Follow her thoughts and act accordingly. At some point, you may need to stop thinking and act on impulse and instinct. Relax and experience your human side."

Noah and Ruth walk back to the dormitory hand in hand.

Back at the dorm, Noah puts on a nice shirt and hustles to Ruth's door to pick her up. They walk to his car holding hands again. Noah senses her thoughts and opens the car door for her. He drives to a nice Italian place with a wood-fired pizza oven, not far from campus. He gets a chuckle from Ruth when he makes a deal with her; she can choose the pizza toppings if she lets him have a beer. She also has beer. The dinner goes well as they chat and gossip about their fellow physics students and all the quirky professors.

They arrive back at the dorm, and Noah escorts Ruth back to her dorm room. She opens the door and turns to Noah. She reaches out to him and gives him a passionate kiss. She pulls him into her room, and Noah senses her deep feelings, wondering what he is supposed to do now. He knows Viera told him there is a point where he must stop deliberating. Then, he gets a reminder.

"Go. Do not overthink this. Do it all; it will come to you naturally. You know what she wants."

She kicks the door shut and pushes him up against the wall as they embrace and continue kissing. As their passion builds, she pulls back. She gives him a look he has never seen before, then takes him by the hand to lead him to her bed. She sits him down on the bed and pulls his shirt off over his head. Ruth takes off her shirt and bra. Noah feels his emotions overtaking his thinking, but senses exactly what Ruth is thinking. It is primal and instinctual. He reinforces her strong emotions with feelings of love, trust, and affirmation. He starts undressing, but she is naked before he gets his belt undone. The sight of her naked body sends his mind into a primitive state. She helps him remove the last of his clothing. They begin writhing in a passionate embrace. Her emotions nearly overpower him, but Noah is still able to sense what she is expecting. He hopes the feelings he is transmitting are appropriate and effective. His mind seems to blur upon penetration; he will never forget this feeling. Upon his subsequent orgasm, his cognitive mind is stalled by the event, but only temporarily. Later that evening, he finds that the third time is much easier than the first, just like his first time drinking beer.

Chapter 18.

A sturdy house cannot be built upon a weak foundation

Noah wakes to find Ruth beside him and feels it is quite wonderful to have her with him. He trusts Viera, who assured him that he is doing the right thing. He is still trying to process last night as these situations are very new to him. He finds it hard to accept that humans must go through such situations alone. He does not believe he could have done it without Viera's guidance. Maybe it is all easier if you let your emotions guide you without thinking.

"Kiss her, say something nice to her, then get to your room. Tell her you have an errand and will meet up with her at the physics building."

Noah follows Viera's orders and is back in his dorm room promptly.

"What did your first intimate human experience teach you about humans?"

"Humans are tricky, subtleties and assumptions rule their world. At first, I tried to decide the correct and proper course of action. I was locked into an internal debate about what I should do. Fortunately, I knew what Ruth wanted and expected. However, your advice was the critical boost I needed to get started and to follow through with the proper actions."

"Your answer is so very clinical and analytical. That is truly Homo Galaxus behavior. Now, try to imagine what it would be like if you couldn't read her thoughts or get advice from me. You would be consumed by doubt and worry as you tried to read verbal and physical cues. Perhaps that is why humans give up on rational thoughts and yield so easily to emotional drives. It simplifies the process but adds great potential consequences. Because humans cannot read minds and can lie easily, all Homo Sapiens relationships are tainted by doubt compared to telepathic species."

Noah stops to ponder. *"Yes, that makes perfect sense. I suppose I have an unfair advantage, since I knew what she was thinking at that moment. I knew she was acting legitimately and not tricking me. I cannot imagine being in a relationship without that ability. Emotions coupled with hormonal drives are so powerful; I see how they can lead to bad consequences due to deceptions and trust issues."*

"Yes, now you are gaining a deeper understanding of Homo Sapiens. Your new experience with Ruth is just a small example. Humans depend far too much on their feelings and, subsequently, much less on their reasoning. Taking action without thoughtful deliberation tends to produce bad outcomes. Thoughtful evaluation and analysis are pushed aside by Homo Sapiens predilection for emotional drivers. Bad decisions are made when

emotions dominate the thought process. This is true for every aspect of life, not just intimate relationships."

Noah sighs and says, *"I am beginning to understand why you wanted me to interact with humans in order understand them better. Their actions and habits are fundamentally different and inconsistent."*

"You said you could not imagine being in a relationship without the psychic ability to know what the other person was thinking. You need to realize humans form all their relationships without telepathy. Also, realize that they cannot detect lies either, which increases the difficulties. Do you see the difference between telepathic and non-telepathic relationships?"

"I see where you are leading me. Telepathic people can form strong, open, and honest relationships because their motivations are clear, and lying is not possible. Non-telepathic people, like Homo Sapiens, form relationships that are always clouded by doubt. They never know what others are really thinking and must build trust slowly through their actions over time. It seems so unstable, especially when emotional drivers can suddenly appear and change minds on a whim."

Viera smiles and nods, recognizing that Noah is learning. She then asks, *"Now tell me what consequences unreliable human relationships generate for society at large."*

"I'm confused. I do not see why emotional bonding habits would be a very serious issue for Homo Sapiens society. What am I missing?" asks Noah.

"The ability to form strong, honest relationships is the foundation of all advanced societies. A civilization is created by the sum of the individuals and their actions. People must form strong relationships in which they subordinate their selfish interests to prioritize the union's mutual success. This demonstrates the acceptance of responsibility for the success of the relationship above the individual's self-interests. A male and female pair must do this to become a successful married couple. A married couple must accept responsibility and subordinate their selfish interests when they have children to build a successful family. Families then form communities that must come together to form societies, governments, and nations. The individual is the foundation of society, and the ability to form strong relationships is the glue holding it all together."

Noah nods, *"I think I understand. If a person is too selfish or corrupt, they can form only defective relationships; strong societies cannot be built on such foundations. This is a difficult concept for me because I cannot imagine dealing with people without being able to read their thoughts. It seems impracticable."*

"Yes, that is the point. Deceitful, unreliable people can only form defective relationships. This failure cannot be the basis of a stable, civilized society. Advanced societies have a complex matrix of interdependent relationships that require a high level of cooperation. Anything built upon

a weak foundation will eventually collapse. As Homo Sapiens civilizations grow and prosper, they reach a point where their weak ability to form honest, effective working relationships starts bringing down all systems. We expect your Homo Galaxus society will not have this limitation."

"It is sad that humans have this inherent limitation. I suppose that a world filled with lies and deceptions should be expected to fail," says Noah somberly.

"Exactly. That is why Homo Galaxus must replace Homo Sapiens. Now, you need to get back to your mission. I want you to go to your office and try to earn your professor's confidence. Also, check with Jesse and see what he knows."

Chapter 19.

He thinks he knows

Noah walks to the physics building alone this morning. He checks into Ruth's mental state and finds a lovely glow, but with a dash of unease. She is nervous because she doesn't know what he is thinking about her after what happened last night. Viera correctly predicted this. Noah acknowledges that the solitary existence of humans is very stressful and triggers bad situations. He sends reassurance and warm, pleasant thoughts to her. It seems to help.

Next, he tries to get to Professor Feingold. The cold, dark aura still surrounds him, perhaps more so today. Noah does not think he can penetrate the dark force shielding the professor. He sees the high anxiety and mania driving the poor man toward collapse.

Noah approaches the physics building and begins receiving a message from an unknown human source. He hears his name being repeated over and over. He begins seeking out the sender and detects the mind calling to him; he accesses the periphery of their psyche. He can see what they see, directly viewing through their eyes. He can see himself being watched from across the street. Two men are looking directly at Noah from a white van parked on the street. Noah stops and turns to look straight at them.

A message from Viera breaks his stare, "*Ignore them now. I will check them out and let you know what you should do.*"

Noah quickly enters the physics building. As he arrives at the fishbowl, he gets more advice from Viera and readily obliges. He goes directly to Ruth's office and gives her a warm greeting. She smiles and gets up from her chair to give Noah a kiss and a big hug. He knows she feels much better now, and her fear fades away.

The rest of the morning is very quiet. Noah and Ruth have lunch in the conference room as usual. Jesse joins later but sits at the far end of the table. He doesn't talk very much, which is unusual for him. Noah cannot help but notice that Jesse is staring at him through most of lunch.

About an hour later, as Noah is back at his computer, he receives a text from Jesse. "Come down to the mech lab, I need to talk to you." Noah senses confusion and unease in Jesse but hesitates to dig deeper into his mind. He leaves his office and heads to the mech lab. It's a large workshop filled with all kinds of tools and machining equipment. It is the place where the experimental physicists build their testing equipment. Noah enters the room and sees Jesse at the far end, next to a large table saw. Jesse turns on the saw when he sees Noah and waves to him.

Noah walks over to Jesse. The whizzing sound of the saw is quite loud when standing next to it.

Jesse leans in close to Noah, "Noah, you know that I am your pal. I just wanted to talk with you one-on-one because there are a lot of things going on right now. So, you and Ruth. It's obvious that you two are a thing now. I just want you to be careful, women can fuck you up. Don't trust them; always keep your wits about you. Deceptive women have ruined many a man. So, I want you to know that you can come to me and talk if you ever need an ear. You seem so young and naïve, so I don't want you to get hurt. I'll help you any way I can."

"Jesse, I appreciate what you are telling me. It is good to know that you are a friend who is ready to help me. It is true that I never lived on my own before coming here and may need extra help. I did have a very good time going out for beers with you. I look forward to doing that again. Also, I have never had a girlfriend before, as you probably guessed. As far as Ruth is concerned, she has been extremely nice to me and genuinely cares about me. We both are feeling that way towards each other."

"Okay, I can believe that. Just keep in mind, women can turn on you in an instant. I say that because I know a guy who is a postdoc at Ruth's undergraduate school. He knows her and has troubling things to say about her. He said that she is a real man-hating, bitchy boss babe. She looks out for herself and no one else. She loathes men and never, ever dated anybody. That does not sound anything like the Ruth we have here. She starts grad school here with you, and she has been rather pleasant for a bitter, man-hating uber-feminist. Now she has started a lovey-dovey relationship with you. It's a bit mysterious."

Noah is starting to feel uneasy vibes from Jesse. "Well, people can change, I suppose."

Jesse continues, "There are other unusual changes around here since you arrived. PIF and I regularly got into a lot of nasty exchanges in group meetings. We would go back and forth with lengthy arguments filled with angry insults. At the last meeting, we barely got started arguing and insulting each other when we suddenly stopped and apologized. That seemed weird to me. It is like you are changing all the people around you."

Noah tries to deflect where this conversation is going, "It's just a coincidence. Nothing stays the same forever."

Jesse presses on, "I wasn't going to ask you this directly, but here it goes. You know I have worked for many summers at top-secret operations for some of the biggest tech aerospace companies. I have a security clearance. I have seen freaky shit and heard about a great deal more. I look at you and see what your presence does to people. I have to ask. What planet are you from? Seriously, you are not just a super smart kid, you are something else."

Noah tries to laugh it off. "Jesse, I was born about 100 miles from here. You can call my mother and ask her yourself if that would satisfy you."

"No, that won't do it. There is something about you. You seem to be in our heads. We all seem to have new influences. There's something going on with you. I have been told that extraterrestrials exist and that they all have telepathic abilities. They walk among us. Now I will deny I said this if you tell anyone I did. You may have been born here, but you are not an earthling like the rest of us. I can't really prove this, but I would sure bet a lot of money on it."

Noah knows he must stop Jesse from going any further. He freezes him and his thoughts. He wipes the thoughts of his extraterrestrial connections from Jesse's mind. He leaves the parts of the discussion about Ruth. He implants the thought that Noah is just an unusual genius kid from Earth, and nothing more. When satisfied, he unfreezes Jesse.

"Jesse, thanks for the advice about women. I definitely will come to you if things get weird with Ruth and me. You are a good friend. I think we should get back to work."

It takes Jesse a moment to collect himself and reply, "Good, you just come see old Jesse if Ruth or any other woman starts giving you trouble. We can go have a beer and talk about it."

Noah and Jesse return to their offices.

Jesse sits down at his computer, feeling a little disoriented. He looks down and sees a note that he obviously wrote to himself. It starts with the date and time, then says, "If you don't remember you wrote this, your mind has been invaded and memories erased. You are going to ask Noah if he is an extraterrestrial. If he is, you won't remember writing this."

Chapter 20.

We are on the same side

Noah awakens to a second morning sharing a bed with Ruth. He can feel her growing emotional attachment, and he knows Viera assures him he is proceeding correctly. Rational thoughts and emotions are aligned, and Noah feels really, really good in this relationship. He wonders why so many guys don't have girlfriends. He wishes he had a girlfriend sooner, if that would have been the right thing to do.

"The two men who were surveilling you will be back. They are from a clandestine government agency. They are allies, I have confirmed this with certainty. Before going to work, speak with them. They may be useful and able to support your mission."

Noah puts thoughts into Ruth, motivating her to want to get to her office early. It is just a little anxiety and scholastic guilt implanting that drives her to feel the need to catch up on her research. She hustles to get an early start to the physics building.

Noah takes his time getting ready. He scans the area, waiting to detect the same voices he heard yesterday. While leisurely finishing his breakfast, he senses that they are back in the parking lot across the street. Noah sighs and admits to himself that he is a bit nervous about this interaction. He knows Viera has never steered him astray. He hears them chanting his name once again.

Noah walks out of the front door of his dormitory and stops. He stares directly at the white van across the street. He raises his hand while continuing to look at the two men in the van. The mental chanting stops. As Noah walks toward the van, he reaches out to them with peaceful intent and says he wants to talk. Noah cautiously approaches the passenger-side window and sees two men in dark suits.

Curt is sitting in the passenger seat and rolls down the window. "Hello, Noah. I am Curt, and this is my colleague, J.T. I think it is time we have a talk, but you probably know that already. We have no ill intent, but you can also tell that. Would you come inside the van and chat with us, or would you like to meet elsewhere?"

Noah calmly replies, "The van is fine. Let's talk here."

Curt opens the van door and steps out. He extends his hand; Noah returns the gesture and shakes his hand. Curt then walks over to the side door of the van and slides it open. Inside are two stools surrounded by computer screens and piles of electronic devices. J.T. stays in the driver's seat. Noah enters the van and sits down; Curt follows and slams the side door shut

Curt turns to Noah, "We are fairly certain that you are not a normal human and likely have off-world connections. If we are correct about that, you should have a high level of advanced telepathic powers. You could make us think, believe, or do anything you wish. Moreover, you would be able to read our minds and know when we tell you the truth or lie."

Noah only nods.

Curt continues, "Very good. With that in mind, I am going to tell you everything. J.T. and I are government agents. We work for a secret agency buried deep inside the intelligence community. Our mission is to suppress the disclosure of the existence of extraterrestrial beings and associated prohibited technology. Our agency was formed shortly after World War II. Contact was made secretly by extraterrestrials with the highest level of our military; treaties were signed with both Presidents Truman and Eisenhower. The same sort of thing happened in Russia also. These agreements were not really treaties. They were our marching orders from the extraterrestrials. If we wanted our species to survive, we had to prevent any disclosure of extraterrestrial existence. Disclosure is not a decision for humans to make; it is controlled by extraterrestrials. Also, we were given a list of advanced physics and technologies that human society was forbidden to possess. It is that simple, do this or be destroyed."

Noah interrupts, "Yes, I understand. Any triggering event must be prevented. I have the same mission. We are on the same side."

"Very good. Let me tell you why we are at this university. We have been following a dangerous person who is trying to expose forbidden physics by using well-known professors to disclose it. This being goes by the name Ulak Tazarachabayev. He was operating in Russia, but our Russian counterparts were on to him. This triggered the assassination of two physics professors. The Russians were ready to go to outrageous means to stop Ulak. They were considering swarms of self-directing killer drones or blowing up entire buildings with mass casualties. We think Ulak sensed their plans and disappeared. He showed up in Canada with Professor Chandra. We sent in two top-notch assassins, and he or someone protecting him killed them easily. We don't know how many were lost in Russia. Now we know he will soon be in Professor Feingold's group, where you work. We tried to stop his visa application but could not. He is a very dangerous creature. Right now, I have no idea how we are going to stop him. It is encouraging to have someone like you here on the same mission."

"I have not seen Ulak yet. The professor told us he will be here soon. I believe Ulak has already passed on forbidden information. Also, Professor

Feingold is acting oddly. He is in an agitated manic state, working long hours, quite out of his normal behavior."

Curt interrupts, "That is good information. Ulak has powerful telepathic abilities. Presumably, you do as well. As mere humans, we cannot lie to you, but you could be fooling us. You could probably wipe this meeting from our memory and convince us you are just a normal kid. Would you be willing to do something for us to prove we are on the same side?"

"Yes, yes, I would, within reason. What would you like me to do?"

"Would you install some tiny cameras and listening devices at the physics building so we could monitor both the professor and Ulak?"

Noah smiles and nods, "I would do that for you. I could start today."

Curt pulls out several electronic devices and explains where and how they should be placed. He puts them in a brown paper bag and gives them to Noah. He then says with a very serious tone, "We will move to a safe location. Now that you have met us, you should be able to find us when you need us. Listen for us, we will call out if we need you. If we cannot find a way to stop Ulak, your professor must be terminated, but that will only delay their operation. Extreme actions are always an option, but no one would like that. Ideally, we take out Ulak and stop him for good. We do not know how we can reasonably do that, but with your help, there may be a way. Let us continue to communicate and work together for mutual benefit. Do you agree?"

Noah does not hesitate, "Yes, let's work together on this. There is something blocking me from getting into the professor's mind. I presume it is Ulak's presence. I will know more when he arrives. I will keep you informed as the situation changes."

With that, Curt and Noah shake hands again. Noah leaves the van with a brown paper bag of electronics and a heightened sense of apprehension as he walks toward the physics building.

Chapter 21.

That is wonderful

Noah struggles at his computer, trying to focus on his research project. He now knows that the entire premise of his project is a waste. Knowledge of the true future of physics makes the current ruse of contemporary physics nothing more than folly. He has learned the secrets of advanced physics. He can see the breakthroughs that need to be made, but he also knows they are forbidden to Homo Sapiens. He accepts that it is his mission to keep humans from acquiring more advanced knowledge, and that important purpose helps him deal with his sham research project. It is in this melancholy haze that he realizes he has not told his mother about Ruth. The thought lifts his spirits, and he dashes out of his office to find a quiet place to make a call. He heads down to the third floor, where the classrooms are found; they will be empty because the next semester is weeks away.

Noah calls his mother, hoping she is not too busy at work. He doesn't want to wait until tonight. He is a little nervous as the phone rings.

"Hello, Noah. I am glad you called. Is everything alright?"

"I am fine. I have some news for you. I have a girlfriend. Her name is Ruth, and she is a physics graduate student who also started graduate school this year. We were in the same classes and became good friends. I finally had my first date. I know you have worried about me having a normal life with social skills, friends, and relationships."

"That is wonderful. You sound happy. I have been worried that you were devoted only to physics and would never have anyone to share your personal life with. I know your father will be relieved to hear this, too. I'm glad she is a physicist; you need to have that in common. This is your first girlfriend, so let me give you a bit of motherly advice. Treat her nicely, but don't get obsessed with your relationship. Many people have been led astray by romance and had a bad time of it. Enjoy it, but do not let it overtake you to distract you from your goals."

"Yes, Mother, I am aware of the dangers when someone follows their emotions without due regard for their rational side. You need not worry about me on that account. I also have Viera, who keeps me on the straight and narrow. I was already overthinking Ruth from the start. I had to stop thinking before I could move forward and start a relationship. I do appreciate your sound advice. Don't worry, I will not give up physics or the other duties that drive me. I made sure I was being rational up front, then I allowed my emotions to fill in."

"I am relieved to know you haven't lost your head. Nowadays, I see young people come in with terrible problems. Young women are lost to promiscuity and have serious emotional issues. Also, a lot of young girls need treatment for nasty, socially transmitted diseases, not to mention all the out-of-wedlock pregnancies. It's not just the girls who are struggling; we get young men who are pale, depressed, and overweight. They have a variety of health issues from living in their parents' basement, playing video games all day and night. It just seems like too many of today's kids are lost in the chaos of the times. I am so happy to hear that you are doing so well living on your own at school. Are you still enjoying graduate school?"

"There is an unbelievable number of incredible things going on here besides getting a girlfriend. It is all vitally important. I cannot really give you details about them."

"That's okay, dear, I wouldn't understand them anyway. By the way, I had government agents stop by and ask questions about you for a security background check. I hope I didn't cause you any problems."

"You did fine. I think I know these agents. Mom, let me ask you one last thing before I let you get back to work. When you met father, was it an emotional transaction only or did you rationally decide that it was a correct decision?"

"Oh, Noah, you are such a scientist. Back when I was young, it was different than today. In those times, people would meet, and if there was a mutual attraction, the romance would take off quickly. Like with your father and I, we were young and didn't have much when we met. We certainly did have sparks flying. Once each of us was satisfied that the other had good character and was trustworthy, we got engaged and married shortly after. It was a much quicker process than today's, because we didn't need gap years to travel abroad to find ourselves and the like. To answer your question, I suppose that the attraction was certainly emotional. The rational part was learning that each other was a good, respectable person. We had to convince your grandfather that your father was worthy enough for me. After that hurdle, our emotions were strong enough to push us to get married as quickly as we could. People were expected to marry young, as long as they could take care of each other. There was a much stronger sense of duty and respect for vows back then. You always make me think. Does that answer your question?"

"Yes, thank you. I never thought much about the emotional aspects of life. You cannot do physics properly and be emotional. It's too bad that most people are emotionally driven and never stop to think rationally."

"Well, dear, I suppose you are right. People usually follow their heart or trust their emotions to guide them. That can cause big problems sometimes."

"Mother, you have no idea how big those problems are." Noah also thinks about how she would not be able to believe all the things he now knows.

"Mother, I have not really thanked you properly for all the things you have done for me. You never gave up on me when I was young and struggling. You watched out for me and always tried to make the best decisions for me. I just want you to know that I really appreciated everything you have done. I am going to do all I can to keep you happy."

"Noah, you are welcome. You have made me so proud of you. Your mother is doing fine; you don't need to worry about me. Now, take care of yourself and stay out of trouble. Maybe we can visit you soon and meet your girlfriend. Call us next week, your father will be back from his latest long haul."

"Okay, thanks, Mom. I love you."

"I love you too, sweetie. Bye-bye."

Noah stands there after the call. His mother is so nice and kind. Why can't more humans be like her? If they were, maybe Homo Sapiens could develop higher societies. It could be that nice people are too nice. That is why the wicked always win in the long run. Noah sighs while feeling sadness for humans.

Chapter 22. Jesse prods again

Calm times can be the most anxious when severe conflicts are looming. Knowing that a single event can change the world forever creates dark stress that looms over everything. Noah easily plants the surveillance cameras around the professor's office and his office areas, including the fishbowl. His task is simplified when you can send people out of the room with your thoughts. He regularly stops by a camera to tell Curt there is no change. There is still the dark barrier around the professor, who is clearly being driven to the point of collapse. Does this mean that Ulak is nearby? The big unknown is Ulak, the mysterious postdoc. Noah awaits his arrival with apprehension and curiosity. Viera has relayed her concerns and those of the council because they cannot track down Ulak either. Dracons are the masters at camouflage.

Noah has been finding comfort these days through his relationship with Ruth. They spend most of their time with each other, including every night in bed together. Today, however, Ruth is spending the day with the astrophysicists to hear about new breaking data that may be relevant to her research project. Noah pretends to work on his project in his office.

Jesse pops into Noah's office, interrupting the solitude, "Hey buddy, got a minute?"

"Of course, come on in and pull up a chair." Noah still likes Jesse quite a bit and misses his flippant comments since Ruth has been monopolizing his time. He hopes that he did not wipe the memory of their friendship from his mind after their last conversation.

"So, you and Ruth. Congrats man. I am happy for you. I think you look much more confident now. You are definitely a changed person, much more confident and self-assured. As difficult as it is for me to believe that a girl can make you a better person, it seems to have worked for you. However, you may have broken the hearts of several guys around here by taking Ruth off the market. They had their eyes on her, but clearly, she only has eyes for you. Good going."

Noah is a bit flustered and unsure how to respond. He quickly reaches out for Viera and gets the needed suggestions. "Thank you, Jesse. I really didn't plan to get a girlfriend. We became friends during the first semester, when I occasionally helped her with her coursework. Suddenly, we just clicked."

"Well, you just never know when dealing with females, good and bad surprises all the time. Hey, I really came down here to talk about physics, but I did want to applaud you on your romantic success, you dog. It doesn't happen that often for us physics nerds."

Noah grows uneasy thinking about their last conversation. "What's your physics question?"

"I know you are smarter than the entire faculty in this department. You know that I think they are just blowhards, wasting everybody's time. I want to see real progress for a change. It seems to me that everybody has it wrong about gravity. Einstein's General Relativity is great, but it is clearly missing something. Also, the Quantum Mechanics dudes seem to raise more questions whenever they think they learn something new. Oh, it's a wave; no, it's a particle. It seems too convenient. Then there is String Theory. They just add another unprovable dimension or something absurdly complicated whenever their mathematics gets bogged down. Noah, I bet you have real insight. What do you think?"

Noah knows that he must be careful now that he has been implanted with the knowledge of forbidden physics; he is supposed to prevent its proliferation.

"I think General Relativity and the overall application of space-time concepts were major achievements of the modern era. So much of the workings of the Universe can be appropriately explained. I am keeping an open mind, as we may have measurement issues. Scientists have only partial data on the Universe; they assume the rest. Each new advancement in measurements pokes significant holes in many accepted assumptions. Ruth is with a group of astrophysicists today to hear about unpublished new data; I'm sure there will be surprises. No one should be shocked that we have incomplete theories because they are based on incomplete data."

"Okay, that is reasonable. So, you don't believe in dark matter or dark energy?"

"I am skeptical, but again I am keeping an open mind. Things that cannot be measured are being proposed because it makes their mathematics work. I could easily believe that dark matter and dark energy are fudge factors, a needed correction for poor assumptions and incomplete data. I am waiting for the experiments that definitely prove the existence of such concepts."

Jesse makes a face, "Alrighty then, you must be in the camp of those pushing conditional gravity. You know, gravity is not constant throughout the Universe; it depends on the surroundings."

"You are making my point for me. The assumption of constant gravity throughout the Universe is being challenged by radical new data. Even the Big Bang Theory is getting questioned."

"Maybe the Universe cannot be described without invoking multiple dimensions? String Theory could be on the right track."

Noah knows he must be careful now. "Yes, there are several positives introduced by String Theory, but its math becomes problematic all too often. The other problem is the inability to experimentally test most of the theory. The majority of the top people in physics are working on String Theory, so they have a good chance to refine the area." Noah strains to keep a straight face, knowing that so much current work is a distraction, heading in the wrong direction on alternative dimensions and the true nature of electromagnetic fields and matter.

"Noah, you are being so diplomatic. Cut the shit. You haven't told me anything. You say mildly positive things about every theory and say we can figure this out. Good men doing good work, blah, blah, blah. You know more than you are letting on. As a matter of fact, I think you know a great deal more about a lot of things. You aren't a normal human at all. I know you are something else. You are an extraterrestrial, or a hybrid being created to infiltrate our society. Don't worry, I am not going to turn you in to the Feds. I just want to know a few of the secrets of the Universe. Just tell your pal something, you don't need to erase my memory again."

This startles Noah. He pauses, waiting for more advice.

Jesse pounces on his pause. "Boom. You just answered me. Noah, you obviously never played poker. Your pregnant pause tells me that I have a winning hand."

Jesse receives a clear message.

"Go ahead and tell him, then ridicule what you told him."

"Jesse, you are a smart guy. You have figured it out. I am an alien hybrid working for extraterrestrials, trying to keep you Homo Sapiens from destroying one another. Your physics theories lack a great deal, but that extra knowledge would only bring about your destruction. Your backward species is not sufficiently advanced socially, culturally, and individually. My mission here on Earth is to prevent the development of knowledge that will lead to the self-destruction of you and your planet. You must be patient until all on Earth has advanced sufficiently to achieve full civilization."

"I knew it. You are just too smart, and your presence seems to change everyone. Look, I am well-connected to the leading aerospace companies. If you help me bring them valuable new concepts, we can both become filthy rich. We could write our own ticket, mansions, yachts, Lamborghinis, and money galore. Come on, let's get out of this crummy university and get rich and powerful."

Noah laughs, "Jesse, I can't believe you bought that story. I was joking. My cynical comments sound more like the plot of a second-rate sci-fi movie." Noah sends a blast of extreme doubt into Jesse.

Jesse freezes as the wave of doubt washes over him. "Well, maybe I got carried away a bit. You are an extraordinary genius, so if you have a breakthrough, I can get it to the right people, and we can get rich. Keep that in mind."

"Okay, Jesse. I will let you know."

Jesse leaves Noah's office meekly, filled with doubt.

Chapter 23.

Ulak

It's Friday afternoon. Noah, Ruth, and the rest of the group wait patiently at the fishbowl conference table to see if PIF will have his group meeting or cancel it once again. Ruth sits close to Noah; she oozes prestige while flaunting her relationship with the brightest star in the physics department. Jesse sits uncharacteristically silent at the far side of the table. Noah is uneasy; he is sensing a growing dark aura, the same one surrounding Professor Feingold.

PIF is fifteen minutes late, and the group is about ready to give up on the meeting. Fifteen minutes is the long-standing time allowed to professors when they are late to a class. Just then, Tim, the senior postdoc of the group, pulls out his phone; after a quick glance, he announces that Professor Feingold is running late and will be here in ten or fifteen minutes.

Jesse sardonically responds, "Great, our prima donna research advisor is cutting into my beer drinking time. It's frigging Friday afternoon. Man, he is losing it. I think he is falling apart and should get therapy."

Ruth tries to inject a little sympathy, "Maybe he is just suffering from the loss of his good friend and that sudden shock. I don't think any of us have been very supportive."

Jesse counters, "Maybe so, but have you seen him recently? He looks like he is living on the street. He's a mess. I think he has had a serious breakdown. He needs professional care and time in a loony bin. He is not right in the head."

Noah jumps into the conversation before things get heated between Ruth and Jesse, "There is certainly something afflicting the professor. It seems he has been overtaken by an outside force, very dark in nature. I believe Jesse is correct; it is well beyond our ability to help him. I hope he gets real help before something very bad happens. Hopefully, his wife or the department chairman has noticed and is working on it. Perhaps the work he has picked up from Professor Chandra is so shocking that it drives people insane. It may have killed him, and now the same is happening to our professor."

Noah's statement halts the conversation, leaving everyone in the room stunned by the idea. Scientists are very good at detecting trends and analyzing data. The logical deduction from this data at hand for Professor Feingold is clear and disturbing. The entire group sits in silence.

After a seemingly long period of silence, Professor Feingold walks into the room. He does look as ragged as described. His hair and beard are unkempt, and he has obviously lost weight. The dark bags under his eyes suggest he is sleep-deprived. Just as the shock of his condition begins to sink in, a large man follows the professor into the room. He is easily six and a half feet tall, with a large barrel chest. He has dark eyes and a stern expression partially obscured by a long beard, yet his hair is neatly clipped in a short crew cut. The two stand at the front of the room.

"I am sorry to be late, but I had to pick up my new postdoc from the airport. He is staying with me for now. This is Ulak. He comes to us from Professor Chandra's group. He and I will be completing Professor Chandra's final project. It will be quite an accomplishment, as you will hopefully see soon. Ulak, please introduce yourself to the group."

Ulak looks over the group from one side to the other and starts speaking with a heavy Russian accent, "Hello, I am Ulak. I am from central Asia, a remote spot that you have never heard of. I was educated at Novosibirsk, Russia. There are many good physicists there because that was a major research center for the Soviet Union. Several other breakthroughs in physics are starting there. Professor Chandra was working on such a project, which is how I came to work for him. Now that work will continue here."

Noah feels a chill go down his spine as Ulak speaks. He reaches out to Viera, and she warns him to be careful.

Professor Feingold asks the group to introduce themselves.

By the time it was Noah's turn, he could barely speak. His head is spinning, and he is having trouble breathing. He can only say, "I'm Noah, first-year graduate student."

As Noah looks into Ulak's dark eyes, he feels a sharp pain in his chest and slumps forward with his head hitting the table. Ruth shrieks and grabs Noah, pulling his head to her shoulder.

Noah can only whisper, "Get me out of here, out of this building."

Ruth yells out, "Help me get him some air."

Jesse jumps up out of his seat and runs over to help Ruth lift Noah out of his chair. They grab Noah by his arms and drag him out of the room. They rush to the elevator, then out the front door. They sit Noah down on the front steps of the physics building. Jesse runs off to get his car to drive Noah to the Campus Health Center.

Noah starts feeling a little better now that he is out of the building. The sharp pain is gone, and his breathing is getting easier. He still feels a bit woozy.

Ruth is sitting next to Noah, supporting him with her arm tightly around him. Ruth softly asks, "Noah, how are you feeling now? What happened to you?"

"I am feeling a little better. I was suddenly having trouble breathing and thought I was going to pass out. Then I started to get this terrible pain in my chest. I don't know what was going on."

"I think you are starting to look and sound better. I am glad you are starting to feel better also. Jesse is getting his car; we are going to take you to the campus infirmary. Maybe you have Covid, they can give you anti-viral meds, and you will recover quickly."

Noah puts his arm around Ruth, "Thank you for taking care of me, again."

Ruth kisses him on the cheek and says, "My pleasure."

Jesse arrives, and all three go to the medical center. They take Noah straight into an examination room while Ruth and Jesse sit in the waiting room.

After about an hour, Noah comes out, "The doctor says he cannot find anything wrong. He thinks I may be dehydrated and prescribes rest and water."

Ruth smiles and says, "Well, that's a relief. We'll take you back to the dorm and put you to bed with a pitcher of water for you to drink."

The trio walks out of the medical center as a large black BMW sedan pulls up. A tall, gorgeous woman steps out of the car, her blazing platinum blond hair shining in the sun.

Noah looks up, "Viera, what are you doing here?"

"Noah, your doctor called me since I am your emergency contact."

"Ruth, Jesse, this is my therapist, Viera. She has taken care of me since I was a small child."

Ruth looks Viera up and down, then nods, showing obvious apprehension, "It is nice to meet you. We took Noah to the clinic as soon as we could. He looks like he has fully recovered."

Jesse smiles and tries turning on the charm, "Very good to meet you, Viera. I am Jesse, Noah's good pal. I wondered why he still sees a therapist; now I understand. You're the best-looking therapist I have ever met. Usually, they look like old rejects from Woodstock."

"Oh, you are the pal that introduced Noah to alcoholic beverages," says Viera stoically.

Jesse quickly replies coyly, "Yes, I am a troubled soul. Are you taking any new patients?"

Viera ignores Jesse and changes the subject, "Noah, I am here to take you to several specialists. I want your brain and heart scanned to make sure there is nothing serious going on with you. I have the first scan waiting for you. We need to go now."

Ruth agrees, "That is a good idea. There could be something serious that this general practitioner would not notice. Do you want me to go with you?"

Viera quickly responds, "No, that won't be necessary. I will take him. It may take a few days to complete all the testing. Noah, we should hurry."

Ruth is a little put off by Viera's tone, but doesn't push back. She kisses Noah and says, "Call me when you get back."

Noah and Viera drive away. Noah senses that Viera is flustered and perhaps a little frightened. That tinge of fear scares Noah. He has never seen her like this.

Viera starts speaking before Noah can further analyze the situation, "Noah, that was a close call. If I had not been in direct contact with you at the time, you would be dead. It took all of my energy to keep you breathing and your heart beating. I could not have sustained it much longer. This Ulak creature must be a hybrid, but he seemingly has more power than expected from a hybrid. He is likely a new tool from the Dracons. They were forced to develop the ability to hide themselves both physically and telepathically. When they are hiding themselves, they cannot detect others like us unless they are physically nearby. When they hide, they are blind to the world around them except at close range. That is why you were not detected until your group meeting. That is an advantage for us in our conflict with them, and we need to use it. We need to fight them with everything possible. They will kill you, me, or any other opposing hybrid. They do not want a positive outcome for this planet and certainly are not friends of anyone on Earth."

"So, what does that mean? I cannot return to school, or what?"

"I am taking you to the Earth Council. They want to put you through a regimen of advanced training and teaching. You are going to be rushed through the remainder of your development. They hope that unleashing your full potential will be sufficient."

"Sufficient enough for what?"

"Enough ability for you and me to take out Ulak. They will explain this and much more for you."

Chapter 24.

Taken up

After leaving the university medical center, Viera drives to the top floor of the parking garage of her office building. She parks her car and asks Noah to follow her, and walks to the center of the lot with Noah following closely behind her. Noah senses something in the air above. It is a new, unique sensation; it feels like an intelligent being, yet not a being.

Viera turns to Noah, "Prepare yourself. You are about to experience advanced beings and technology. Do not panic and do not worry. You will be among allies who want the best for you and Earth."

Suddenly, they are surrounded by a cylinder of golden glowing light. An instant later, Viera and Noah are no longer in the parking lot.

Noah awakens in an unusual room with curved metallic walls. Soft light is somehow radiating directly out of the ceiling. He is lying on a small bed, one more comfortable than any he has ever been on. Viera is sitting in a large chair beside him, staring at a video projection that emerges from the wall, fully three-dimensional. It is an image of Earth from low orbit, with dots of light in different colors scattered across the land. Strange texts scroll across the image; he somehow knows they are the Pleiadian language.

Noah sits up, and Viera turns to him. He sees she is wearing a tight-fitting jumpsuit, glowing with a deep blue color. Physically, Noah feels quite well, but he is a little lightheaded.

Viera speaks calmly to him, "Noah, welcome to the Earth Council vessel. You have been in a healing trance and should be fully physically fit. The council has removed all blocks and screens from your abilities. You may feel somewhat disoriented, but that is expected. You have full access to the collective and all your telepathic abilities. This is a large change, you will need time to equilibrate. You should restrain your movements and allow the new mental powers to come to you slowly."

Noah nods and rubs his head, "Where are we exactly? I do not recall anything since we got out of your car on the top floor of the parking garage. Also, what is the Earth Council, and what is the collective?"

"I took you up into my spaceship. I then rendezvoused with another vessel in high Earth orbit. This vessel now resides in an alternative dimension, detached from the space and time constraints of Earth. You are here to undergo advanced training. It is unknown how long your training will last, so placing you here will allow you to be returned to Earth without a time lapse relative to Earthbound observers. You are now in a completely new world outside of the quarantined Earth. It is complex, massive, and filled with extraterrestrials. Your training will be conducted by three members of the Earth Council, all extraterrestrials. The Earth Council is the official overseeing body created by the Galactic Confederation. They have many duties and usually orbit Earth, though some are found on the Moon. One important task is to monitor the planet for illegal visitations and unsanctioned interference in human development. There are criminal activities taking place from time to time involving Earth's resources and living creatures, including humans. They have full authority to intervene. The Earth Council has a longer-term mission to observe life on Earth and help promote human advancement. You will learn about the collective very soon, and it will help inform you about the galaxy."

Noah puts his hands on his knees to steady himself as he leans forward and lets out a deep sigh. He tries to tell himself it's just a dream, but he knows it is real. His mind is spinning. He then feels Viera's comforting presence. Her presence is the only thing keeping him from total collapse.

Viera tries to steady his thoughts and ward off hysteria. She fears that she may need to put Noah back into a healing trance and call for help from a council member. Instead, she decides to try reasoning with him. Viera projects a new message, "*Noah, you are resisting acknowledgement of your situation. Why? Denial of reality is a false remedy; it breeds anxiety and sadness. Acceptance of your circumstances is the only logical solution. Only then can you move forward and grow stronger. You are on the verge of advancing into a new, incredible stage of your life. Seize your amazing future.*"

That message works: it pushes the emotional trauma aside and gets Noah thinking again. He begins to calm down and breathe normally. As his rational mind returns, he starts to imagine what it will be like to travel through space and meet off-world beings. He knows he was able to believe that he is a hybrid species; this is just the next rational extension of that revelation.

Noah responds, "*Yes, I see. It is all there in my head, as if it had always been there. There is just so much new stuff in my mind now. Who are these extraterrestrials who are going to train me?*"

"*Three members of the Earth Council are here to train you and help you reach your full potential. They are friends and wish to develop an advanced civilization on Earth. One is a Pleiadian, a very sensitive and spiritual being who looks something like you. Another trainer is Arcturian. He is tall, with bluish-purple skin. Your other instructor is from Zeta Reticula and should be familiar. He is what is called a Gray on Earth by the UFO communities. The revelation of Grays to humans was caused by a series of illegal*" *visitations and abductions. It nearly caused a triggering event, but our human allies who abide by the treaties were able to discredit the events."*

"Reach out with your mind, and you will see three bright spots on this vessel; those shining points of energy should be your trainers. Do not try to interact with them yet. You should also sense the vessel itself and several lower beings. Pab is the ship's name; it is sentient. There is very little background psychic energy in this dimension, so there is little interference."

"I am still a bit overwhelmed, but I think you have pulled me through my panic attack. I feel fear when I think about all this weird stuff around me, it feels like falling off a boat in the ocean and looking into the frightening deep blue depths."

Viera switches to verbal communication, "I suggest you focus on your immediate surroundings. Do not try to think about this gigantic galaxy that has been suddenly revealed to you. You are here for training; keep your mission as your absolute priority. The councilors that you will meet soon have extraordinary mental powers. Their minds work much faster than even our advanced hybrid brains. They can work on multiple complex problems simultaneously. As I told you previously, they must slow down their minds just to communicate with us. Remember, we are just one step above park squirrels compared to them. They are our allies, here to help us complete our mission. They expect you to pay attention and work hard. Do not get distracted."

"Yes, I understand. I cannot help but feel overstimulated. I know you are working to keep me stable; I feel your presence and appreciate it. I must try to keep my composure and not lose my mind. I hope I will be able to do that without your constant telepathic mental support."

"It is very challenging for you to go through this enormous transition in such a short period of time. I understand the difficulty, but there are serious problems on Earth that have forced all this upon you. After your interaction with Ulak, you now understand the high stakes involved. Across multiple locations on Earth, potential triggering events are unfolding at alarming rates. The disclosure of the existence of extraterrestrials has occurred recently, as you may know, but it was not substantiated. Disinformation campaigns have dulled the Homo Sapiens reaction to this round of disclosure, but pressure is building once again. The power of our psychological operations is limited, so we need to complete our current missions as quickly as possible to move on to other ones. You must work as hard as you can to quickly reach your full potential. We must get back and defeat Ulak to keep advanced physics secret."

"There was a point during Ulak's attack when I thought I was going to die. It felt like I had a sword shoved through my chest. The pain was unbearable, but then there was a moment of tranquility and clarity.

Perhaps it was a state that one enters before death; I don't really know. Regardless, at that moment, I realized my life up to then had been frivolous. I was living a sheltered, juvenile life in an academic crib. You then showed me a new reality with purpose and potential dire consequences. I wanted that new profound reality, and that desire gave me the strength to fight through the pain to live on. My soul merged with my new path at that moment," said Noah in an uncharacteristic, solemn, serene voice.

"I sense that change. You have accepted your new life. It can be considered your rebirth. I am glad to know that you have accepted your mission."

"Will I be able to face Ulak without being killed?" asks Noah solemnly.

"Yes, I think so. You will be much stronger, and I will be with you. A councilor will be watching us more closely from now on."

Viera's statement lifts Noah's spirit. The thought of Ulak did bring back frightening memories.

"Very well. What do I do now?"

"You need to prepare yourself to meet your trainers. Can you sense the vessel? It is its own entity, named Pab. Go stand in the middle of the room. Reach out to Pab and ask it for your jumpsuit."

Noah stands up and goes to the middle of the room as directed. He easily connects with the vessel and asks for his jumpsuit. A door then appears in the wall beside the bed. The door opens, and a jumpsuit like Viera's is hanging there. He walks over, grabs it, and returns to the middle of the room.

Viera continues, "You just need to ask the vessel, and it will respond to your needs. Now ask for a bathroom and a shower."

Noah complies. Immediately, the bed folds up into the wall. Within a couple of seconds, a new floor slides out, and a fully functional bathroom emerges from the wall. Noah turns to Viera with an astonished look on his face.

"Yes, you are no longer on Earth. Refresh yourself, then ask for something to eat. You must keep up your strength; you will need it for the training. Let me know when you are ready, and I will take you to your first training." With that, Viera stands up and leaves the room.

Noah looks at his unbelievable surroundings. He appreciates Viera's psychic support because he could easily imagine that the sudden revelation of his hybrid DNA, extraterrestrials, and galactic reality of fantastic proportions would drive him to psychosis or outright insanity. Following awareness, the choices are acceptance, denial, or mental breakdown. Denial is a harmful mental state, so Noah knows acceptance is the only rational choice. The near-fatal attack by Ulak put it all into mortal perspective. It forced him into immediate acceptance of the bizarre circumstances into which he had been thrust. Noah focuses heavily on his rational mind to conquer runaway emotions in the face of his incredible circumstances. Thinking back, he always has. He now knows that, after these recent extraordinary events, his preference for rationality sets Homo Galaxus apart from Homo Sapiens.

Chapter 25.

I am Briel

Noah signals Viera that he is ready. While sitting in this room alone, he felt panic attacks building, but Viera and other powerful beings are calming and reassuring him. He is still nervous thinking about what may be beyond the closed door of this room, but his fear is mostly under control now. He has been careful about exploring new psychic abilities because there is a limited number of astonishing shocks that anyone can take. When he searched for Viera, he avoided the powerful energy radiating from the advanced beings on the vessel for the same reason. He noticed that the constant flow of Earth consciousness is nowhere to be found, which is troubling itself. In this dimension, he only senses the beings on this vessel. Occasionally, he senses a passing vessel with other advanced beings, but only briefly.

Noah is nervously standing in the hallway. He jumps a little as the hiss from the opening door breaks the silence. Noah is immediately comforted when he sees Viera standing there in her shimmering blue jumpsuit. He is dressed in his new jumpsuit, which looks just like Viera's, and he feels a little self-conscious.

Viera, standing in the doorway, sees Noah and asks, "How do you like your new jumpsuit? It is much better than shabby Earth clothing, is it not?"

"It is amazing, but I feel a little weird wearing it. At first, I did not think that it would fit, but as I put it on, it adjusted itself to me. I suppose I will get a new surprise every time I turn around."

Viera senses a rising anxiety in Noah. She sends stronger calming feelings and says, "Relax, but stay sharp. All the beings in this vessel are friendly and here to help you. You are about to meet your first true extraterrestrial being. You are starting the most challenging and incredible teachings you have ever had. I know you will do well. Stay focused and keep an open mind."

Noah feels a little relief, but he is both excited and terrified. He replies, "Thank you, I will do my best. Let's get going, the suspense is only increasing my nervousness."

"Follow me," she says in a reassuring tone.

Viera turns and starts walking down a long hallway. The walls and ceilings of the hallway look just like those in Noah's room, composed of brushed metallic material with soft light radiating from the ceiling. Noah anxiously keeps looking left and right, waiting for his next shocking surprise, but only sees bright lights in the distance at the end of his visual range. Along the hallway, closed doors are spaced evenly, with no signs or markings anywhere.

As they approach the bright light, Noah can see that the hallway opens into a large room. There is a circular arrangement of six chairs protruding from the floor, surrounding a large metal projection that resembles a giant aluminum toadstool. There are two lines of three chairs, facing the walls to the left and right. A swirling projection of colors appears on the wall facing the chairs to the left; it reminds Noah of the Northern Lights.

Viera walks forward to stand next to the chair directly in front of them, where they entered. Noah receives a message, "*Pleasant greetings, Noah. Welcome. My name is Zizzletik.*"

The chair next to Viera swivels around. A being with a large pear-shaped hairless head is sitting in the chair. It has large almond-shaped black eyes, a tiny nose, and a small mouth. Its exposed skin, not covered by a black jumpsuit, is a mottled gray color. The being is small, maybe four feet tall, and is very slender with long arms and legs. Its hands are large and nimble, with five long fingers and a curved thumb on each. Noah supposes that this is obviously a "Gray" alien he heard about in all the UFO buzz that pops up regularly in the media. Noah Shock is tempered by irony, thinking about all those UFO people have been right all along.

Zizzletik continues, "*I am the captain on duty. This is the control room. We are parked here, so I do not have much to do until we decide to leave this dimension. Please contact me if there is anything you need that Pab cannot supply. Also, if you have time, I would be happy to give you a tour of Pab.*"

Noah replies, "*Thank you. I would very much like to tour your ship.*"

"*The vessel's name is Pab. It is happier when you address it by name,*" says Zizzletik.

Viera cuts in, "*Yes, perhaps some other time. Noah has an appointment and a great deal of work ahead of him. Best regards, Zizzletik.*"

"*Nice to meet you, Zizzletik and Pab,*" says Noah as he turns to follow Viera again.

Noah tries to stay calm after meeting Zizzletik, but he can feel his heart pounding like a bass drum in his chest.

Viera senses this and projects to Noah, "*Relax, that was a bio-engineered being created to do the menial jobs for their creators. You will soon meet someone incredibly special, a being with exceptional kindness and spirituality.*"

Viera leads Noah around the circle of chairs to the hallway on the other side of the control room. The hallway looks identical to the first one, except the doors are bronze-colored. Viera continues a long way down the hallway until she stops in front of a door on her right.

She turns to Noah, "Here we are. I will take you in, then leave you to your training. After you are done here, ask Pab to guide you back to your room.

The door slides open, sending a wave of apprehension through Noah. Viera walks in with Noah following closely as his pulse races. She motions for Noah to step forward to stand beside her. The room looks like a larger version of the one he has on the vessel, but at the far wall, a man floats two feet above the floor. The person is suspended in the air, legs crossed, in a pose reminiscent of the Buddha. He has shining, shoulder-length blonde hair, neatly coiffed, with a dark headband holding it back. His skin is a gleaming creamy white color. He is wearing a tight-fitting jumpsuit similar to Noah's and Viera's, in the same lustrous blue, except for one silver-sheen sleeve. He has a glittering white shawl around his shoulders. Noah can sense the raging river of thoughts flowing through the mind of this floating individual. He cannot follow any of those thoughts as they are multiple streams of images and thoughts all flashing by simultaneously.

A message is transmitted to Noah and Viera, "*Noah, welcome. I am pleased to finally meet you. I would like to interact with you verbally now. It is easier for me to slow down my communications when I interact verbally. Viera, please stay with us for a while.*"

After that message, two large chairs emerge from the wall and slide to the middle of the room. The floating man motions with his arm to invite them to sit. As Noah moves closer to the chairs, he feels an intense energy, as if he were standing before a roaring fire. He and Viera sit down, and the impressive being floats closer.

"Noah, I am Briel, one of the members of the Earth Council. I am a Pleiadian Elder. Viera, it is good to have you here in person once again. Noah, I hope my levitation is not too disturbing for you; I am wearing a levitation belt that creates a field that allows me to comfortably hover without the painful effects of gravity. I am over 600 of your Earth years old, and I find it easier on my body to float in the air rather than sit," says Briel.

Noah's pulse is racing again. He struggles to respond, but then a powerful wave of calm washes through him. He clears his throat and says, "I feel honored just to be here. The last several days seem like some kind of fantastic dream."

"I completely understand. It is a shame you must be rushed through so much in such a brief period of time. We prefer to slowly disclose the unknown realities to our special hybrids. Circumstances, however, dictate that we move quickly. Homo Sapiens are hurtling toward a critical juncture with grave consequences. I have been a member of the Earth Council for two troubling centuries. We have worked to assist Homo

Sapiens toward the development of a higher civilization. In recent times, we have placed hybrids like Viera and you on Earth to provide positive influence. You are a new kind of hybrid, mostly human, modified with a medley of galactic-derived changes that finally may lead to a species with Earthen DNA and suitable improvements to ultimately lead to a healthy civilization. A premature triggering event would scuttle our preferred course of action. A frightening number of different triggering events are nearing actualization. Your mission on Earth involves one such critical situation. Your encounter with this being, Ulak, was curious and changes the dynamics of your mission. Luckily, Viera was there, with just enough strength to save you. For your self-preservation and the success of your mission, we have unleashed your full potential and brought you here for direct training. Previously, we were attenuating your powers to allow you to slowly develop and to incrementally discover your true self. There is no longer any time for slow, orderly development. We are currently in an alternate dimension, detached from space-time constraints. We should be able to spend sufficient time here for your training before the effects of this dimension begin to cause physical problems for us. This will give us enough time to fully train you and bring you to your full potential. We can return you to nearly the same time that you left so there is no suspicious missing time. Viera, do you have anything you would like to add?"

"This Ulak being had more power than expected. I do not understand how this is so. Obviously, he is not merely a mind-controlled human; he is a Dracon creation, a powerful hybrid of some sort. I was barely able to do enough to get Noah away from the situation. It was quite draining."

Briel responds, "Agreed. The council is actively exploring the incident; a galactic code violation is suspected. It is likely that other Dracon hybrids are at the university and working with Ulak. We plan to be more directly involved, without violating galactic edicts ourselves. We are hopeful that Noah's training will exceed expectations, boosting the chances of success. Additionally, we will add another hybrid to your team to increase mission support. Viera, we have planned an advanced healing therapy for you as well."

"Noah, are you reasonably comfortable allowing Viera to leave and meet with another councilor?"

"Yes, I am. I am starting to feel significant positive energy here with you," says Noah while showing a nervous smile.

With that answer, Viera stands and walks out of the room. Her chair slides back and disappears into the wall from where it came..

Briel stares at Noah in silence. Noah can sense him exploring every part of his psyche. Noah is still nervous, but he knows he is being supported by powerful waves of calm directed at him.

After a long while, Briel speaks, "Noah, you have had all our remaining constraints removed from you. One of my goals is to help you access all your capabilities. You have untapped telepathic powers with full access to the collective. The collective is the amassed knowledge of the galaxy placed in an incorporeal entity; you may think of it in human terms as the living psychic version of the internet. It is a resource you can access to gather information. Just as access to the human internet does not make one a wise person, the collective will only provide information, not knowledge or wisdom. Information can be both good and bad. You will never gain wisdom if your knowledge is corrupted or tainted by bad information. Therefore, information should never be considered knowledge. Information becomes knowledge from rational analysis and validation; knowledge becomes wisdom through the comprehension of the interconnections of the Universe. Do you know how information becomes knowledge?"

Noah is a little perplexed, having never thought about information and knowledge this way. In physics, everything always appeared straightforward and logical. Philosophy always seemed like a game of self-consistent logic puzzles. Generally, he paid little attention to the social sciences or politics; they were just irrelevant and boring. Then, he considers the forbidden physics he has been shown. Conventional physics has been stalled in its progress by incomplete or tainted information secretly advocated by extraterrestrial agents. The prior schemes were implanted in his mind along with the details of the forbidden physics. His mission back on Earth is to continue disrupting the advancement of physics. Physicists who adamantly cling to bad knowledge will never discover advanced physics. Homo sapiens cannot gain this knowledge because they are constrained by misinformation. Briel smiles as he follows Noah's thoughts.

Noah slowly replies, "Information is merely a starting point. It must be evaluated to prove its worth before any valid conclusions can be made. One must be educated in the basic fundamentals to be able to evaluate information. Validated information may be compiled and organized to form legitimate theories, which in turn yield true knowledge. To hold a strong opinion without a grasp of the fundamentals and subsequent validation is foolish."

"Very good. You understand an important concept. When you return to Earth, you will find that most humans hold strong, unverified opinions that only lead to wasteful folly. If you look more closely into Homo Sapiens societies, you will see that most people form strong opinions based solely on emotion and corrupted information. Such impulsiveness accelerates societal collapse. There is an enormous amount of information in the collective that will be useful in your development.

Primarily, it will help you build knowledge, but you should keep a healthy degree of cynicism even with the collective. Proving theories for yourself builds the strongest knowledge. Keep in mind that there are many areas of disagreement in our advanced galactic civilizations. Let me now guide you through an initial exploration of the collective."

Noah feels Briel joining into his thoughts. *"Relax your mind, calm your thoughts, and allow me to show you the way to access the collective."*

Noah closes his eyes and tries to pause his thoughts. Soon, he feels the tug of Briel. The sensation sends his mind into a state that feels like trying to pull up an old memory from deep down. Then, Noah connects and follows Briel. Noah has never reached out like this with his mind. Suddenly, he senses something immense: a giant mass, like an enormous pulsating cloud. Briel heads straight into it. A vast energy vault of knowledge surrounds them. It is an incredible experience to contact the collective for the first time.

Briel sends a command, *"Show images of the Pleiadian capital planet."*

Noah concentrates with all his might to stay with Briel as incredible images begin to pass by. Large gleaming buildings with steeples and spires stand above a bustling city. Unusual vessels fly down avenues with people like Briel hovering everywhere on the streets below. Noah is astonished and completely overwhelmed by the show.

Briel interrupts the exploration, *"Very good. You may go sightseeing later. Leave the collective with me now."*

Noah breaks his mental link with the collective and opens his eyes. The look of astonishment on Noah's face is obvious. Briel is smiling at him, seeing the results of Noah's discovery.

Briel speaks, sounding very pleased, "Noah, you accessed the collective with my help. This is a very good sign. Now I want you to go back to the collective on your own. Return to it on your own. Once there, ask it to teach you the Pleiadian verbal language.

Noah closes his eyes again and tries to access the collective. Briel floats calmly and makes no attempt to help. After about 30 minutes, Briel comes back to aid Noah. Briel directs Noah to leave and once again try to access the collective on his own. This process is repeated through several cycles. Finally, Noah succeeds and opens his eyes after a long while, alone in the collective. Using only the Pleiadian verbal language, Briel asks him if he was successful. Noah responds in perfect Pleiadian.

"Very good, that is enough for now. I want you to ask Pab to direct you back to your room. Explore the collective to delve deeper into the Pleiadian civilization. I want you to know what a truly civilized and advanced civilization looks like. Then, get some rest and have something to eat. Make sure you try the nectar; it is delicious and very good for you. Your next

training session will be with Gilmesh in three of your Earth hours. You will find it to be more physically rigorous."

Chapter 26.

Replacement is the only solution

After Viera leaves Noah with Briel, she is summoned to another room in the same hallway. She only walks a short distance until a door that slides open as she nears. She enters to see a familiar large being sitting in an equally large chair. It is Gilmesh, the Acturian representative on the Earth Council. If standing, Gilmesh would easily be seven feet tall. His head is elongated, with a distinctive narrow-oval face, small, blazing green eyes, and a large mouth. His nose is just two vertical grooves, partially covered by folds of skin. He has large feet but rather small five-fingered hands for his size. His skin color is very distinctive; it is an interesting mixture of purple and blue pastels. His body is lean and imposing, his movements fluid and graceful. His overall appearance suggests strength and power.

Gilmesh welcomes Viera, "*Please come in. I am pleased to see you in person once again.*" A chair slides out from the wall for Viera.

Viera walks in and sits down, "*It is good to be back here with the council. I must admit that I need time to recover. I have exhausted myself tending to Noah over the last several days. The accelerated development is draining for both of us. There were just too many massive disclosures put to him in a very short period of time. I had to stabilize his mind constantly. I am surprised that he did not have a severe collapse. The incident with that Ulak hybrid nearly took me down also. We were very lucky. I feel I need an extended healing trance.*"

Gilmesh clasps his hands together and tilts his head sympathetically, "*Yes, we agree. Your effort is greatly appreciated, and after this meeting, we will rejuvenate you fully. We are pleased that you and Noah were able to escape permanent harm from the Ulak incident. That was a surprising event, certainly caused by the Dracons. They have deployed more hybrids than we thought. Their ability to hide their telepathic presence makes it nearly impossible to fully monitor their activities. I suspect the Dracons violated galactic codes again and are accelerating unsanctioned, illegal activities on Earth in earnest. We conclude that there must be at least one other Dracon hybrid at the university. We are determined to find the Dracon squad that is behind these new violations.*"

Viera knows that the Arcturians are very strict. They demand firm enforcement of codes, treaties, and laws. Their philosophy drives them to readily enforce rules and punish violators with all the appropriate means necessary to invoke justice. They do not hesitate or lament over violent actions in support of galactic rules, unlike the Pleiadians, who are more spiritual and sensitive in this regard. The Arcturians have the power and proper attitude to regularly act as the primary police force for the galaxy.

"*Yes, something is not right with that Ulak creature. No hybrid has ever shown so much power. Either he is himself a Dracon, or there is another, or a group of hybrids, tightly coordinating efforts. They are illegally interfering in Earthling activities through Ulak, who obviously is the nexus of this operation.*"

Gilmesh replies forcefully, "*We believe there is a concerted effort on a global scale. The forces of the Dracons are driving multiple efforts simultaneously to bring about a triggering event. The push to unveil forbidden physics is just one scheme of their overall strategy. The situation you encountered with Noah is just one of several such operations in this area; there are others at advanced stages. It is becoming increasingly clear that the Dracons believe a triggering event at this time will secure their claim of sovereignty over the Earth and give them a fertile new home planet again. Sadly, they may be correct. Support for continued development of the current Homo Sapiens species of Earth is waning for more and more galactic representatives.*"

Viera is saddened by the undeniable realization that Homo Sapiens are a lost cause. She has worked for more than one hundred Earth years aiding their development and has an attachment. "*Homo Sapiens are a stubborn species. There certainly are many lovely humans with warm emotions and kind natures. However, they lack the character to suppress the omnipresent degenerates, let alone any devious hybrids. The wicked majority continue with their mass violence and corruption. After every atrocity, the wicked blame others for their violence and wickedness. The good humans cannot overcome the continued barbaric nature surrounding them. They are too few in number and too weak to take necessary actions; they are unable to stop the truly vicious. As a human society develops, they reach a point where they become overly sympathetic due to their prosperous, pleasant lives. They are tricked into feeling sorry for selected groups; this causes rules and laws to be ignored, which eventually leads to a downward spiral and the eventual collapse of the social order. Tolerance of anti-social behavior is a toxic product of their soft emotions. We have seen this process play out several times with the same result.*"

Gilmesh comments with resolve, "*We Arcturians have a strict moral code about anti-social behavior, corruption, and degeneracy. It only seems harsh until one becomes a victim. I cannot understand how Homo Sapiens can forgive those who commit horrible offenses that shred the fabric of their society. It makes no sense. There cannot be any real civic duty, only oblivious self-interest, laden with destructive denial.*"

Viera knows that Gilmesh is correct about Homo Sapiens. She adds, "*It makes no sense because such actions are driven by emotions sparked by lies. To make matters worse, groups of humans incensed by emotions reinforce each other's wrath. This often leads to large-scale violence.*" Viera adds, "*Corrupt humans have used emotional arguments to create mass hysteria that is used for control and the acquisition of political power.*"

"*Yes, well said. Homo Sapiens become more emotional and less rational when they are isolated in groups. Emotional incitement can powerfully intensify degenerate attitudes. This proclivity is a major hindrance to cultural advancement. Even in this current era, angry mobs are all too common. The less developed areas of Earth are frighteningly vicious and completely corrupt. Homo Sapiens seem unable to move beyond those barbaric tendencies. Homo Galaxus replacement is the only solution,*" says Gilmesh.

Viera quickly agrees, "*Indeed. This first generation of Homo Galaxus is impressive. They are showing the necessary advanced traits. It is sad to realize that Homo Sapiens cannot evolve into anything as promising as Homo Galaxus, but I am very encouraged and happily work to develop this new species.*"

Gilmesh pauses to consider Viera's comments. "*Once you get past your remaining emotional attachment to Homo Sapiens, you will see that you are justifiably frustrated. I, too, am very encouraged by Homo Galaxus. You have seen Noah grow and develop, and this you know better than anyone else. Your other apprentices show similar positive attributes. Noah certainly has many positive characteristics that we have been hoping to create in our hybrids. Do you think he and the other Homo Galaxus can assert themselves and start controlling the Earth?*"

Viera quickly replies, "*Noah has the intelligence and telepathic abilities necessary for an advanced civilization. He typically uses logical cognition before emotion for his decision-making process, which is always a requirement for advanced civilizations to survive. I am certain that he does not have the emotional problems inherent in Homo Sapiens. We will soon know if successful reproduction is possible. There is still another aspect that has not been assessed. He has led a soft, sheltered life. It is to be seen if he has the fortitude to withstand conflict and difficult situations. I think he is capable, but this trait has not been demonstrated. Also, it should be noted that he was totally unprepared for his first encounter with Ulak.*"

"*That is useful information. I will make certain to prioritize it in my instruction plans for Noah. I will definitely challenge him. I will find out if he carries any Acturian disposition. Now you may go back to your room, and we will give you a well-deserved healing session.*"

Gilmesh analyzes the information from Viera. Other Homo Galaxus hybrids have shown stronger personalities, but Noah has the most advanced intellect of the first-generation hybrids. Every Homo Galaxus hybrid possesses a high degree of telepathic ability, the most essential characteristic for advancement. Gilmesh is optimistic and knows he would welcome a Homo Galaxus world. He hopes they get the chance.

Chapter 27.

Gilmesh and the Arcturian Way

Noah is back in his room, still in awe of the incredible feeling he had just being in the presence of Briel. He has not rested as Briel recommended; he is too stimulated to rest. He has been accessing images and information of Briel's Pleiadian civilization. He is in awe, viewing scenes that make him wonder if this is what a society of angels would be. He takes a short break to eat a plate of interesting pastes and cubes of food washed down with a delicious nectar-like liquid supplied by Pab. Next time, he will see if Pab can make pizza. Now he is back searching the collective. This activity is interrupted as he receives a message.

"Noah, this is Gilmesh. I will come to your room soon to start your next training session. Prepare yourself for self-defense training."

Noah hears the message but ignores it to lie down on his bed to return to his exploration of the collective. Suddenly, his room door slides open. Before Noah can even look toward the door, he feels a blast of energy enter his mind, triggering all the muscles in his arms and legs; he begins to flail uncontrollably. The muscle contractions are so severe that they hurl him onto the floor from the bed. He ends up on the floor, face down and quite helpless. As the tremors subside, he manages to look up and see a towering bluish-purple being standing over him. He next feels two strong arms grip him and set him back on the bed. Noah slowly sits up and looks at the alien. His mind is equally assaulted as he looks in shock at the towering bluish-purple being standing before him.

Gilmesh introduces himself in a loud, booming voice with an odd-sounding accent, "I am Gilmesh, your instructor. I am an Arcturian. I detect that you have not downloaded the Arcturian language, so I will speak in your tongue. I am here to prepare you for conflict. You have lived a soft, sheltered life and are totally unprepared for aggression. The event you just experienced was merely a demonstration to get your attention. I could have easily killed you, because your guard is down, leaving you constantly vulnerable. You are weak. That is why you failed in your first encounter with Ulak. Thankfully, Viera was able to intervene. You grew up on a very violent, dangerous planet, yet seem to be unprepared for conflict. We have much work to do."

Gilmesh stands uncomfortably close to Noah who sits on the side of the bed and is still a little unsteady. He feels immediate embarrassment. He dislikes failure, and it bothers him to be called weak. He responds defensively, "In school, I was always surrounded by others who were much older and bigger than me. I suppose my teachers always looked out for me. I never had to fight, so I am not used to being in a physical conflict."

"That is an excuse for children. Arcturians are taught self-defense and physical fitness along with their scholastic subjects. An advanced, civilized society is maintained only by strong citizens who are ready and able to defend it. A resilient moral code must have formidable people to preserve it. Arcturians feel strongly about enforcing the rules. To allow aberrant behavior in individuals and groups is to initiate the downfall of society. If you want Earth to develop an advanced society, you will need to do as the Arcturians do. I am here to teach you how to be a defender of society, not a soft, over-protected dependent."

Noah, recalling the Ulak incident, knows Gilmesh is correct, and it is time to stop making excuses. "Very well, what do you want me to do now?"

Gilmesh asks Pab to slide out two chairs facing each other. One is very large for Gilmesh, the other is sized for Noah.

Gilmesh motions to the chairs, "Please sit, and then we shall begin."

They both sit down. Gilmesh stares at Noah intently. Noah can feel the telepathic projection of Gilmesh into his mind.

"You must be constantly alert for contact from others. You must keep this posture at all times. That is how Ulak so quickly incapacitated you. He sensed you were not paying attention and went straight for the kill. The first step for self-defense is awareness. You must know how to maintain this feeling. It is your psychic radar, to use an Earth term. I am going to pull back from you and then come back in. Raise your arm as soon as you feel my contact."

Noah concentrates and feels Gilmesh pull back. He sits and tries to sense Gilmesh trying to enter his thoughts. He feels an approach and raises his arm.

"Very good. Familiarize yourself with that mental state. Let's continue this exercise to reinforce the learning."

Gilmesh and Noah continue to practice this exercise for quite a while until the point where Noah has become bored with the exercise.

Then Gilmesh stops and asks, "Noah, do you think you have learned how to be on guard now?"

"Yes, I think I know how to sense..." Suddenly, Noah's right leg kicks out uncontrollably.

Gilmesh interrupts, "I did that to you. You just learned to use your radar, but you dropped it when you were distracted by speaking. I attacked; you did not see it coming. You must learn to keep alert no matter what else you are doing."

"That is going to be difficult. How can I function normally while holding a defensive posture?"

"It only seems difficult because you have not practiced it. No one has pushed you to work hard enough to reach your potential. You will never discover your limits until you are compelled to find them. A good coach will teach you a great deal about yourself. You will be surprised by your abilities that you cannot imagine at this time. I am the coach who will give you the push you need. From now on, it will attack you at any moment. You will quickly learn to have your defenses engaged at all times."

Noah only nods with trepidation.

"Now for your next lesson. Detection of an incoming attack is futile unless you can repel an attacker. Once you detect someone making contact, you need to be able to block their improper attack on your body. Thought-to-thought contact is just an exchange of information. When foreign thoughts try to take over your physical functions, that is an assault. You must learn where that point is and how to defend it. I will come into your mind and then pull back. Then I will enter again, but make you raise your arm. I want you to feel the difference."

Noah sits with his psychic radar on, feeling Gilmesh come and go. Then he feels him return and has his arm raise uncontrollably.

"Do you feel the difference and detect the point where none should be allowed to cross?"

"Yes, yes, I think so. The first approach was felt in my head, while the second approach seemed to move further and extended down into my core. I did feel the difference."

"That is good. Now you must start focusing on the area before the point where it gets to your body and put up a mental barrier. Consider it equivalent to a boxer putting up his guard rather than letting his arms dangle at his side. Let us try this exercise again while you try to put up your guard."

Noah concentrates and focuses on the spot to protect. He senses Gilmesh and pushes back. His arm only twitches slightly but does not rise.

"Very good. Let us repeat this."

Gilmesh continues the exercise for a long time until he senses Noah has improved his technique.

"You have recognized how to wield your defensive posture. I want you to practice keeping your radar on and your guard up. I will make attacks on you at any time, so be prepared."

Noah sighs, "This will be exhausting. I don't see how I can keep my guard up constantly."

"You don't think you can do it, but you have never tried. It takes discipline to put in the work necessary to develop skills and strength to their fullest. Discipline separates the winners from the losers, and sometimes the living from the dead. Your easy life has made you soft. These tasks will seem difficult until you strengthen yourself. You have shown me that you are able to do these things, now work hard and make them part of you. I will not stop testing you because your opponents will not stop either."

"You mean Ulak, right?"

"No, I mean the Dracons and their allies. Ulak is but one of their tools. The Dracons were part of the last intergalactic war. Earth was one of the planets swept up in the conflict the Dracons had with the Nibiruans, or the Anunnaki, as humans call them. The Dracons believed they had an ancient claim to Earth, though they ignored it for a very long time. The Anunnaki came in many thousands of your years ago to mine for gold and other heavy elements. They also broke galactic codes by conducting unsanctioned genetic manipulation of the indigenous hominid species. They modified the DNA of humans to make slaves who could do the work for them. The Anunnaki on Earth were few in number and found that a society of slaves could increase their mining results. Also, their inflated egos enjoyed being treated like gods by their human slaves. Homo Sapiens were made more intelligent and obedient in order to be more useful slaves. Telepathic abilities were purposely stunted to keep humans from advanced development. Long after that, the Dracons started a vicious war with the Anunnaki. That is why the Anunnaki left the Earth. They had to go fight the Dracons. The Dracons destroyed the Anunnaki planet and wiped out all remnant populations in acts of savage brutality. Their victory came at great cost, as most of their population and their planet were destroyed by Anunnaki counterattacks, aided by some of their allies. The Galactic Confederation formed after this war; they punished the Dracon's aggression by taking control of their colonial planets, including Earth. They exist on their devastated home planet, in small clans embedded with sympathetic civilizations, and in pockets as fugitives hidden on protectorate planets. We know they are infesting Earth, and we are fairly certain that they are interfering in the development of the planet. Their thought patterns are divergent from most of the other galactic civilizations, which helps them hide and prevent detection. We believe they would like to cause a triggering event and use it as an opportunity to control Earth. They exploit exemptions in the Galactic Codes to spread their reach. The Dracons are aggressive and unsympathetic, yet they have cleverly leveraged several members of the Confederation to secure a measure of political protection. That is why we need local populations and our implanted hybrids to rid themselves of the Dracons. If we move directly on the Dracons, we would be violating the same Galactic codes. That would spark serious conflicts within the Confederation, giving the Dracons more power. Our advantage is that we can use our fully sanctioned hybrids to avoid violation of Confederation rules. This may help you understand why we created you and are now putting you through this training. Consider the notion that you are fighting to have your own planet."

Noah starts rubbing his temples, "This is far bigger than I originally assumed. I thought I was just working to prevent Homo Sapiens from doing something stupid. Now you tell me that there are galactic ramifications, alien conflicts, and an existential issue for Earth."

"Yes, exactly. Now you understand. Let us get back to your training."

Chapter 28.

Uhlt and harsh, blunt reality

Noah is alone in his room, feeling the full impact of his situation as Gilmesh shows him the danger he must face and the immense consequences. It seems like eons ago that he was living an easy life of physics classes that posed little difficulty for him. His biggest challenge was living away from home and his mother. How trivial and embarrassing his old life seems now. He knows he must accept this duty, but questions if he has enough courage to meet the challenge. Bravery is the fuel that drives the righteous toward victory; he hopes he has it. His carefree childhood is over, and he can only wonder if he can successfully engage in mortal conflicts with savage enemies. He begins to feel overwhelmed once again. Suddenly, he is contacted.

"This is Briel. I volunteered to help you because Viera is in a well-deserved healing trance. I have great confidence in you and your abilities. You have surpassed expectations. However, you have much to learn and more to do before we return to Earth. Focus on improving your abilities in preparation for your mission; hard work will calm your nerves and give you confidence. Close your eyes and take slow, deep breaths."

Noah obliges and can feel powerful calming energies from Briel flowing through him. He feels his pulse slow and begin to return to normal.

"Now that you have calmed yourself, I have a short exercise for you. I want you to find Viera and see what she is doing. You are connected to her, so you can reach out to actually see her."

Noah easily detects Viera's familiar energy pattern but struggles to see any images. Then, he feels a nudge from Briel, and a mental image appears. He can see Viera lying quietly on a bed. He can pull back and see the whole room. He pulls back further to see that she is across the hallway from him.

"Yes, Noah, you have the ability to do long-distance psychic viewing. It takes considerable practice to fully develop this ability. Humans call it remote viewing, but only a few have the ability, and their vision is weak. This exercise you just carried out was easy because we are in hyperspace and not in the psychic maelstrom of the galaxy. As you develop your ability, you may reach out for specific people or places; moreover, you can peer into distant places that you can see or sense. Practice this, and you will find it quite useful for your missions. I will now tell your next instructor that you are ready. Ask Pab to direct you to the room of Uhlt. He will expect you."

Noah is fascinated by the way this vessel, Pab, can communicate with him. Pab leads Noah through the control room, where he exchanges greetings with Zizzletik, who is still there. He is directed down the same hallway with the brass-colored doors where Briel is found. He stops in front of a door that Pab specifies. The door slides open to expose a dimly lit room. The light from the hallway makes it more difficult to see anything in the room, but Noah again senses a powerful being inside. Noah hears a command.

"Come in and have a seat. I prefer telepathy to verbal communication. I can slow myself down so as not to overwhelm you."

Noah walks in and, after his eyes adjust to the low light, sees a simple chair in the middle of the room. He sits down and can now see his instructor as his eyes adjust to the low light. The being looks like a larger version of Zizzletik, except he has a more substantial build. Also, his face has more lines and wrinkles, a larger mouth, and a much more prominent chin. His eyes are similarly menacing, large, dark, and almond-shaped.

"Hello, Noah, I am Uhlt. I am a Zeta Reticulan, as you would call me. I see that you think I look like Zizzletik, but it is he that looks like me. Zizzletik and those like him are bio-engineered beings that do most of the labor for us. They are friendly, loyal, and enjoy working for us. They have but a fraction of our mental powers and intellect. I own him and many others, in case you were wondering. We dumped a considerable amount of new information into you during your last healing trance. Are you familiar with the basics of our technologies that allow us to traverse dimensions, utilize gravity, and create unlimited energy?

"Yes, I now understand the basics. The nuclear physics that enables the fusion of heavier elements to release massive amounts of energy in a very small space is fascinating. Human theories of the nucleus with protons, neutrons, and meson exchanges are so backward. The use of the same fusion method to produce ultra-heavy elements is the key to gravity manipulation and interdimensional travel, and is well beyond human capability, but I understand the process. The mastery of advanced electromagnetic fields and hyper-dimensional energy barriers remains somewhat confusing to me. I will need time to study that area."

"Very good. That should be enough for you to understand why all that and more is forbidden for Homo Sapiens. Unlimited power can be used to create immense good, but can also bring immense evil when in the wrong hands. The Galactic Confederation will not hesitate to act when a triggering event threshold is reached. The destruction of Homo Sapiens will not be done due to any malice. It is necessary to prevent a dangerous civilization from entering the galaxy, bringing conflict and destruction."

Why can't the Homo Sapiens be given a chance to prove themselves worthy? The Earth continues to improve with each generation," asks Noah defensively.

"I disagree. Every day, the Earthlings have a chance to show they are worthy, but they do not make any cultural progress that would give the Galactic Confederation a tangible reason to remove the quarantine. Advancing technology has led to greater devolution within individuals and society. Have you had a chance to familiarize yourself with the prominent galactic beings and their planets?"

"I have been in nearly constant training, but did have a chance to explore some of the Pleiadian civilization. I found the things I saw to be incredible and amazing."

"You will be equally amazed by the other advanced galactic civilizations. Advanced states are not achieved by accident; they are maintained only by strict rules and rigorous enforcement. I want you to know up front that I do not think Homo Sapiens can achieve advanced status. Most importantly, all advanced civilizations have a high degree of telepathy. Without it, beings are trapped alone in their physical shells. I can hardly imagine such solitude, or its horrible side effects. If nothing else, it promotes destructive selfishness with anti-social consequences. This also leads to mania, mass hysteria, and high levels of insanity. Self-absorbed beings have weak connections to others and their communities at large. They feel only a duty to themselves, which causes degeneracy in large percentages of the overall population. This explains the ubiquitous corruption and lying. Telepathic societies can detect lies, so corruption cannot be hidden. Stark honesty may seem cruel at times, but it creates a stable, honest society. All Homo Sapiens societies are barbaric and corrupt, no matter how benevolent their outward appearance is. Homo Sapiens have forced us into action as they now have suitably potent weapons to destroy themselves. If we had not already stepped in, the Earth would be a nuclear wasteland. There is also another human characteristic that dooms them. Homo Sapiens have not evolved sufficiently beyond being biochemically and emotionally driven animals. They rarely rely on logic or intellect to make decisions. Emotions, driven by hormones and pleasurable neurotransmitter stimulation, bring on behaviors akin to those of vicious animals in the wild. Once cognitive thought is overrun by emotional obsessions, it is nearly impossible to recover. Homo Sapiens are doomed to create an emotional reality that will ultimately destroy their society. Telepathic connections prevent such issues as you can see in our stable, superior civilizations. We have studied this in multiple other planetary beings."

Noah counters, *"My mother is a good, honest person who makes her community better. Are you not condemning the species by overlooking all the good people?"*

"*Your mother may be a very good person, but she, even with a billion like her, is no match for corrupt, selfish people. Because lies are not easily detected by the non-telepathic, there is no hope for them to conquer the corrupt. Good Homo Sapiens cannot help but be fooled by the wicked.*"

"*Why do you tell me these horrible things about humans?*"

"*You need to know this because it is possible that a triggering event may soon occur. I want you to understand the reasoning behind the horrible consequences of a triggering event. In the prehistory of Homo Sapiens, there have been multiple triggering events. Human development has been reset several times. Rebel off-worlders have come to Earth and lived among the people. It once resulted in nuclear conflict eons ago. Large meteorites were directed to crash into the oceans, unleashing a global flood to purge the planet of corrupted civilizations. Later, other rebel extraterrestrials came to Earth and lived amongst man once again. They practiced wanton, unsanctioned genetic manipulations on Homo Sapiens to create a servant race who would worship them. Their reckless genetic experimentation created an unplanned race of giants. The giants were a true abomination. They were very intelligent but very evil. Advanced societies were springing up with these giants as their kings. The Galactic Confederation moved the moon into orbit around Earth, causing gigantic tidal waves and incredibly high winds. The few Homo Sapiens that survived had their memories wiped away and started over in another Stone Age. Homo Sapiens have little recollection of these times. Now humans are approaching their own triggering event by attaining technology that is beyond their cultural maturity.*"

Noah continues to plead the case, "*If humans were advanced enough to develop higher technology, shouldn't they be given the chance to catch up with cultural developments?*"

"*The Homo Sapiens had help, unsanctioned help. That is the problem. We are certain that there is a Dracon influence behind numerous recent events on Earth. They have accelerated their efforts in the last century of Earth's history. The Dracons were likely a major force behind the world wars and helped them develop new weaponry for more effective killing. We were slow to intervene to stop them. Therefore, after the Second World War ended, we did make contact with the United States and the Soviet Union. We require that the existence of extraterrestrials be kept top secret in exchange for some minor technical innovations. Also, strict warnings were given about the development and use of advanced technology, which we deemed forbidden. The Dracons, however, corrupted many agencies inside these governments; they also infiltrated most major aerospace, military, and technology companies. The real Cold War is between the galactic human partners who abide by the treaties and the Dracon human partners. A triggering event threshold would likely benefit the Dracons, and they seem*" *to be pushing harder and harder for it. Many others in the Confederation have lost faith in further development for Homo Sapiens. This could potentially lead to Earth being ceded to the Dracons."*

"So let me see if I understand. The Earth will either be flooded to eliminate all Homo Sapiens, or it will be given to the Dracons. What would Draconian ownership mean for Homo Sapiens?"

"Dracon history provides a good idea of what their actions would be. The Dracons are few in number now, so they would likely keep humans as slaves. They would eradicate much of the population, however. The old, weak, and superfluous humans would be eliminated at once. They would keep the remaining population as humans keep sheep and cows. The females would be kept in groups with a few males who would be used to impregnate the females to maintain the slave population. The other males would be used as slave labor. I feel I must tell you that a certain amount of the human population would be food for the Dracons. They do enjoy consuming human flesh and are certainly at this time, consuming many people who go missing or are abducted and sold to them."

"What's the point, then? The future options are horrible. I am sickened thinking about the Dracons butchering and eating my mother."

"Do not despair, there is a wonderful alternative. You and others like you are the alternative. The creation of the Homo Galaxus species is a recent accomplishment. It changes everything about the Earth's future. Homo Galaxus has shown all the attributes necessary for successful societal development. We just need more time to answer the remaining questions, but I am confident the results will be positive. Soon, the transition of Earth from Homo Sapiens to Homo Galaxus can begin in earnest. A planet filled with the Homo Galaxus species would be welcomed into the Galactic Confederation."

"But what about the Homo Sapiens? Won't another flood take out Homo Galaxus also?"

"The Homo Sapiens will be allowed to fade away. Their weaknesses are already being exploited. Populations around the world are collapsing; it is happening slowly now and will accelerate in a few decades. Substance abuse, destructive selfishness, video addiction, and the corrupt human nature will cause the population to reduce itself to a small fraction of today's numbers. The females, being more emotional, have been easy to influence, and their actions control population growth. Also, their evolutionary tendencies lead them to imitate one another and to engage in self-promoting flocking behavior. Their breeding instinct has been largely thwarted. When the males are deprived of purpose, responsibility for loved ones, and sexual propagation, they turn to depressed solitude, substance abuse, and debauchery. The resulting effect is the loss of their drive for societal maintenance and sexual reproduction. Populations are now below

sustainable rates of reproduction and will continue this decline exponentially. Homo Galaxus hybrids are already being seeded around the world while the Homo Sapiens fade away into history. You need to understand that the creation of the Homo Galaxus is the righting of a wrong done long ago. The Anunnaki unethically altered the course of human evolution. Homo Galaxus puts the Homo genus back on track to develop advanced, peaceful, and prosperous civilizations."

Noah is filled with overpowering thoughts and emotions. He cannot say anything.

Uhlt continues, *"I understand this is a lot to take in. These outcomes are tragic if you are a human, but they must be done. A barbaric civilization must be extinguished to protect the peaceful, advanced civilizations of the galaxy. Do you understand?"*

Noah can only manage a slight nod.

Uhlt senses Noah is unsettled by their session. He suggests, *"You will need time to think through this. Go back to your room and verify everything I told you through the collective if you need more proof. The collective has everything you will need. Also, practice your other assignments. We need to get you back to Earth fully prepared to vanquish the Dracons."*

Noah silently stands and walks out of the room. After the door closes, Noah's arm flies up into the air. Gilmesh caught him with his guard down on his first sneak attack. Right now, Noah is too consumed by Uhlt's revelations to care about self-defense training. Noah shakes his head, knowing he'd better pull himself together if he can.

Chapter 29.

Emotional distress can destroy the soul;
resolution produces wisdom and strength

The stark reality presented by Uhlt now weighs heavily upon Noah. The thought of billions of human beings going away in one sudden, horrible event struck him like a speeding bus. Enslavement of humanity by the Dracons is an equally disturbing idea. There is little comfort in the plan that allows Homo Sapiens to fade away into history. He cannot reason away feelings caused by the knowledge of the ultimate fate for all Homo Sapiens. This means his mother will be included in the grim possibilities. He has never felt so troubled and struggles to understand why. He barely remembers walking back to his room and ignoring two more psychic attacks by Gilmesh that sent his arm flying up in the air. Noah can only plop down on his bed in a numb haze. He longs for his carefree prior life but knows there is no going back. All the knowledge of the true state of the galaxy has locked him into a dark place with no obvious way out.

Suddenly, from out of the gloom, Noah senses a familiar bright energy. It is Briel. Just feeling his active presence provides enough of a spark for Noah to sit up.

Briel calmly mind-speaks, *"Noah, I know you have been traumatized by Uhlt's disclosure of the imminent Homo Sapiens extinction. You have been subjected to a series of shocking revelations and have accepted them quite well, but everyone has a breaking point. Do not despair because you are not alone; I am here to help. You will find that in your new life in a telepathic society, there is incredible support from your surrounding community. Your friends and the surrounding community are now part of your essence, and you are part of them. A telepathic bond is real and purposeful. You are never alone or left to suffer by yourself. I felt your pain, and I'm here to help you. Psychic connections are inherently therapeutic.*

In an advanced telepathic society, a group would be drawn to you to help you through your issues. There is a genuine communal existence in which one cannot hide pain or sadness. Homo Sapiens, on the other hand, are trapped in their physical bodies, alone and isolated. They must attempt to heal their mental traumas on their own. Verbal support has at best a limited effect. Usually, this is not sufficient, and the lonely soul of the human all too often descends into silent misery or self-destructive psychosis. Telepathy binds individuals and provides strong community ties that stabilizes all.

Briel pauses and transmits uplifting energy. *Take a deep breath and calm your emotions. Now, please share your troubled thoughts, honestly and slowly, one at a time."*

Noah takes a deep breath and tries to untangle his depressing feelings. *"I think the triggering event details were very difficult for me to hear. The knowledge that Homo Sapiens are doomed is deeply troubling. Knowing they will either be driven to societal collapse to fade into oblivion or to become a herd of slaves is horrible. I am especially disturbed to think about this happening to my mother, to Ruth, and to my other friends."*

"You may not find this immediately helpful, but there are worse possible scenarios. Briel somberly continues. *We have seen the result of nuclear destruction on a planetary scale. We have also seen the horrors produced when planetary societies rapidly crumble to drive the population into barbaric savagery. I assure you that the level of suffering is much worse. Let me redirect us to a larger, more hopeful topic that may put this into a greater perspective for you."*

"Our material world in which we physically exist is only a part of the comprehensive reality. There is a natural part of existence, the things we can touch and measure with scientific instruments. The other part of existence is the supernatural, existing beyond our senses, unseen and unmeasurable. Telepathy, your inherent ability, is beyond scientific measurement and should be a clear example for you to understand the intangible. Our existence extends beyond the physical; there is a duality of existence in all of us. What Homo Sapiens calls a soul is one's supernatural essence. We believe it is more akin to a spiritual life force, which can be understood in more technical terms, such as a wave function or an energy field. Upon conception, a physical body captures a conscious life force from the Universe or the Creator, if you will. Individuals may grow and improve their individual wave functions throughout their lives. However, if a being lives contrary to the positive energy of the Universe, degradation of their wave function produces inharmony to send them ultimately into negative chaos. The death of our physical self frees our metaphysical wave function to proceed to its next plane of existence. If one's wave function is aligned with the Universal Good, it transcends to an enlightened dimension. If one's wavefunction has corroded into misalignment with its frequency out of synchrony, it is driven to inharmonic chaos and suffering. I assure you that your mother, being a good person, will transcend upward to an incredible realm of splendor."

Noah responds with perplexity, *"It sounds like you believe in good, evil, heaven, hell, and an omnipresent being. Does your highly advanced society with extremely powerful telepathic ability hold essentially the same philosophy as the first-century human Christians?"*

"Yes. Absolutely yes. Perhaps our psychic ability has allowed us to sense the connectivity of the almighty Universe and the pervasive positive energy inherent in all things; nevertheless, the overall message is the equivalent. We may use different terms and details, but it is essentially describing the same concepts."

Noah continues, *"So then, God exists. All my secular human professors are wrong. God created everything in his image, even though I am now aware of a wide variety of beings in the same universe that differ greatly in appearance. Aren't there too many variations in intelligent life for a single image of God?"*

"Noah, you are looking at the Creator using human terms and concepts. Earth people ascribe human characteristics to God and use names like "king" and "father". We do not use terms that humanize the Creator. Our view is esoteric, an abstract vision of a supernatural presence pulsing through the universe, not a man in the sky. We hold equal reverence and recognize objective truths without using human terms. You referred to sentient beings created in God's image. We view it more broadly and abstractly, but with the same notion of creation. It is true that there are many types of beings in the universe. However, you should know that beyond the superficial features, there are more similarities than differences in the beings across the galaxy."

"A more appropriate question to ask is just who created chemistry and physics. Ask who created the planets with the proper conditions for life. Such planets can be considered test tubes, with the same physical laws, chemicals, and conditions that would produce the same molecules under the same universal physical and chemical laws. Chemicals have identical properties and will undergo the same reactions under the same conditions, no matter where in the universe they take place. Living beings are a result of the laws of chemistry and physics in action, not a random production. Living beings are a complex extension of carbon chemistry. Chemicals do what their inherent properties force them to do. There is a chemical driving force that produces molecules, which eventually give rise to life forms and DNA. The DNA will then produce beings through the inherent driving force of carbon chemistry and subsequent biochemistry. It is naturally governed by thermodynamics and kinetics. Therefore, the phrase, created in God's image, would mean the creator of chemistry and physics would be responsible for the ultimate production of living things because God wrote all the rules for how the Universe runs. All the beings are manifestations created from the same guidance."

Briel continues with a heightened glow, *"I must humbly admit that even with all our advanced technologies, the creation of the universe by intelligent design cannot be disproven. The supernatural part of living beings comes from the Creator Universe and is not defined by physical laws.*

The universal laws of physics and chemistry create the physical life forms. Supernatural events place the soul into the living beings. It is the merger of the tangible with the intangible. I have taken you down this roundabout discussion for one reason. You should not fear physical death because there is another plane of existence for your supernatural self. If your wave function is aligned with the Universal Essence, we believe it will be an amazing next step. You can feel better about Homo Sapiens' extinction with this larger scope of existence. The good shall continue existence on the next plane, while the wicked are cast into painful chaos due to their misalignment with the Universal Goodness."

Noah pauses to consider Briel's message. Noah slowly responds, *"Your presence has certainly lifted my spirit. I have rarely considered such concepts; I have never focused on any supernatural matters in my entire life. We will need to discuss this in more detail after I have had the time to truly consider all that you have just told me. These thoughts are powerful and make me think about doing the right thing for a good purpose. I do not want to lose myself in this emotional trauma that is tormenting me right now."*

Briel responds quickly, *"Certainly not. I have tried to instill some hope in the greater good and true purpose of existence, both material and supernatural. Hope itself is therapeutic; progress dies without it. You should focus on your role in a much larger mission. If the triggering events can be put off, you will be part of a wonderful transition of Earth into a Homo Galaxus Earth. You will still carry the legacy of Homo Sapiens into the future of Earth rather than cede the planet to the Dracons. You and the other Homo Galaxus hybrids have the Sapiens' legacy and can carry that into a great future. The successful results for Homo Galaxus will end the quarantine of the planet, lift the constraints of forbidden physics, and bring forth astounding technological advances. You can help drive changes that will allow the Earth to become part of the Galactic Confederation. All this is possible in your lifetime. That should be immensely motivating?"*

Noah feels his energy level rising, *"Yes, I wish to live in such a world. Now that I know of such things, I want them. There is no going back now. I was falling into an emotional trap and grieving about a future that could not be. I was acting like a backward Homo Sapiens, not a proper Homo Galaxus. I do have a role in building the fantastic new world that you describe."*

"Very good, Noah. This conversation has taught you something else to remember. Once reality becomes too emotionally painful, one can distort perceptions to create a more acceptable false reality of delusion. Delusion is like an addictive drug for the emotionally compromised. Living in a world of delusion will eventually cause terrible problems. The creation of an artificial emotional reality is self-destructive for both the individual and

society, especially when mass hysteria is produced. When you feel lost, your noble purpose should always guide you back."

Briel pauses to do a deep examination of Noah. "I can sense your renewed focus. It makes you stronger. I will now go. Return to your assignments. Strengthen yourself and refine your new skills. Always keep in mind that you have a critical mission on Earth to complete. The vision of the new civilization you can help create should always be a powerful motivator for you."

Chapter 30.

Frustration is resolved by acceptance

A coach who sparks self-motivation to drive performance is a treasure; a telepathic coach is even more so. Briel's intervention has pulled Noah out of his dark place, flipping his attitude completely. With renewed zeal, Noah is practicing his newly discovered powers. He now successfully blocks all the sneak attacks from Gilmesh. Noah has a clear vision of a galactic future for a Homo Galaxus planet, which greatly boosts his determination. His telepathic outreach is exponentially greater. He senses Viera has come out of her healing trance and is preparing to stop by. He surprises her with a preemptive invitation to visit whenever she is ready.

As Viera leaves her room and starts to cross the hallway to Noah's room, the door slides open before she reaches it. Noah has two large chairs already in place in the middle of the room. She senses that her connection with Noah is markedly different. It has become an equitable two-way linkage. Viera, now curious, tries a deeper probe into Noah's mind and finds a defensive block in place protecting his physical autonomy.

Viera enters the room, and Noah greets her in the Pleiadian way, right hand on the right shoulder, followed by a gentle touch of their temples. They both sit down, and Viera initiates the conversation, "Noah, it is good to see you. Let us speak verbally. I wish to get the full story from you slowly, with all the details. It is obvious that your first round of training has changed you considerably. Your psychic presence is impressive. I feel we are now full teammates, no longer a trainer/trainee relationship. This is good, because that encounter with Ulak nearly took me out with you. I have been in an extended healing trance while you started your training."

"It has been quite an experience so far. Briel has been more than supportive. We had quite the philosophical discussion a short while ago. I suspect he was moderating some of my deeper thoughts while we were talking. He first taught me how to access the collective. I wish I had more time to explore it. My brief time exploring the Pleiadians has been incredible, and I would very much like to visit their planets. I know there are hundreds more civilizations to see, and I can hardly wait. More importantly for the mission, Gilmesh is teaching me self-defense; I am embarrassed after discovering how wimpy I was. He also started filling in the background and the overall aspects of our mission. Later, Uhlt gave me the brutal truths about Homo Sapiens, Dracons, and triggering events.

It did depress me quite a bit. Briel had to intervene. He is such an inspirational, positive influence. By the way, are all Pleiadians so spiritual?"

"Yes, they may have the most sensitive attitudes and telepathic abilities. As they age and gain deeper insight, as Briel has, they may actually be sensing the divine, supernatural part of the Universe. The truly advanced elders can hardly communicate with others because of their deep connection to the Universe. I cannot really describe it properly, and I have only experienced it through the memories of one of my trainers years ago. To get back to you and your training, I can tell that you no longer consider yourself a Homo Sapiens. When I first told you, you knew I was not lying, but you kept clinging to your human roots. I no longer sense any of that in you."

Noah cocks his head, then replies after a short pause, "Yes, you are correct. I have learned too much, including many things that Homo Sapiens will never know. I feel different about myself and about them. I have deep feelings for my mother and humans in general, but now that I know the truth about my true identity, I'll never think of myself as anything other than a Homo Galaxus being."

Viera nods, then asks, "Will you still go back and complete your mission?"

"Yes, especially now that I know the consequences and the alternatives. Anything other than defeating the Dracons and making the Earth into a Homo Galaxus planet is unacceptable," says Noah in a strong, bold voice.

"So, you have come to terms with the inevitable conclusion that Homo Sapiens must fade away. As you see more of the advanced galactic civilizations, it will be perfectly clear that humans will never be allowed to travel through space to infect galactic peace with their corruption and violence. It was a mistake on my part to shelter you from Earthly history, news, and current events. I made it harder for you by letting you ignore the Earth's brutality. Acceptance of your true nature would have been easier for you if I had. You may have realized or seen it in the collective that there have been several initiatives to help bring on population collapse, including some less sympathetic Draconian schemes. The self-destructive nature of Homo Sapiens would have ultimately caused violent population decline, but we believe that there will be less suffering if Homo Sapiens fade away slowly.

Noah cocks his head and asks, "Is a slow, controlled decline in the Homo Sapiens population possible? The chaotic nature of human society and the Draconian schemes make me think that this will be difficult to achieve."

Viera takes a deep breath. Noah senses a large swirl of negative thoughts and frustration in Viera. Viera looks at Noah with a very conflicted expression.

She replies after a tense pause, "You make a good point. It will not be easy. Nothing has been easy with Earth and Homo Sapiens. I have worked for more than a century to help manage the development of their civilization. I have been dedicated and hopeful, but disappointment after disappointment has curbed my optimism. I have seen multiple bloody wars, genocidal slaughters, and all types of horrendous behaviors. I admit that on many occasions, my supervisors had to step in and save me from mental trauma due to what I have seen."

Noah sends Viera sympathetic feelings and asks, "Was it not possible to use mind control on the leaders to force positive changes?"

Viera sighs, "If only it were that easy. Homo Sapiens' society must come together as individual entities, but they lack telepathic connections. Without telepathic abilities, civic duty is weak because of poor personal connections among the population. Lies and corruption taint all of their societies from the bottom up. If top leaders are changed, they are just tossed aside by the corruption and emotional mass hysteria of the masses. A limited number of hybrids and the Earth Council's constrained actions have not been sufficient. Even when a society shows positive progress, its offspring become soft. They allow their sympathies to empower the wicked to destroy the improved society they have just created. With Homo Sapiens, the flawed individual is the building block of civic order. When individual discipline and restraint are lost, social order crumbles."

"Wasn't there a way to suppress the bad to let the good people flourish?" asks Noah hesitantly.

"We had success after success as some countries made progress and they became more civilized and prospered. However, no society has been able to sustain their gains for very long, let alone spread their improvements around the Earth. Homo Sapiens become weak and soft as their lives get comfortable. They lack the necessary discipline to enforce rules to maintain society.   The good people create comfortable communities for themselves, but allow the rest of the world to exist in violence, decadence, and disorder. Eventually, their good communities are swallowed by the bad. Their sympathies eventually bring about destruction as they ignore the wicked, allowing the deviant to prey upon their good nature. You are now exhibiting the same destructive sympathy as you defend Homo Sapiens. It is probably just lingering contamination from your human upbringing."

Noah is disturbed by Viera's comment about him.

"I suppose you have a point. I don't like the insinuation, but I am just getting used to the idea that I am different. Also, I have known mainly good humans and think that they could change their civilization if they were in charge," says Noah very defensively.

"All Homo Sapiens carry the possibility of good and bad behavior, so the bad people just keep appearing, no matter if good people take charge. Good leaders have only held power temporarily. There has never been a Homo Sapiens society that was not filled with lies and corruption. Advanced civilizations require strict, rigorously enforced guidelines to endure. Maintaining civil order with strict guidelines may seem harsh, but it is absolutely necessary for an advanced society. Perhaps the emotional side of Homo Sapiens is too dominant, and that sympathy is mistaken for virtue to always become a fatal flaw."

"I understand what you are saying. Their society softens, becoming overly tolerant and nonjudgmental. Collectively, they forget the value of discipline and the need to preserve the qualities that made their success. They essentially get soft and crumble from the inside. They adopt a false reality based upon human sympathy that disregards the consequences. The barbarians take charge."

"Yes, it has been a continuous cycle of frustration. Now that you and the other Homo Galaxus hybrids have grown up, I am optimistic about the future. I am very certain that you and your fellow Galaxians can produce a true civilization worthy of the Confederation. I hope you avoid the mistakes of your ancestors."

Noah replies at once, "I am confident we can succeed. However, the Homo Sapiens will be a constant issue as their population collapses. It will be messy, but it will be easier as the Homo Galaxus population increases. I assume that the Dracons do not want any Homo Galaxus on Earth. They can enslave the humans but not us. There will be constant conflict with them through the transition. Why can't the Confederation do something about them?"

"The Dracons have been clever. They exploit gray areas in their treaties and in the galactic codes. They have been gaining sympathy from several significant Confederation members. Homo Sapiens continued failure to show any signs of progress leading to future assimilation into the Galactic Confederation has been well noted. This has eroded much of the support for Homo Sapiens. Many think the overall Dracon problems would be solved if they once again had a healthy home planet, and the Earth would be an easy answer. Luckily, most members of the Confederation prefer native species to inhabit and develop their home planets, but a triggering event at this time could sway many to the other side. The successful launch of Homo Galaxus has destroyed the Dracon arguments. We suspect that is why the Dracons have launched so many schemes to cause a triggering event. Noah, your successful training here at full capability could be a major boost in the final acceptance of the new plan for the Earth. You and the others like you have a few final questions to answer, but I am very confident in your success."

"So, I am engaged in a battle for control of the Earth. That would explain why the Dracon hybrid tried to kill me as soon as he identified me."

"Yes. I am afraid the conflict between Dracons and all Homo Galaxus hybrids is real and will not go away. I do have exciting news for our mission. A new person is being added: she is a Homo Galaxus hybrid like you and a physicist. Her name is Aditi. She just completed a smaller mission with a team of particle physicists. She will be joining us here soon to have her full abilities unleashed. She will join you in your future training sessions and will be another fully empowered hybrid helping us defeat Ulak."

Chapter 31.

Spread doubt to temper runaway emotions

Noah suddenly feels exhausted after his meeting with Viera. There is no day and night cycle on the spaceship, so Noah has lost track of his sleep cycle. He has no idea how long he has been awake. His dominant cognitive side is excited about further exploring the vast information in the collective, but his weariness comes from deeper down, perhaps emotional exhaustion combined with just plain lack of sleep. He hopes his exhaustion is due to sleep deprivation rather than emotional stress. He does not want to appear weak or emotionally compromised any longer. Regardless of one's mental fortitude, an avalanche of paradigm-disrupting disclosures is going to land a staggering blow at some point. Perhaps Briel knows this and is compelling him to rest. Noah relents and lies down to sleep in hopes of regaining full strength. Before falling asleep, he wonders what Aditi is like and how soon he can meet her.

Noah is awakened from a very deep slumber by a message from Briel, *"Good day. I hope you are now well rested. Come to me for another training session as soon as you are refreshed and have eaten something."*

Noah opens his eyes and replies, *"Yes, thank you. I feel quite well. I will be there shortly."*

Noah sits up and takes a deep breath. He feels very good, filled with energy. He grins, knowing that his sleep session may have also been enhanced by a healing trance from Briel.

Pab guides Noah through the spaceship to Breil's room after exchanging greetings with Zizzletik in the control room. Noah gets a pleasant welcoming vibe from Zizzletik and is starting to like the little guy. Noah enters Briel's room to find him once again floating in the lotus position. Noah sits in the chair placed in the middle of the room, and once again, gets a warm feeling as if he were sitting in front of a fireplace in the winter.

Briel speaks telepathically this time, *"Noah, we have decided to scrub your mission and destroy the Earth's population."*

Noah is stunned and feels a cold shock running through his body. Anger, fear, sadness, and other powerful emotions course through his veins. He feels his fists tighten and his jaw clenches. He is about to shout in protest, but then senses something. *"That is a lie. You are testing me. I can tell, even you cannot lie to me."*

Briel smiles, claps his hands, and speaks verbally, "Yes, very good, Noah. I was lying. I had no doubt you could detect the ugly stench of falsehood. I want you to think about your emotional response. I could feel the eruption of powerful emotions streaming through you. I know you well enough to know that your emotions are secondary to your cognition, as in all Homo Galaxus individuals. However, your emotional response was significant, was it not?"

"Yes, I must admit that my emotions flared. I am disappointed that my emotions nearly triggered an angry outburst. Luckily, I was able to detect that your statement was untruthful."

"Very good, Noah. That is the point of this lesson: deceptive lies can inflame emotions. This is an uncommon, insignificant experience for telepathic people because lies are easily detected, as you have just shown. Now consider Homo Sapiens and their inability to detect lies. Lies become powerful weapons for the wicked and for the Dracons. It is very possible you may need to start or stop a campaign of mass hysteria as part of your mission, so you need to fully understand it. Assuming the Homo Sapiens 'fading away' strategy continues to its ultimate conclusion, there could be many challenges arising from a collapsing population. There is also no doubt that the Dracons will take devious measures to oppose Homo Galaxus's development. The succeeding Homo Galaxus generations will certainly need to understand and deal with emotionally charged situations. Coordinated lies can be crafted to generate emotional responses. Repetition of the lies will corrupt the isolated human mind and create an emotional shell that repels any contrary ideas, no matter how obvious it is that their emotionally held beliefs are disproven. You and your peers must remain vigilant to mass hysteria flare-ups in the Homo Sapiens society. A deliberate effort to emotionally compromise a large group of humans may result in an emotional reality, a reality based on deceit. The wicked perpetrator of an emotional reality creates an agitated army protected by a shield of passionate denial, and they may set this army against you. At this point, logic and actual truths are meaningless to a mob like that. Violence, destruction, and death are produced when the emotionally compromised mob targets enemies as directed by their corrupt leaders. Human history is filled with mass hysteria events fueled by unrestrained emotionalism."

Noah thinks back to his attack by Ulak. The thought of Ulak producing an irrational mob to support his efforts sends a chill down his spine. "So, what can be done? It seems like extraordinary actions are needed."

"You now have the power to terminate human life simply by concentrating on their heart or lungs and compressing them. That is unacceptable and usually ineffective against a mob. Martyrs are created, or animosity toward you is produced, if you are identified as the cause of mass casualties. However, you can implant competing emotions. The most potent emotion to negate toxic mass hysteria is doubt. Without telepathic connections, humans become self-righteous and intolerant when wrapped in a fortified emotional reality. Put questions into their minds they had never faced, thanks to their smug emotional armor. You will be accessing their psyche from the inside; this is almost always successful, while words and information are not. It can be done quite effectively. Do you understand?"

"I do. An emotional mind can easily become a closed mind when manipulated. Doubt must be created to burst their inappropriate emotional reality. Hysteria will not be extinguished until the mind can open itself to pursue rational evaluation of the world."

"Well said, you clearly understand the theory. Let us see if you can put the concepts into practice. Follow me."

Briel drifts toward Noah and appears to stand up, but his feet are several inches off the ground thanks to his levitation belt. Briel moves to the door, and Noah stands and follows. The door opens, and Briel turns right and heads down the hallway, passing by door after door. A long distance down the hallway, the line of doors stops. Briel opens the last door and enters a large room with a high ceiling. The ceiling casts bright yet soft light. A large table in the center of the room holds a human female lying on it. A tight-fitting blanket covers the female up to her shoulders. A large pod that obviously held the human is floating just beyond the table. Noah sees a long row of similar pods stretching down the length of the room.

Noah is shocked by this sight; his anxiety flares. Anticipation about what Briel has planned sends a shiver down his spine. He blurts out, "Is that a human? Did you abduct her for experimentation? This is a bit disturbing."

Briel points toward the female. *"Let us communicate telepathically here. Remain calm, it is not what you think. This is one of the Homo Sapiens we recovered from a Dracon ship. We detected the unsanctioned abductions and captured a Dracon with a cargo of humans. Do not be upset; we will remove their abduction memories and return them to Earth when we return. We suspect this Dracon was conditioning these humans to spread targeted hysteria on Earth. The Dracon insists otherwise, but it is also illegal if he were poaching humans as food. It is difficult to abstract anything from a Dracon, but all the humans have memories of their participation in violent riots and were clearly directed to do so. They are also suffering from multiple other traumas and emotional instabilities. They have been implanted with a very negative emotional reality. I had this female removed from the suspension pod a little while ago. The table and blanket have her immobilized. I now have her believing that she is sitting in her apartment. I want you to access her thoughts and see if you can detect the emotional constraints that are in place."*

Noah looks closely at the woman. Her hair is cut in an unusual style, with one side clipped short and the other long, flipped to the side. Bright pink streaks run through her brown hair. She has multiple piercings on her ears with more in her nose and eyebrow; there are others lower on her body that he cannot see but can sense. She has several neck tattoos, with others over much of her body. Noah reaches into her mind to glimpse her thoughts and inner foundations.

Breil joins Noah, *"Do you sense all the rampant, unrestrained emotions? Go past those to find the core that they surround. What do you see?"*

"I see fear, great fear of the wealthy and powerful. There is also self-loathing and envy of others. Confusion and frustration abound. I see hatred for many, but unrestrained love for others. There seems to be little tangible reasoning to support the strong feelings. It is like a steel box, but empty inside. The dream of violent revolution is prevalent and seems out of place. There are so many contradictions and disorder, yet there is strident absolutism."

"Now, spread doubt deep down into the center of the emotions."

Briel observes, then interrupts, *"No, use more force. It should be a command, not a suggestion. Push very hard and do not stop until you sense the implanting of your commands and the changes you demand."*

Briel senses the increasing force of Noah's mind. Then, finally, the contour of the woman's mind shifts. The conglomeration of her emotional shell collapses to leave her true internal matrix awash in therapeutic doubt. Briel and Noah pull back.

"Did I finally do it properly? Was that how it feels?"

"Yes, I think you did complete the assignment with minimal help. I have seen in your past that you have redirected thoughts and even wiped away recent memories in humans. It is sad observing Homo Sapiens as they live with the idea that they are the pinnacle of creation and the most advanced creatures in the universe. If they only knew that their minds are weak and subservient to advanced telepathic beings. Now I want you to try it again on another specimen."

Briel summons two grays who look like Zizzletik but are wearing white jumpsuits. They are bringing forward another pod from the back half of the room. Noah sighs with mixed emotions about re-arranging another human's mind.

Chapter 32.

Healing trances

After discovering his power to profoundly manipulate human thought, Noah's opinion of Homo Sapiens has dimmed further, as has his bond with them. He no longer thinks of humans as equals. Transformations of this magnitude produce an extensive reorganization of one's perspective. There is no going back except by the false reality of severe denial. He wonders just what kind of being he is becoming. The extensive mental changes he forced on the humans in his last session with Briel have troubled him. Has he merely replaced bad ideas and beliefs or has he changed their souls? He is not sure he wants to know the answer.

Noah is back in his room after the lesson, which seemed to last a very long time. Briel told Noah to have more food and drink, then rest because Uhlt would contact him soon. Noah hopes he recovers sufficiently before the next session with Uhlt.

The psychic manipulation of humans was draining at first. It could have been due to the stress he was feeling because he was manipulating a living human, immobilized and strapped down to a table like a lab rat. Maybe it was the thought in the back of his mind, imagining his mother being strapped to a table like this one and fertilized to create him, a Homo Galaxus baby. However, by the time he finished practicing on the last human, he found it much easier. Does he have any boundaries to his ability?

Noah asks Pab for a large nectar drink and a reclining chair with a cup holder. Pab readily supplies him with both. Noah sips his alien nectar and tries to make sense of it all. Having grown up in a Homo Sapiens world as one of them, he feels a strong connection. Just a short while ago, he was a boring, nerdy human, but suddenly, he learns that he is an alien creation. His perspective is in turbulent disarray. Now he knows he is an advanced species and that the Homo Sapiens era must end. The idea that a new Homo Galaxus future will dawn and that he will be part of its founding generation is what motivates him to accept his new reality. However, the emotional connections remain. Maybe his attachment is mere naiveté, based on a childlike idealization of human society. He wishes he had paid more attention to current events and the history of humanity. The more he thinks about wars, lies, riots, corruption, genocides, and criminal behaviors that are routine for Homo Sapiens, the more he understands the Galactic Confederation viewpoint. Also, after seeing what a truly advanced society looks like, he realizes how ignorant and arrogant most

Homo Sapiens really are. They indeed are like park squirrels who want to drive a car. That idea would be funny if it wasn't so true to life. Perhaps if he can delay any triggering event until after his mother completes a long, happy life, he will feel better about it all. Noah eventually dozes off into a light sleep.

Noah is awakened by a message from Uhlt. *"It is time for your next lesson. Come to my chamber."*

Noah gets up and tries to prepare for Uhlt as best as he can. The last lesson was a rough one. He asks Pab to direct him, and he starts the long walk across the vessel. After blocking two more sneak attacks by Gilmesh, he soon sits in the same chair in the dimly lit room of Uhlt. He is still a little unsettled looking at Uhlt; it is odd considering that he gets the opposite feeling with Zizzletik, even though they have similar appearances. He must be sensing Uhlt's mind and feeling another round of disconcerting information.

"Welcome back. I will show you more of your new abilities. First, you have healing trance powers. You may put yourself in a mild healing trance and can enhance healing for others. Please close your eyes and relax. I will start a healing trance for you. I want you to focus on the part of your psyche that is activated. To master the technique, you must be able to access this area on demand. Relax your mind and body, and then I can start your healing trance."

Noah sits with his eyes closed, trying to relax. Then he feels the soothing sensations of a healing trance. He concentrates on the sensation. After a few minutes, Uhlt stops, and Noah looks up to see Uhlt staring at him with his large, almond-shaped, black eyes.

"Now I want you to put yourself in a healing trance. Relax and find that same area in your mind to start it yourself."

Noah struggles and fails to do it.

Uhlt interrupts his effort, *"I will start another healing trance. Pay closer attention. You will try again afterwards. We will repeat this cycle until you succeed."*

After the fifth or sixth attempt, Noah manages to initiate a healing trance.

"Very good. Now, to heal others, you must project yourself into their mind. Then just activate the same area, and you will start a healing trance for them. You may also enhance one that is in progress in the same manner. You cannot do that for me because my mind is too powerful. Our mismatch is too great. Soon, you will be able to practice with another Homo Galaxus who is now on board."

"That will be interesting. I have never met another Homo Galaxus, which seems odd now that I have met several extraterrestrials. I feel confident that

I could block an equal from starting a healing trance just as I learned about self-defense from Gilmesh."

"Yes, that is correct. Beings with comparable powers must agree and allow. That is the next lesson. You can use the healing trance on weaker beings like Homo Sapiens to essentially hypnotize them. I know that in your last lesson, you were able to implant broad ideas and emotions, but there are additional actions you may take. You may put them in a trance using the same technique. Then you may implant specific actions for them to do. You may find it helpful to hypnotize a human to perform an action for you. Also, you may have a human commit an act unconsciously at a later time when they hear a triggering word or phrase you give them. Humans can become your own remote-controlled devices. The action cannot be too objectionable, otherwise it damages the human mind. For instance, you cannot make someone kill another unless they are already willing to kill. Exceeding one's moral codes can cause mental breakdown and insanity. Be aware that repeated manipulations can eventually produce a person who is willing to kill. The Dracons do not hesitate to employ this tactic. Do you understand?"

"Yes, all that makes sense. I have realized that the human mind is easily controlled and that telepathic beings can influence them with implanted messages. It does make me wonder how many awful events on Earth were prompted telepathically by the Dracons. I do have a question along those lines. Do you think I can withstand attacks from Ulak after all this training? I have been told all blocks on my abilities have been removed, and I am learning so much."

"I was able to learn the details of your incident with that creature, Ulak. You should keep in mind that Viera, even in a weakened state, was able to fight back enough for your friends to get you away from him. Your abilities are approaching hers. I do think you, at full strength, could hold off attacks from other hybrids. Another Homo Galaxus is being added to the mission, and the combination should be effective. Ulak is very likely a Draconian hybrid. Be cautious; there may be something else going on with him; he may have other hybrids around him secretly. If there is a Dracon getting directly involved, the Earth Council will intervene quickly and severely. Ulak did make a mistake attacking you that way, so he may have called for support. Always remember that Dracons don't fight by any honorable rules. He exposed himself as an unsanctioned hybrid who is also getting involved in Homo Sapiens society. It is a severe violation if he is trying to cause a triggering event. We would like to capture Ulak as evidence to present to the Confederation. The Earth Council or our allies could abduct him ourselves, but that action could possibly cause greater sympathy for the Dracons. It would be better for your team of hybrids to capture him and turn him over to us."

The thought of a potential battle with Ulak frightens Noah, as it causes the vision of his near-fatal collapse to run through his mind.

Uhlt senses the anxiety and responds, *"Do not despair. You have a larger team now and will be given special equipment. Gilmesh has more training for you that will be useful. Most importantly, we will be following you closely. I was told you have government support. Use them as you can, but be careful. Remember what you were told. Part of the government is on our side of the conflict, while others have been trading allegiance with the Dracons for advanced technology and weapons. Screen them all carefully. Also, be wary of friends and colleagues; they may have been corrupted by the other side and the Dracons. Never trust a human, always verify."*

"I have already experienced that. A good friend is tied to advanced aerospace and military corporations. He has certain secret knowledge concerning extraterrestrials and guessed that I was not human. He tried to coerce and bribe me into divulging higher technology for his contacts in the super-secret programs of those companies."

"It would be safe to assume that those companies are allied with the Dracons. Those humans have traded their allegiance for advanced technology. Unwittingly, they are helping to bring about devastating consequences from a triggering event. It is good to hear that you have recognized their intentions. We are done training now. However, Gilmesh wishes to spar with you so that you may practice your defensive skills. After that, you will need to put yourself in a healing trance. Arcturians are a demanding race. Please go to his chamber now."

Chapter 33.

Aditi joins in

Noah is happily back in his room, flat on his back and exhausted after a training session with Gilmesh. He had to repel sustained telepathic attacks from Gilmesh, the much more powerful Arcturian. The session continued until Noah was exhausted, but he did learn advanced deflection techniques. Noah is mentally drained and has no interest in exploring the wonders of the collective. He decides to use his new skills to put himself in a well-deserved healing trance.

Hours later, Noah is rousted from his healing trance by Viera. She wants to introduce Aditi, the new team member, and another Homo Galaxus. Noah had enough time in the healing trance to help his depleted state, but not to fully recharge. After a short while to wake up fully and straighten himself, Noah messages Viera that he is ready. He tries to stay cool but must admit to himself that he is somewhat excited to meet another of his kind.

Noah senses their approach and opens his room door. Viera walks in first, still looking impressive in her jumpsuit. Closely following is Aditi. Noah is surprised by his first look at her. His expectations were off the mark. She has lovely caramel-colored skin and thick, shimmering black hair dangling down past her shoulders. Her eyes are a bright hazel-green, which Noah finds almost mesmerizing. Aditi is a few inches shorter than Noah and looks very athletic in her matching blue jumpsuit.

Viera walks up to Noah and exchanges the Pleiadian greeting. Aditi confidently steps up to Noah to initiate the same Pleiadian greeting. Noah feels her pleasant energy as their foreheads touch. Also, it feels very natural.

"Noah, this is Aditi, Aditi, this is Noah. Aditi has recently completed her first mission at Cambridge involving a CERN project. I have been supporting her since she was young, just like you. Also, I have brought her up to date with Ulak and the rest of our mission. She has just been through her first round of training with the Earth Councilors. I told her about her real identity well before her last mission, so she has had a head start adjusting to that disclosure. You both have your full abilities; all earlier blocks and screens have been removed. Good thing too, it may take all our collective powers to thwart Ulak and complete our mission. You will take the remaining training sessions together. Now that I have introduced you, I will step back and give you a chance to get to know one another. I am confident that you two will make a powerful team." Viera nods to each of them and heads out the door.

The pair stares nervously at one another for an instant, then Aditi breaks the silence, "Why don't we sit and talk for a while? Maybe have one of those nectar beverages…"

"Yes, certainly. I should have made the offer already. I'm not used to hosting visitors," says Noah with a hint of embarrassment. He directs Pab to slide out two chairs and two glasses of nectar.

Noah grabs the two glasses of nectar that float to him on a gravity-defying tray. He walks over to the chairs and hands Aditi her drink. Aditi sits and takes a long drink, and Noah follows her lead.

Aditi breaks the silence again, "So, you are the pretty boy that I have heard so much about. I can sense that you are a very nice person, so I should warn you that I am very direct and very blunt. I grew up in Seattle with strict, conventional parents. It forced me to toughen up starting at a very young age. I hope my personality doesn't put you off, because I really am very excited to join you in this mission and the greater Galaxus objective."

Noah smiles, "I am really excited to meet another Homo Galaxus. I can sense your energy and boldness. It doesn't bother me at all. If anything, I am a little jealous as I tend to overthink things at times. I grew up in a relatively quiet, mid-sized city you've never heard of, not too far from the university. My parents and Viera probably shielded me a little too much. I was able to devote most of my time to physics and studying."

"That sounds like a dream. My father forced me to do chores before he let me study. If I wasn't cooking or cleaning our house, I was working at one of my family's gas station convenience marts. Thanks to Viera, I was sent to a boarding school where I was able to zoom through the grades early, then on to college. I had my Ph.D. in short order. As a postdoc at Cambridge, I completed my first mission, stopping a very small aspect of forbidden physics from Sapien discovery."

Noah continues, "Viera only very recently told me about Homo Galaxus, psychic powers, forbidden physics, and extraterrestrials. I still am processing much of it. I see the reasoning and wisdom in the Confederation's plans, but I may care too much about Homo Sapiens, especially my mother, who took such good care of me when I was a child. As a toddler, I was overwhelmed by my telepathic abilities, and everyone else thought I was brain-damaged. My mother always believed in me, and then Viera straightened me out and got me functioning properly. I fully accept my mission and the galactic plans, but I may be a little conflicted," replies Noah.

Aditi laughs, "I have no such conflict. I found it liberating when I was told I was an upgraded species of human. I always felt like a stranger while living among the Sapiens. Even as a young child, I was very annoyed by the arrogance of their strong opinions when they were so obviously ignorant. I think I was more intelligent at four years old than the rest of my family put together. Sapiens leap to strong conclusions based only upon their feelings, not rational thoughts. They say stupid things like 'Oh, that feels right or that seems good to me'. They latch onto comfortable emotional realities and shut out any contrary information or conclusions that could be gleaned from a minimal amount of analysis and deliberation. I found it highly frustrating. I sensed that something never added up as I was growing up. All the details fell into place after Viera told me how things really are in the galaxy. It makes me wish for a triggering event."

Noah winces, "I would be troubled if there was a catastrophic annihilation. I prefer to have the Homo Sapiens fade away. We may need human helpers until the Homo Galaxus population can grow rapidly enough to reach acceptable levels. By the way, a triggering event may give the Earth to the Dracons; I find that totally objectionable."

Aditi nods, "Yes, of course. The future of the Earth is a Homo Galaxus future. We do agree strongly on that. I suppose you will be the sensitive member of the team. You can keep me from being too brash and inconsiderate, and I will keep you from being too soft and indecisive."

"Yes, it looks like we have complementary personalities. That does seem like an intelligent decision for whoever put us together on the same team. Are you joining my research group at the university?"

"No, I have a postdoc position with the particle physics group one floor below yours. I am a little older than you and already hold a doctorate. Also, it would be too obvious for me to be in your group. Maybe this Ulak creature won't take notice of me until I start fighting him. However, I will be near and in constant contact with you."

"That is good to know. Ulak seemed unusually powerful and should not be underestimated."

"I was told you have one group member with ties to the bad side of the military-industrial complex. We will need to keep an eye on him as well. They are the deceitful ones who have dishonored the secret treaties with the Confederation. They are despicable in their personal ambitions for money and power, as they gather forbidden alien technology. They don't realize that they are pushing for their own doom. They lie to themselves as much as they lie to everyone around them."

"Jesse, the one you mention, has been a good friend. I think the ground-level people like him do not know about the treaties and certainly do not understand the terrible consequences possible."

"That may be, but that is also the reason the Sapiens are doomed and need to fade away as fast as possible. Their violent, corrupt nature and inability to do what is necessary to maintain an orderly society are unacceptable. Such a culture always ends in collapse. They lie constantly, and without telepathic abilities, honest people are easy to fool. Liars offer soothing deceptions to the masses, who construct an emotional reality they staunchly defend. Ignorant, emotionally charged fools are not proper building blocks for an advanced society. I am amazed that society has come this far. When you mix ugly lies with their emotional predilections, it is a disaster waiting to happen."

"It sounds like you have already met with Uhlt. I cannot argue with your logic, especially after using the collective to see what a truly advanced society looks like," says Noah with a hint of sadness.

Aditi makes a bold suggestion, "We should connect telepathically now. We can be totally honest and get all thoughts out in the open. We are in good alignment after our discussion, so we should take it to the next level by making a strong psychic connection now. This way, we can form a much tighter team. What do you say?"

Noah is caught off guard and feels a little nervous. He takes a second to consider the phony relationships of Homo Sapiens versus the starkly honest ones of telepathic, advanced civilizations. He wants the best for a future Homo Galaxus world. "Yes, let's have a direct connection and have no secrets with one another. Homo Galaxus society needs to establish this standard. Let's do it."

Aditi smiles and nods in agreement. Both close their eyes and reach out to each other's minds.

Noah connects readily with Aditi, as if it's instinctive. Being a Homo Galaxus and meeting an equal is a new and welcome experience. Connections with the extraterrestrials are difficult because of their overpowering mental powers. The power of the superior mind always dominates the inferior. He had the same feelings with Viera in the past, but maybe that will be different with her now.

Noah comments first, "*Our connection feels good, very comfortable. It is good to have another Homo Galaxus around. I have not had such a pleasant connection.*"

"*Yes, agreed. I think this bodes well for the future of Homo Galaxus. I can sense your high levels of physics and mathematics. You have obviously spent a great deal of time studying. You are certainly a genuine scholar, as Viera described. However, you need to do something with your shaggy hair. You are a representative for all the Galaxus people, so your looks should match your stature, especially around the Sapiens. Don't panic, I think you are cute, but with a real haircut, you would be quite handsome.*"

"*I am sorry about my hair, but I have never paid much attention to it. Now I am glad our eyes are shut; I may be blushing. You surprised me when you walked in here. Viera had only told me your name, nothing else. I thought all Homo Galaxus would be blond like me. It was a pleasant surprise*" *to see you. I think you are beautiful with your glistening black hair and hypnotic green eyes, highlighting your gorgeous caramel colored skin. You are obviously in top physical shape and look incredible. I will need to improve my looks, get in shape, and get a haircut to keep up with you."*

"Noah, you surely are a sweet one. I understand why the Sapien woman is having sexual relations with you."

Noah is flustered. *"Oh, you see that. I am just..."*

"Don't worry, I am not judging. It is just another part of your mission. We need to know what the offspring of a Sapien and a Galaxus would be like." She pauses, recognizing Noah's surprise. *"You didn't know?"*

Noah is shocked. *"I never thought about it like that. Viera was encouraging me, but it didn't seem like she was actually directing me in another aspect of my mission."*

"Hybrid males can be just like human males when hormones start spiking; their brains stop working properly. Also, it was your first interaction with a woman; of course, you were overwhelmed. You know, if the Earth Council did not want you to do something, you would not be allowed to do it. I forgot that you were only recently told about your true nature. You are still catching up. I had that disclosure some time ago and probably had more screens removed earlier than you. I read it in Viera's mind. It is important to the fading Sapiens plan that you find out what a Galaxus/Sapiens child is like."

Noah is still panicking, *"I don't know if I am qualified to take care of an infant."*

"You won't, the council will take the fetus at 10 weeks and incubate it on their vessel. Your Sapien woman will not need to give birth, and her memory will be erased, leaving only a few mysterious scars. You will not need to become a responsible father yet. The council will give the infant to a suitable couple for observation. This is standard practice; look it up in the collective when you get time."

Noah exercises his newfound powers to regain his composure. *"Well, that makes me feel somewhat better. I still don't know how I feel about it all. Intimate relations always carry associated emotions,"* thinks Noah, still somewhat embarrassed.

Aditi sends a blast of objection, *"Noah, you must break from the bad habits you have picked up from the Sapiens. You are afraid and embarrassed to reach out and read the thoughts of those around you. That means that you are holding back and trying to create a shell around you, just like the way the Sapiens live. They have no choice, but you do. An advanced society must be completely open and honest. If you have anything to say about me or what I do, let it be known. If I am an advanced being, I take it as honest feedback without an emotional response. You should reach into my thoughts, and I should reciprocate. That way, we have an optimal relationship of openness without secrets. I understand this is new to you. I have been aware of my special Galaxus powers and have interacted with Viera as an equal, sharing minds for some time now. We are out of time; you need to advance your thinking. Do not be afraid. You will like the new way."*

Noah feels more awkward, but knows Aditi is correct. He reaches deeply into Aditi's mind. It still feels natural, but it brings on a lingering hint of self-consciousness. He feels like he is walking into someone's room without knocking. He senses her mixed emotions for him right now. She wants him to step up and act more like Homo Galaxus than Homo Sapiens. He sees her good intentions toward him and her focus on the future. He discovers many memories of Aditi's life, including a recent boyfriend in England. Suddenly, he feels her psyche touch his; she flows into his memories. His memory of his first sexual encounter with Ruth rises out of his memory, and he is sure Aditi is seeing everything.

Noah messages, *"I'm sorry you have to see this with Ruth. I don't know what to say."*

"What part of an open and honest society do you not understand? I want you to probe all of my thoughts. It will give us a comprehensive relationship that is resilient."

"I suppose I am used to the closed social interactions of humans. Openness is a new concept for me."

"Relax, Noah. Remember, no secrets. Don't feel as a Sapien would, think like a Galaxus. It is important that you finish that part of your mission; I totally agree. You really didn't think that the Earth Council would let you settle down and marry a human. That makes no sense at all when the plan is to create a Homo Galaxus civilization. Think about it, and you will know what your next mission of this type will be. You and I will partner and produce many Galaxus/Galaxus babies. I look forward to our joining together to create our new species. I am honored to be the mother of a new society. I can tell you are interested in sexual relations with me."

Noah suppresses his feelings of embarrassment again. He wants to act more appropriately for a Homo Galaxus. *"Yes, you are very beautiful. I would very much like that. I also want to bring on a Homo Galaxus Earth. However, you did see that Ruth triggered an emotional response from me. I do have feelings for her now. Does this bother you?"*

"It does not bother me at all. If you look further into my past, I, too, have had sexual relations with a Sapien. A fetus was created, and the council took it for incubation and fostering. We both have duty requirements. I found human relationships lacking. I think we will find that true psychic and physical intimacy between fellow Galaxus partners will be far superior to the physical-only Sapien bonding. More importantly, you and I know we have civic responsibilities for our species. When our advanced society is formed, duty will be a priority, as it is in all such societies. Look at the selfish

Homo Sapiens trapped in their non-telepathic shells. Duty to society is an afterthought. Happiness is getting a hormone-induced dopamine spike, brought on by selfish actions or artificially by the use of recreational chemicals of one type or another. They lie constantly for self-satisfaction, no matter what they tell you. If they were culturally advanced at all, civic duty would influence their definitions of happiness. Achievement and positive productivity for society would be the core of happiness, not frivolous physical or emotional thrills. Humans never ask themselves to define happiness; they just chase primitive biochemical stimuli or selfish ego enhancements without regard for the greater good and the creation of a truly advanced civilization. That is why they are doomed, while we will progress. Ask Briel if you want further confirmation."

Noah reaches deeper into Aditi's mind. He lets down his guard and opens up. He senses many ups and downs in Aditi's memories. He can now feel a surging partnership as their link strengthens.

"I can think of no greater reward than bonding with you and creating a Homo Galaxus society. I hope we can survive the coming battle with Ulak, and we can start our society."

"We are in this together. If we stick together, we will prosper," says Aditi with a big smile.

Chapter 34.

Zizzletik helps out

Noah and Aditi were instructed to rest before the next round of training. However, Noah cannot stop thinking about his meeting with Aditi. The shocks to his system keep coming. He now realizes that he must stop being a telepathic introvert; he is missing too much. Life was much simpler before he started interacting with females. Now he discovers he has a double mission: impregnate Ruth, then partner with Aditi to help start the Homo Galaxus species. The most comforting aspect of his situation is the flawless logic of the plan. Noah can only wonder if he is being too emotional and, therefore, a poor example of a Homo Galaxus. His deepest concern is that his human emotional leanings are merely bad habits picked up by years of association, not a fundamental flaw in himself.

Noah yields to his restlessness and leaves his room to walk the hallway. He walks to the far end of the vessel, then turns around to go the opposite direction. He passes by his room and keeps walking. He can sense Zizzletik as he approaches the control room.

"*Welcome back, Noah. I sense that your anxiety level is high right now. Can I provide any supportive items? Pab has a large selection of accessories that can be helpful. Would you like a beverage, perhaps?*"

Noah looks at the alien and realizes it no longer shocks him as it did during his first encounter. Those large black eyes were frightening at first, but now he feels an odd kind of fellowship.

"*Thank you, Zizzletik. I felt I needed to get out of my room for a while. May I sit here?*"

"*Of course, I would enjoy some company besides that of Pab.*"

Noah walks over to one of the chairs circling the large metallic mushroom-like thing in the middle of the control room.

"*I could use a large glass of that delicious nectar beverage that I have been drinking with my meals.*"

Zizzletik nods, then a levitating tray carrying a large glass appears from the far wall and floats over to Noah. Noah lifts the glass and takes a large drink.

"*Zizzletik, how do you like working for Uhlt and the other Earth Council members? Do they treat you well? Do you trust them and their plans?*"

"*It has been a privilege to be assigned to Uhlt. Many of my type are sold to other beings as laborers. I have worked for him, and no other, for a long time. I was created to work for my owner, and it is rewarding to do my assigned tasks. After many seasons of loyal duty, Uhlt trained me to be a starship captain. I am very happy to serve. Also, the Earth councilors treat me very well. I trust them to do the right thing always. They take their mission very seriously."*

"That is helpful to hear. I have found some longer-term council plans for myself from discussions with Aditi. I suppose I was not prepared for that; maybe I should have been. I have trusted Viera my entire life, but the scope of my mission continues to grow and grow. Now I am introduced to Aditi, another like me. That is exciting, but I have come to find out that they have selected her to be my life partner. This is an arranged marriage, essentially. I don't know if it is just the shock that bothers me, or if I'm being obstinate. Maybe I am just feeling inadequate or just clinging to my childhood. Aditi seems stronger and more mature; she certainly is better looking than me. She did make fun of my hair."

"I am a simple creature and lifelong servant. I can tell you that I have great trust in Uhlt and the other councilors. You should, too. They appear to have great trust in you. I am not trained to help relieve this type of anxiety, but I can do something for your hair."

A large device floats over to Noah. It looks like a large, oversized helmet that rests on the shoulders. Zizzletik walks over to Noah and the helmet-thing.

Zizzletik continues, *"This is a Pleiadian device that they use to maintain their hairstyle. All you need to do is put this on and lower the visor. The device will show you a variety of haircut options. Select the one you want, and it will cut your hair accordingly."*

"Wow, another amazing device. You know, maybe a new look would help give me a boost of extra confidence."

Zizzletik places the device over Noah's head and lowers the visor to activate it. Noah is presented with several hairstyle options, each accompanied by a video simulating what it would look like on him. He selects one and smiles.

Chapter 35. Stingers and a fright

Gilmesh summons Noah and Aditi to a large room they had not visited before to continue their self-defense training. They meet in the hallway outside of their adjacent rooms.

Aditi sees Noah and his new look. His hair is combed straight back with a small flip at the base of his neck. She smiles and says, "Noah, you cut your hair. That is a very good look for you. I think you look like a serious Galaxus representative now. Also, that is a sexy look too."

Noah suppresses embarrassing feelings and responds, "Thank you. You set a high standard, and I am trying to keep up with you."

Noah faces Aditi and puts his hand on her shoulder to initiate a Pleiadian greeting. This time he reaches out with his mind to make a deep mental connection as they touch heads.

Aditi reciprocates, *"Now that is a proper telepathic greeting. I look forward to keeping this habit. Now let's see what Gilmesh has in store for us."*

They are directed by Pab to walk down past the control room to the far side of the vessel. It is near the examination room where Noah practiced his telepathy on human subjects. He still has reservations about that lesson, but knows it had to be done. He is now concerned about today's lesson as they reach the designated door, and it opens unexpectedly, making him jump. They walk into a relatively small room with Gilmesh standing at the far side. The small room makes him look even more imposing than usual; he looks tall, muscular, and purplish blue.

"Come in. I have taken you to this small room because I wish to show you a couple of close-contact defense moves. You both have learned to fend off telepathic attacks to your psyche and your key physical processes. You must have a defense against actual physical attacks if your opponent can block your telepathic defenses. I will show you what I mean."

Suddenly, Noah feels a sharp pain in his arm and clutches it as he gasps in surprise. A second later, Aditi does the same.

Gilmesh responds, "What you have just experienced is what I call a stinger. The vast array of nerve endings in your skin is there to sense the environment surrounding you. It is very difficult to defend all of them all the time, but it is possible to repel an attack of this kind. Battle suits block this kind of mild attack, but you are not going to a battlefield. The pain of a stinger attack can be maintained by the attacker if not repelled. Luckily, it is easy to repel. You may use the same technique you have learned to protect your vital body parts to stop a stinger attack. Noah, I will sting your arm until you repel my attack."

Before Noah can respond, his arm feels a sharp point of pain. It goes away only after he figures out how to repel it. Before he could celebrate his success, another sting hit him mercilessly. Grimacing, he strains to quell a series of stings. It is a painful lesson, but soon he is able to stop the attacks nearly instantaneously. The stingings then cease.

"Good, that is correct. That is exactly what should be done. Aditi, it is your turn. I hope you were following along."

Aditi winces, grabs her arm, and shrieks in pain. She learns to block the attacks faster than Noah did.

Gilmesh nods his head in approval, then says, "Very good. You can now defend yourself against this kind of attack. Now I want you to go on the offensive. Aditi, you will go first. I want you to pick a spot on Noah, then recall the feeling of the stings I hit you with. Project that feeling onto the spot of skin to deliver a sting.

Aditi turns to Noah and concentrates. Noah feels a sting on his arm and then blocks the attack.

Aditi responds, "This trick could really come in handy. I could have used it in some of those rough streets in England."

"Noah, it is your turn," says Gilmesh.

Noah looks at Aditi's ear and stings it. She repels it promptly and shoots Noah a dirty look in jest.

I have one more maneuver for you two. Gilmesh holds out his arms and says, "I want you to grab my arms."

Noah and Aditi give each other a puzzled look, then step toward Gilmesh and grab him. Each has a firm grip on Gilmesh's forearm. After a second, Noah and Aditi feel an intense heat on their palms and quickly pull their hands back.

"That is a hot spot technique. No one can grab you if you master this method. It is essentially the same process as the stinger, just with the thought of intense heat. Now you have techniques to thwart physical attacks. You can use the stinger to force people to drop weapons or get them to back away. The hot spot prevents anyone from seizing you. Consider the size and strength differences between yourselves and Ulak. A telepathic standoff can lead to an equally dangerous physical attack. I want you to practice these techniques here until I return. I will have something else to show you to reinforce this lesson."

With that command, Gilmesh leaves. Noah and Aditi start their practice. They quickly figure out how to use the hot spot, then practice stinging one another. It is fun at first, but the constant sting becomes annoying. They stop practicing when their speed to sting and block becomes second nature.

Gilmesh must have been observing. He arrives shortly after they stop practicing. He takes a couple of steps into the room and says, "I see you are both proficient now. I will now show you a reason to keep training in self-defense. Follow me."

Gilmesh leads them to the last door at the end of the hallway on this side. Noah is sure that the examination room is across the hall. They all step inside to find a small alcove with transparent walls made of thick, very imposing-looking glass. There is a door on the far side of the alcove that leads to a large room that looks like the examination room. Gilmesh unhooks a small rectangular device from the belt of his jumpsuit. He holds it up to a similar device on the door. The door pops open, and Gilmesh motions them to enter. Once inside, the door slaps shut, making Noah a little nervous. He sees a long, glass-lined hallway extending away from the door. Gilmesh walks down the hallway a short distance and stops.

Noah and Aditi follow and see a door to the left with a room with transparent walls. This room's only opening is the one door. In the center of the room is a bed with a large alien on it.

Gilmesh points with an open hand, "This is a Dracon. He is the one we captured who was transporting humans illegally. I wanted you to see what you are up against on Earth."

The Dracon is humanoid, wearing a highly colored, brindled jumpsuit in green and yellow on a black background. The boots are very odd-looking and certainly cover long, triangular feet. Noah imagines a dinosaur foot. The head and hands are exposed. The skin is a dark olive color, with faint black lines that give the appearance of scales, but it is not truly scaled. There is a prominent triangular crest covering the forehead and extending down to a small nose, essentially just nostrils. There are fleshy tufts with points that sit above each eye. The being has no ears but instead has openings shaped like the letter "G," where the ears should be. The jaw extends out beyond the nose, almost like a small snout. A long mouth without lips adds to the menacing look. The hands are large and powerful. Each finger has a short, thick claw. A metallic cable encircles the Dracon's neck; a large metal rectangle hangs from the center cable. Noah and Aditi stare with incredulity and shock.

"I will have the Dracon stand up to give you the full effect. Do not worry, the mechanism around its neck is a tether, a restraining collar. It keeps the Dracon in a trance, essentially a partial coma. It cannot use any telepathic powers and is very susceptible to commands. You are quite safe."

The Dracon sits upright, sending a chill through Noah and Aditi. Then it stands up. The Dracon is very tall, maybe seven feet tall. Its physique is impressive and looks very powerful, with an athletic body, thick legs, and arms.

"Now I want you both to reach out and sense its mind. You will sense a great difference."

Noah feels an immediate aversion and says, "It seems so odd and rather dark. I'm not sure what I make of it."

Aditi agrees, "Yes, it is unusual. I have never sensed anything like that."

Gilmesh warns, "Keep in mind that this Dracon has been dulled by the tether. A fully functioning Dracon would have many times your power. However, they have developed the ability to hide themselves and can be difficult to detect. One must be in close physical proximity to sense them. Remember this feeling that Dracons generate; it may be your only clue that they are around. They have underground bases on Earth and a fleet of advanced vessels. They are in the mountains and in subterranean caverns they carved out deep underground. Their presence is sanctioned because they have refugee status. Their only requirement is to hide themselves and not interfere with human activities. They have been warned and then punished in the past for their transgressions. We need to prove beyond doubt that they have violated these terms once again. We believe, at the very least, that they have hybrids in powerful positions in Homo Sapiens society. Now that we are getting more Homo Galaxus hybrids in place, we can begin to expose and remove the Dracon presence. You two must take out Ulak as your first assignment. I think you now have enough power to do that."

Chapter 36.

Abolitions and other weapons

Noah and Aditi walk back to their rooms after the exhausting training session with Gilmesh. They are in good spirits and feel a surge in confidence, having acquired skills that make them formidable opponents for the Dracon hybrids. Confidence from true accomplishment is always a great reward. Their training has transformed them, and they feel the changes.

As they approach their rooms, Noah asks Aditi to join him for dinner. She agrees with a smile, and they enter Noah's room. Noah requests that Pab provide a table with two chairs and a full dinner for two. A floating tray holding a variety of squishy cubes in different colors, each with a delicious herbal aroma, appears from the wall and lands on the table. Noah is happy to see a large bowl of crunchy chips and two glasses of nectar on the tray as well.

As they sit and begin to eat, Noah asks, "Can you believe all the things they have taught us? Although it has been only a short time, it seems like years have passed. I am embarrassed by my old self after gaining all of these new abilities."

"It has been quite a crash course in many regards, for sure. Keep in mind that we both have had blocks and screens on us for our entire lives until now. I suppose they wanted to give us our full abilities only after they thought we could handle it. Aditi pauses, and Noah feels her reaching into his mind. "I'm ready, ready to join your battle," she says boldly.

Noah feels the unspoken question hanging between them and says slowly, "You sound ready. I guess that we may have nearly completed our training here in hyperspace. I don't know what else they could teach us. I suspect that we will be going back soon."

"I hope so. I am getting anxious. I want to start my new mission as soon as possible."

Noah lets his guard down and opens up to Aditi. He sighs, "I wish I had your confidence. Ulak nearly killed me in our first meeting. I still have that memory haunting me. I would love to give him some payback, though."

"Noah, you are not alone. You have me with you now. You really need to start reaching out more. I am right here. You should not be embarrassed about connecting minds. We need to establish a deep, permanent connection. It will make both of us better Galaxians, and I suspect that it will be a delightful experience. A connection between us will make us stronger psychically, emotionally, and physically. We must be open and honest if we want a new society built on openness and honesty."

"You are correct once again. I start over-thinking then pull back in embarrassment. Teams are always more powerful than individuals."

Also, you should realize that you are greatly enhanced since your incident with Ulak. You must acknowledge that you have substantially more abilities and power after all this training; it should give you confidence. Have any of the sneak attacks from Gilmesh gotten through to you lately? I don't think so. Keep that in mind. Payback is on the way."

Probing into her mind, Noah weighs her words and then quickly surveys his own feelings of confidence and self-awareness again. "You are right, I have you and Viera on the team; I also have new abilities that I never before could even imagine. Besides, the council is now aware of Ulak and will keep an eye on us as a backup. I do appreciate your energy; it gives me strength. Also, I enjoy having you nearby."

Aditi only smiles and sends a warm telepathic blast to Noah.

They finish their meal without further discussion, yet savor their extended psychic connection with each other. There is a pleasing psychic glow between them, and they find it relaxing and soothing.

Aditi breaks the silence, "That was a nice meal. I suppose it is time to get some rest. I would like to take a nap here with you. I think I would rest much better if we are together."

Noah responds without a pause, "I would like that very much. It was very good to have dinner with you. It makes me realize how much time I have been alone. I also think it would be good to rest with you; it could be the next best thing to a healing trance."

"Just to make things clear, we will only sleep. We will not have sex. It is not our time for that. Also, Viera told me that procreation in hyperspace can produce bad results."

Noah smiles and nods, "Of course. Right now, I am thrilled to be here with you. I agree completely, we both need serious recuperation before our next training session. Who knows what that will be like?"

Noah has Pab take away the table and chairs and has the bed sent out. Aditi jumps onto the bed, and Noah lies down next to her. She scoots closer and deepens their telepathic connection, adding more soothing thoughts. They both drift off to sleep side by side, shimmering with affection.

Noah and Aditi are awakened by a request from Uhlt. He wants them to join him in the examination room. Noah feels a little discomfort trying to imagine what they will be doing to human subjects there.

Aditi returns to her room to clean up and get ready for the next training session. They meet up in the hallway, then make the long walk across the vessel to the examination room. The door slides open, and they see Uhlt standing at the end of the examination table, his stern expression intensified by his large dark eyes. Two smaller grays stand quietly behind the table.

Noah feels an ominous foreboding when he sees a man secured to the table by a restraining blanket. The man has a rough, weathered look, with unkempt, wavy brown hair reaching his shoulders. His neck is covered in odd tattoos. Noah knows, with mixed emotions, that he will do something to this person.

Uhlt projects to both of them, *"Yes, this will be our first exercise. Do not feel remorse for this one. You will find that a thorough examination of his memory is very disturbing. This is a violent man who has seriously harmed many people. He has led a troubled life and has an acute antisocial personality disorder. The Dracons have implanted ideas and emotions to create an enhanced street thug to do their destructive, antisocial bidding. The implants have created an emotional reality of righteousness for false causes. We believe he is a full sociopath who has been driven to this state by Dracon manipulation. Civilized societies do not allow such a corrupted being to live among them in such a state. Telepathic civilizations have methods to permanently treat the unredeemable antisocial mind."*

Noah replies, *"Human societies do the same using pharmaceuticals, therapy, and prison."*

Uhlt disagrees, *"The Homo Sapiens efforts to curb their violent and truly corrupted individuals are not effective. Also, without telepathic powers, a sociopath may lie and fool the therapists to get released into society to bring violence once again. I will teach you a method that is harsh, but effective. You may find it useful in difficult situations. Now, you must master what is known as an abolition. An abolition is the removal of memories, but much more severe. It causes total amnesia. I know both of you have wiped memories from humans. To perform an abolition, you must delve deep into the subject's mind. You must go all the way down to the edge of the conscious mind. You both have shown that you can find the area of protection for your involuntary controls; the abolition target is located just before that spot and centered within the memory control locations. It is at this point that you wipe the conscious memories and plant a heavy screen. I will guide you to this area, where it is also possible to implant information and commands. You may leave them their name or give them a false one. I find it useful to leave a command, perhaps to suffer a life of penance, such as undertaking life-long tasks of reparation for their prior heinous acts."*

Noah baulks, *"That sounds like we are erasing a person from existence. Are we killing a personality and effectively purging a life from a body?"*

Uhlt calmly replies, *"Yes, you are correct. Keep in mind that an abolition is used in extreme cases. I believe you would choose to conduct an abolition* on someone who was determined to initiate a triggering event. I know that an abolition is preferred over life termination for someone who is a violent murderer. You must understand this."

Aditi asks, "Is the process reversible?"

"An abolition is not reversible when done properly with appropriate force. Occasionally, limited memory returns, but usually not. Are there any other questions before we start?"

Noah once again has a question: "Why would we ever use this in our missions?"

"That is a good question. Use this on a dangerous, relentless opponent who will not stop opposing you and your mission. If you feel truly charitable, you may leave them their name and, if they have one, information about their family. Another potential use would be against someone who has gained too much knowledge of forbidden subjects and remains a persistent threat. When a simple, short-term memory removal is not enough, use the abolition. It is a severe tactic, but necessary at times."

Aditi comments, "I think I see what you are saying. If people learn only a few forbidden things, we can erase their memories. If their minds are thoroughly corrupted, we may need to erase it all, especially if the person is emotionally destabilized to the point of violence."

"Homo Sapiens are easily corrupted by highly charged emotional manipulation. That often leads to irreversible antagonism and belligerence toward whoever they are directed to oppose. If left unchecked, it can turn into social contagion. Such circumstances can severely compromise your mission if a mass hysteria movement is created and directed against you. Often, there are only a few provocateurs with severe mental corruption who may need an abolition to stop them. That is how deep emotional damage can be in humans. We are certain that Dracons are behind many social contagions that would help their cause to take possession of the Earth from humans."

Noah understands and can only agree with the logic. He nods in acceptance.

"Very well, let us begin. Noah, you will go first. Aditi, I see you have a mind link with Noah. Please join him even more closely and follow along. Your turn is next. Noah, you will feel me following along and directing you. Go with my guidance. Now project into the subject's mind and go deep. The location is just before the area where you can stop their life functions."

Noah concentrates and goes into the man's mind. He finds it as dark and disturbing as Uhlt described. He reaches deep into his memory and psyche, layer by layer, yet feels the push from Uhlt to go deeper and deeper. Noah passes through a void area and then feels the beating heart, the lungs, and other involuntary functions. Uhlt pulls him back to the void at the base of the memories and signals to Noah that this is the spot. Uhlt prompts Noah to burn a screen in place, then start wiping all the memories he has passed through. It is a much harder task than wiping out a couple of recent memories. Noah feels further prodding from Uhlt and continues the process. Finally, Uhlt stops him and suggests that he leave a false name and mission. Noah tells the man that his name is John Nill and that he must work in peace to comfort the destitute, atoning for his sinful past. Uhlt signals approval and pulls away. Noah leaves the man also.

"Very good, Noah. That required less direction than I was expecting. When this pitiful creature is returned to Earth, he will only have the name you gave him and a suitable quest. You would be surprised to know how many homeless people on Earth have been through an abolition. Those who are illegally abducting Homo Sapiens for research or other unsanctioned activities will usually use a full abolition on their victims. Sadly, others just drop their victims from a height to their death to cover their illegal activities. Aditi, it is now your turn."

Noah and Aditi each perform three abolitions. Uhlt compliments them both, but it does not lift their somber mood.

Uhlt breaks the dour moment, *"You have successfully added another telepathic weapon to your arsenal. You have become formidable defenders of your world. You two have impressed me and given me great confidence in the Homo Galaxus species. I will now give you a supply of valuable devices for missions."*

Uhlt sends the two Grays down the hallway of the examination room. They return with a large floating tray holding two metal cases that look like large aluminum briefcases. The assistants push the tray over. Uhlt opens the two cases and directs Aditi and Noah to approach. *"Grab the handles and make telepathic contact with the cases. This will bond them to you and you alone. No one else will be able to open the case, and if they try to break into it, it will destroy the contents. These are yours forever."*

Aditi and Noah step up and grasp the handles, then each steps back, examining the contents with curiosity.

Uhlt reaches into one of the cases and pulls out a length of thick cable with a large rectangle on one end. *"This is a tether just like you saw on the Dracon prisoner. Put it around a hybrid or outworld being to control them. It will put them into a stupor and a state that makes them controllable. Just push the free end of the cable into the rectangle; it will self-activate and secure itself to your prisoner. Each case has two of these."*

Uhlt then pulls out a black fanny pack. *"This is a levitating belt disguised as a common fanny pack used on Earth. You could walk off a cliff and float safely while wearing this device. I want you both to put one on now. It must be controlled telepathically; make contact with it to use it."*

Noah and Aditi pick up a fanny pack. Noah stares at it, then unzips the pack to find another rectangle inside. He looks over to Aditi and sees that she already has her belt on and is floating a foot off the ground. He quickly puts his fanny pack on and levitates himself.

Aditi floats herself up to the ceiling and back down, "Radicle, this is the coolest thing I have ever used. This is awesome."

Noah responds, "Yes, this is amazing. It would make the walk to the physics building much more enjoyable."

Uhlt warns, "*This device must not be used in front of humans. It could lead to a triggering event, quite possibly. If someone sees you levitating, you must erase their memory of it.*"

"*Yes, certainly. I was joking. We will be discreet and only use it to defeat Dracon hybrids,*" Noah replies sheepishly.

Uhlt picks up a small circular device. It looks like a thin metallic hockey puck with a button on the side. He holds the device in front of them and presses the button. Both Noah and Aditi wince and grab their head. They feel their telepathic abilities blasted and scrambled with random sensations. Uhlt presses the button, and the annoying sensations cease.

"*This device is commonly called a flare. It can be a signal to draw attention if you become injured or partially incapacitated. It can also be used to inhibit telepathic actions and communications. Think of it as a telepathic smoke bomb. It can be helpful if you are telepathically outnumbered or outgunned: drop a flare to give you a chance to break away and escape. There are several of these in each case.*"

Next, Uhlt pulls out a black cylinder from each case and hands them to Noah and Aditi. Each cylinder is about six inches long and less than an inch in diameter.

"*Now hold your device and make a psychic connection. This will bond it to you, so it will only work for you. This device is a stun gun. You will notice that one end is textured. That is the handle side. You then point the cylinder at an opponent, squeeze the handle, and give the mental command to fire. Be aware that it has a limited range. Your opponent will be rendered unconscious for several minutes. It is not painful; it simply causes one to lose consciousness promptly. It works on anything with a brain. Lower forms of life will be repulsed but may not become unconscious. My two assistants have agreed to let you try it on them.*"

The two Gray assistants walk out from behind the tray.

"*Now I want you to face them and try your stun gun on them.*"

Noah asks, "I don't know about this. Are you sure it won't hurt them?"

Noah barely gets the sentence out of his mouth and sees that Aditi has stunned one of the assistants, who is now crumpled on the floor unconscious.

"Come on, Noah, don't be a wimp. Trust what Uhlt has told you," teases Aditi.

Noah slowly points the cylinder at the assistant, who is still standing. Then he squeezes the handle and sends the command to fire. The second Gray hits the floor. Noah looks at the device in amazement, unsure what to make of it.

"Noah, your sensitivity is admirable, but can be perilous. You seem to have a little extra Pleiadian sensitivity in you. These devices are not harmful and can be very useful to your success in your missions. Keep in mind that you can kill humans and other weaker beings with your mental powers alone. Your Dracon opponents will not hesitate to use such weapons and much worse ones on you. I see that Aditi does not hesitate. If you want your own planet, you will have to fight for it."

Noah frowns and says, *"Yes, I am still haunted by my soft, peaceful childhood, I suppose. I realize that I had better toughen up quickly. I must not hesitate or overthink during conflict. I think Aditi will be a good influence on me. I promise I will keep working to improve."*

"Very good. I realize you have been pushed much faster than usual. I think you are doing well and have the proper attitude. Now take your devices and return to your rooms for another rest period. Briel and Gilmesh have more for you. This is my last training session for you. You have done well, and I expect successful missions. You now have sufficient skills and weapons. Be advised that your opponents may have equal weaponry. A direct attack often will only lead to a stalemate. You must find clever ways around your opponent's defenses. Sometimes the shortest distance between two points is not a straight line. Deception can be your best friend. Good luck to you both. We will be watching."

Aditi and Noah send thoughts of gratitude to Uhlt. They leave the room and head back toward their rooms. After a short distance, Aditi stops and turns to Noah. He reads her thoughts at once and smiles in agreement. They put down their cases, open them, and put on the levitation belts. They float back to their rooms feeling like children riding their first roller coaster.

Chapter 37.

An Arcturian final exam

The weapons cases from Uhlt broke the distasteful feelings leftover from the abolitions. For Noah, the abolitions almost felt like he was killing a person. The organic portion of those people was left intact, but the personality and life memories were erased. That existence is gone. Even Aditi's brash personality was muted by the experience. Have they purged the human's soul with an abolition or wiped away a lifetime of experiences? Maybe they have done both.

Both Noah and Aditi have recovered after the kick they got from the new devices and the test ride with their levitation belts; they feel confident and focused once again. More excitement is building as Uhlt implied that their training is nearly complete and that they would be returning to Earth. Their battle to create a Homo Galaxus Earth has become a burning desire. Some goals are so large that one must become a fearless warrior to achieve them. Otherwise, it is merely a fanciful wish or just a dream.

Noah tries to rest but is unable to sit still. It is undeniable that his deep psychic connection with Aditi has brought an exhilaration unlike any he has ever felt. Aditi's effect and the summation of all the new abilities and gadgets are certain to enhance his excitement level.

He projects to Aditi, "*I am restless. How about you?*"

"*I feel the same. I am ready to get off this vessel and back to our home planet. Should we contact Briel and Gilmesh to tell him we are ready for the next lesson?*"

Before Noah can answer, Gilmesh sends a request, "*Please go to the examination room for your next lesson. Do not bring any of your new devices.*"

Noah and Aditi meet in the hallway again.

"I wonder if they did not like us using the levitation belts after the last lesson," asks Noah.

Aditi responds, "I don't care; it was a lot of fun floating back to our rooms. I suppose fun time is over; Gilmesh sessions are always a chore. I cannot imagine Gilmesh will have an easy lesson for us now. Let's get it over with."

The pair starts the long walk across the vessel to the dreaded examination room. They pause in the control room to exchange greetings with the ever-present Zizzletik. Noah recalls with a chuckle the shock of first seeing him; now he looks forward to each encounter.

As they walk down the hallway past the control room, Noah stops and points to a door.

"That's Briel's room. I can sense him there now," says Noah.

"Yes, I sense him too," replies Aditi.

She heads on down the hallway, and Noah follows.

Aditi turns her head back to Noah and says, "I think we are approaching Gilmesh's room."

As soon as she finishes the sentence, she shrieks and flies backwards into the wall. Noah feels a powerful telepathic assault on Aditi and knows she is overwhelmed by it. He immediately concentrates and sends his full energy into Aditi to help repel the attack. His energy gives Aditi a chance to collect herself and push back in tandem with Noah. Their combined energy is barely fending off the attack. As they wonder what to do next, the attack stops abruptly. They stand in the hallway panting and looking at each other, not knowing what has just happened.

A door slides open, and they can see Gilmesh standing there with his imposing frame and the bluish-purple skin glowing. He makes motions for them to come into the room with his strong sinewy arms and bluish-purple hands.

Aditi and Noah enter the room to find Gilmesh already seated in a very large chair, with an overstuffed sofa waiting for them. They sit side by side and take deep breaths to steady themselves.

Gilmesh cocks his head and says, "That was an attack from a full-blooded Arcturian. You two did quite well. We estimated that a Homo Galaxus would have about a quarter of my telepathic power. Noah, you instinctively paired your energy with Aditi's, creating an enhanced force against me. If I had continued my attack, I would have worn you down quickly. However, your defense would give you time to drop a flare and flee. I already knew you two shared a reciprocal bond. I assumed you would respond at once to attacks on one with support from the other. That is excellent. Did it feel that way for you?"

Aditi answers, "Your attack instantly put me in a helpless situation; I was instantly overwhelmed. I didn't feel that I could do anything, but then I felt the energy surge from Noah. I was then able to recover a little and push back on your attack."

Noah adds, "I felt and saw what was happening to Aditi. I did not even have to think about it. Instantly, I sent her everything I had to help defend against your attack. It felt automatic."

Gilmesh nods, "That is exactly the connection you will need to maintain back on Earth. You will provide cover for one another, and Viera can also join you when she is present. You have a formidable team now. Also, this test showed me that you have your guard up at all times. Otherwise, you both would be unconscious now. Do not lose that habit. Never forget that an attacker can pick his moment, but a defense must be in place at all times. I encourage you to check on each other regularly. Use an active connection when one of you is in a potentially dangerous situation. Also, you should test each other at random times to help keep one another vigilant. I would recommend regular workout sessions with each other to help build strong powers. This is my final lesson for you. Do you have any questions?"

Noah quickly asks, "What is your advice for us regarding Ulak? My first encounter didn't go so well. I don't want to mess up like that again."

"I am glad you asked. We do not know how much power he has. I would face him right away and do it with confidence. However, I would have Aditi and Viera connected directly at that time. If he has more power than the three of you, pull back and contact us at once. The Earth Council can act at that point, as it is evidence that a Dracon is directly involved. I doubt that he has that level of power, however. Once you prove that your combined energy is enough to keep him at bay, you can make plans to bring him down. You should always carry a flare because you may need to make an escape; a flare can stop an attack and give you a chance to get away. Uhlt gave you several flares each. Make clever plans, be flexible and elusive. Please consult with us as need be. Keep in mind that most direct attacks have poor results. Does that make sense?"

"Yes, it does make sense. I feel confident that I can face him now that I have had your training and a new team with me."

Aditi interrupts, "Why can't we just walk up and shoot him with our stun gun?"

"That direct assault would fail. He will sense your intentions once you are close enough to use the weapon and be able to defend himself. Ask Noah to tell you what the friendly government agents told him about their assassination attempts," replies Gilmesh.

"Great, can't wait to face him again. We will just have to out-think him," says Aditi cynically.

A tray with three glasses floats over to Gilmesh. He removes one and sends the tray over to Noah and Aditi.

Gilmesh stands and raises his glass. In a loud voice with his Arcturian accent, Gilmesh says, "Let us toast the end of your training. Respond by shouting 'victory' after I say the warrior's toast. To courage, to fellowship, and to victory over evil."

All three shout 'victory' together and take a long drink. Noah is grateful his glass holds that delicious nectar, but thinks a warrior toast should be made with beer.

Chapter 38.

Sympathy is not a moral code

Gilmesh sends Noah and Aditi back to their quarters to recharge themselves. They have been told that Briel will summon them soon and that he wants them both to be calm and rested. Noah has invited Aditi to his room for pizza. Pab has tried, but flavor is an impossible thing to digitize. The pizza came out as a round disc of the crunchy chip stuff they had been getting, topped with two layers of red-and-white spongy stuff. Aditi laughed when she saw it. It was tasty, but it was not pizza.

After eating, Noah requests two recliners with vibrating massage inserts. It takes Pab a couple of minutes, but two exceedingly comfortable chairs have been produced. The vibration add-on works perfectly. Aditi and Noah lean back in the chairs and let them vibrate away muscle tightness and mental anxiety.

After a long while, Briel interrupts their relaxation by contacting both, *"Now that you have relaxed, please come to my room. Wear your levitation belts."*

Noah and Aditi are thrilled to be using the levitation belts again. They are soon floating down the hallway to Briel in great spirits. His sessions are always pleasant and thought-provoking experiences.

Briel has the door slide open as the pair arrives. They float in and see Briel floating majestically in the lotus position at the far side of the room. His bright platinum blonde hair hangs down perfectly to his shoulders, matching his glistening shawl around his body.

"Please, float closer. Assume a comfortable sitting position here in front of me. I would like to tell you about greater things and where our true motivation is derived," says Briel with a solemn tone.

Noah and Aditi float over to Briel and try their best to mimic a lotus position like Briel.

"You have wondered why advanced beings like us spend our time struggling to help the lower beings on Earth. We could be living extremely pleasurable, comfortable lives, supported by all our advanced technology and devices. There is a critical component of an advanced civilization that must exist at its core. That critical part is purpose. A society needs a virtuous purpose. Without it, even the most advanced civilization will flounder and collapse. We ultimately derived our purpose from the omnipresent energy of the Universe, the supreme natural and supernatural. It is the great intangible at the center of everything. It is the creator of all. It is omnipresent and all-pervasive. All beings in our physical Universe are merely temporary manifestations of this great intangible. A spark of the universal energy is captured at conception for every being. The physical half of a sentient being is a temporary manifestation; the supernatural part is not. Call it a soul, a wave function, or an energy field; that part of a being may be considered an infinitesimal isolated vibration in a universal chorus. The goal of a being's physical existence is to align their soul, wave function, or energy vibration with the frequency of the Universe.

A synchronized vibration will lead to harmony after the physical part has ceased to function. When a being has learned the truth during their physical life, their soul is then aligned with the Universe. It is in this way that a higher level can be achieved with greater rewards in the next realm. A wicked life in the physical world creates a vibration that is out of synchronization with the Universe; the wicked soul will be torn apart and shredded by the mismatch.

The Universe craves increased energy from the creation of enhanced synchronized vibrations developed in our physical realm that ultimately will be merged into it. That gives our advanced civilizations a clear purpose. Create and maintain enlightened societies aligned with the Universe. We must spread life throughout this galaxy and help it develop properly into a righteous, advanced civilization. That is our motivation and our larger purpose. Do you understand?"

Noah responds, "I think I do. There are certainly parallels in Earth religions that are probably paraphrases of your statements. There is more than our physical life, there is an afterlife for our supernatural side. Our souls, wavefunctions, energy fields, or whatever you may call it live on after death. If we live righteous lives, our souls are aligned with God and may join with him on a higher realm. Wicked souls will be cast down and tormented. These are common aspects of many major religious beliefs on Earth. You have added the part about spreading life throughout the galaxy."

"Your psychic abilities can help you discover the higher truths and increase your understanding of the true nature of the Universe. It is something that Homo Sapiens are, for the most part, unable to do. You can reach out with your psychic ability to project diffusely out in all directions; strive to reach out as far and wide as possible. Imagine you are melting into the all-powerful energy of the Universe. When you reach this state, open your mind and meditate while using all your sensitivity. You will begin to perceive this universal energy and feel a sense of harmony and synchronization. The inharmonic parts of your essence will become obvious; aligned aspects will glow with pure splendor. You should meditate every day. If you do this for hundreds of years, as I have, you will know. I want you to try it now. Take deep, slow breaths, and relax all your muscles, then your mind. Reach out wide and far. Strive to sense the background energy by reaching out in all directions."

Aditi and Noah try to follow Briel's request. Aditi struggles to calm her mind, while Noah hesitates to reach out. Briel tries to steer them, with limited success. After struggling to achieve the proper state, Briel calls them back from their attempted meditation.

"That is enough for now. A proper meditation is not easy to achieve; you must work at it diligently. I want you to practice your meditation; you will find the proper state with time. Please reach out to me for help as you need it. Remember to practice this every day. Eventually, you will understand. I sense you now have questions."

"So, you seed life on suitable planets and help them develop into proper societies that can bring more positive energy to the Universe. Did you seed life on Earth?" asks Aditi.

"Not exactly. Life had begun on Earth before we discovered it, thanks to the planet's isolated location in the galaxy. Mammals with promising cranial aspects had taken over as the prominent creatures by then. We helped hominids develop higher consciousness from time to time. We want a planet to have its own creatures based on its natural DNA, so we do not seed new beings; we assist existing domestic life. However, the natural development of humans was interrupted. The Anunnaki came and seized the Earth. This was tens of thousands of years before the Confederation formed, and the codes that protect developing planets were not yet in place. The Anunnaki were aggressive, greedy, and violent. They were among the civilizations that brought extreme violence to the galaxy. They came to Earth to plunder resources and exploit domestic creatures. They corrupted the DNA of the developing hominids to create a slave race. They used selective breeding and genetic manipulation to prevent any telepathic development. They also shortened the lifespan and reduced the amount of information transmitted to newborns. They wanted a pliable, ignorant population that would not grow or evolve into a threat to their power."

Aditi interrupts, "So these invaders warped human development to produce a planet of slaves. That is really sad."

"Yes, very tragic. This situation lasted for a very long time. The Anunnaki then entered into a territorial conflict with the Dracons, another violent civilization. When the conflict grew severe, the Anunnaki left Earth to consolidate their forces, even though it stood on the edge of the disputed area. The Dracons eventually brought great destruction to the Anunnaki empire, including their home world. A small number of the Anunnaki returned to Earth, desperate for key resources and precious metals, and to maintain their historical claim. This happened many thousands of years ago. They found their old slaves had developed new attitudes and were more difficult to control. The Anunnaki reluctantly helped humans further develop agriculture, engineering, writing, and other civilizing technologies because they needed more and more resources. They were desperate, badly losing to the Dracons. They found that the more civilized humans could produce more for them. Also, they were preparing a planet of exile for themselves if they lost the war with the Dracons."

"As their galactic conflict wore on, they began to lose badly to the Dracons on their home planet. The Anunnaki were recalled and left Earth in a futile attempt to save their world from the Dracons. The Dracons eventually wiped out the Anunnaki, a true genocide. Nevertheless, the Anunnaki had corrupted the development of the Homo genus. There was an interim period between the Anunnaki's occupations, when rogue extraterrestrials came to Earth and conducted other unsanctioned genetic experiments. The genetic corruption was so severe during that period that it triggered a catastrophic act, a massive flood that was needed to eliminate artificially created genetic abominations."

"The Galactic Confederation has worked for centuries to correct the genetic corruption of human development. It has been very difficult, but now we have your species, Homo Galaxus. Your species must replace Homo Sapiens to build a truly advanced, civilized society. So, you see, Homo Galaxus is still based upon Earth-based DNA; your species is our solution to the genetic corruption of the past. Homo Galaxus still has the Sapiens lineage. Your species will achieve a truly advanced planetary civilization that may join the Galactic Confederation."

Noah thinks of his mother and other human friends and asks, "I have seen many amazing things using the collective, and have seen what a truly advanced civilization looks like. I do want the Earth run by Homo Galaxus, but is there no way to share the Earth with Homo Sapiens? I find it depressing when I think of their extinction."

"Noah, you have a big heart, and that is commendable. It is good to see that you are thinking about your feelings rather than allowing them to automatically drive you into destructive behaviors. Your compassion is admirable, but you need to realize that sympathy can be destructive. An advanced civilization must have more rules against antisocial and deviant behavior, not fewer. Sympathy is not a moral code for an advanced society. Enabling bad behavior is not a virtue and only promotes delusions. There are clear examples on Earth of the destructive power of undue sympathy in society. Many of Earth's more civilized countries have created prosperous, relatively peaceful societies, but they grow soft and overly benevolent from their easy lifestyles. Their destruction begins when a majority of the population starts excusing violent, antisocial behavior, allowing it to enter their society. Flaunting sympathy as a virtue, assuming the badge of moral superiority, is a certain path to civic collapse. With good intentions, hoping to elevate the downtrodden, they give their streets to corrupt and violent deviants. It is true that the path to Hell is paved with good intentions, to quote an old Earth phrase. This is the beginning of the end for a civilization. The social order is first warped, then eventually destroyed. Noble acts from sympathetic hearts lead to an unstoppable societal collapse because they lack the will to enforce the standards that sustain their society. That is why the fusion of Homo Sapiens with Homo Galaxus into a single civilization would be a certain failure, because Homo Sapiens would only bring destructive emotionalism and corruption. The influence of Homo Sapiens is toxic. A truly advanced society worthy of the Galactic Confederation cannot be attained with Homo sapiens' involvement."

Noah counters again, "Perhaps with a little more guidance, humans could eventually reduce the amount of bad behavior to levels that would have minimal effects on society."

"Noah, you must never lower your standards because you feel sorry for others who cannot abide by the necessary civic rules. Unconditional sympathy will never actually help anyone, but it will enable more bad behavior. It always leads to ruin. Never forget that Homo Sapiens are inherently violent, untrustworthy, emotionally controlled beings because they lack the telepathic connections that bind advanced species. If you do a detailed survey of all the Homo Sapiens societies, you will find that there is more deviance than excellence. Just because many are good does not mean they can control the corrupt majority. Soft hearts are fodder for the corrupt, malicious deviants. If you wish to have the quarantine lifted and the Earth able to join the Confederation, Homo Sapiens must fade into extinction."

Aditi comments, "Noah, it is like children that are raised without discipline and are spoiled rotten. Those parents end up with little monsters who make their life terrible."

Briel responds forcefully, "The disciplined shall inherit the Earth. This is a very important concept to remember. Keep this in mind because in your future, you will build a society from the ashes of the preceding one."

Noah concedes, "I suppose that I must not surrender to destructive sympathy. Aditi, you will need to let me know when I start getting too soft and mushy. I will do whatever it takes to bring on a Homo Galaxus planet."

"I am glad to hear you say that. You will need to control the human population around you throughout the transition. You both have learned to erase memories, implant thoughts, and to conduct a full abolition. I am certain you will need to use all of those techniques. The Earth Council has been conducting several large-scale operations to drive society. We initiated multiple social contagions throughout the female population to reduce their desire to procreate. Other major shifts are driven by humans themselves, by their inherently corrupt nature. The Homo Sapiens population is collapsing now. The drop in population is accelerating. There are issues you will need to face. You will be tasked to manage the social breakdowns and subsequent disorders; accelerating population decline will certainly cause major calamities. If the chaos becomes too great, a minor catastrophic event may be needed to rapidly reduce the population. That option is not preferred, as it may benefit the Dracons, but it remains a possibility. You will be informed of any plans from the Earth Council, and you may need to contribute to Confederation actions from time to time. My advice for you upon your return is to actively influence the humans around you to your benefit and to achieve successful results for your missions. You may need to use humans to defeat Ulak."

Aditi comments, "I understand. A slow transition allows us to keep infrastructure and resources. A catastrophic event brought on by a triggering event or violent chaos would destroy most everything, and this would delay the development of the Homo Galaxus replacement population."

"Yes, a smooth transition would be good for us and bad for the Dracons. Most likely, many of the violent eras and major anti-social mass-hysteria events can be traced back to the Dracons. Chaos is their friend," Noah adds.

"I believe you two grasp the situation that you will face back on Earth. There are certainly Dracon-friendly forces in your government. You must root them out and never stop fighting their forces. The Earth will be a Homo Galaxus planet or a Dracon planet. The future belongs to the victor. Discipline, courage, and unyielding determination will bring you victory."

Aditi asks in her typical blunt manner, "It sounds like you think our training is complete. I thought it would have lasted much longer."

"Recall I told you that the Anunnaki reduced the amount of information that is automatically transferred at birth. Homo Sapiens are born with essentially an empty brain. They must learn everything, starting from nearly zero inherited knowledge. Humans must toil and struggle to learn the basics over their first decades of life. They spend the next few decades learning how to apply their hard-earned knowledge. By the time they become effective, they begin to physically break down due to their shortened lifespans. It is not an efficient process for an advanced society, but it works for slave labor."

"We have been able to remove these constraints for your Homo Galaxus species. For example, you two think you learned mathematics quickly. You watched your human classmates struggle, while you found it quite easy. Actually, mathematics was already hardwired into your brain. Consider it akin to how birds instinctively build nests and salmon swim upstream to mate. They did not have to figure it out. Similarly, you were born with your full mathematical abilities; you merely needed to learn the nomenclature used to describe the calculations."

"Noah, you thought you learned the Pleiadian language in thirty minutes; actually, it was already there. I suspect you have substantial Pleiadian DNA in your Galaxus half. Aditi, I think you have several Arcturian characteristics. You both learned all your lessons from us so quickly because your abilities are already in you; we just had to bring them out. More importantly, both of you have primary reactions based on cognitive analysis and rational, logical thought. Emotional responses are secondary. This is the opposite of human behavior; emotions are the primary driver for Homo Sapiens. Above all, that is what dooms them. These genetic improvements give you the ability to create an advanced society."

"Our advantage is that we require less time to learn because we have so much imprinted in our brains at birth. That characteristic gives us more time to apply our knowledge," comments Noah.

"Exactly, and I have news for you that you will be very happy to hear. We estimate that the average lifespan of Homo Galaxus will be at least 300 years, probably significantly longer. You are part of the first generation, so we cannot know for certain, but we have strong biochemical evidence for this number. You will have a very long time to apply your knowledge."

In their surprise, Noah and Aditi are speechless. Briel breaks the silence, "Yes, your training session is over. You have done well and are excellent representatives of your species. You and your fellow Homo Galaxus have a planet to win. We will soon be leaving this dimension to return you to the Earth at nearly the same time that you left. Viera will then transport you back to your university and your mission."

Chapter 39.

I am so proud of you two

Noah and Aditi decide to have a nectar in Noah's room and unpack all the things Briel has told them. Briel always drops such heavy topics and concepts on them. He is highly intelligent and has been around for a long time; ignoring any of his advice would be incredibly foolish. He has certainly made the journey from information to wisdom. Noah has two regular chairs sent out with two glasses of nectar.

"I think we failed miserably trying to meditate and get in touch with the Universe," says Noah with a tinge of humility.

"Agreed. That will take much more time and effort. I suppose if it were easy, it would not be that special. On the plus side, we have 300 years to practice. That is quite a pleasant surprise. I wonder how I will feel when I am a spry 200 years old. It is a weird thought for me right now."

"Yes, I should have taken the hint when they said that I would see a Homo Galaxus Earth in my lifetime. I hope it is sooner rather than later so we can enjoy being part of the galaxy and not quarantined on Earth."

Aditi adds, "For sure. When do we get our own space vessels? That will be too cool. At what age do we get our driver's license?"

"That is a good question. I do want to travel to other planets, not just see them on the collective. I am just glad the Anunnaki are no longer around. I need to look back at the last 500,000 years of Earth's history. They really sound like they were bad guys."

Aditi warns, "Just keep in mind that they may have been bad and dangerous, but the Dracons wiped them out. The Dracons are the ones left on Earth and want it for themselves."

Noah pauses and sighs, "Yes, good point. We are now fully engaged in quite a nasty conflict."

Noah and Aditi sit in silence, thinking about their future challenges. The mood is broken when they both sense a familiar presence.

Viera projects from outside the door, "*Hello, Noah and Aditi. May I come in and speak with you?*"

Noah slides the door open and projects warm greetings.

Viera enters, and both Noah and Aditi rise and walk over to greet her. They exchange the Pleiadian greeting with her. Viera holds each one a little longer than usual.

"I am so proud of you two. Your trainers updated me on your progress and gave you many compliments. You are no longer my trainees; we are now equals. Noah, I like your new hairstyle," says Viera fondly.

Noah smirks and says, "I still feel a little like a novice, but I have learned many new things and have an entire case filled with very interesting gadgets. I am ready to go back. There is a score to settle and a mission to complete."

Aditi adds, "I want to see this Ulak person for myself. I had no hybrid foes in my last mission. I am very curious now after seeing what a full Dracon is like. Our longer-term future is likely to involve conflict with many other Dracon hybrids and maybe a few full Dracons."

Viera agrees, "Yes, that is most certainly true. There are only five Dracon outposts on Earth. If they show themselves to the humans, the Earth Council can call in forces that will remove them for good. They know the rules, so they will not confront you directly. They may have abducted a large number of humans to corrupt and create many hybrids; we have no way to know just how many, given their cloaking ability. They also have allies in the governments of the world, the militaries, and most multinational corporations, especially tech and aerospace. Currently, hundreds of hybrids like me are helping bring thousands of Homo Galaxus allies to you. You two are part of the first wave. Your successful development has prompted a decision to produce and develop more generations of Homo Galaxus at maximum production. That is why it is so critical that we prevent triggering events and expose the Dracon hybrids to remove them from positions of power in the Homo Sapiens world."

Aditi responds boldly, "That sounds like quite a chore. We need to get back and start battling."

"We will leave this dimension very soon. Pab will assume a high Earth orbit. I will take you back to Earth in my vessel. We left on Friday afternoon. They tell me that we should be back on Saturday night. That will give us time to settle back in and make plans. Monday morning, we need to confront Ulak and see what his powers really are. Noah was a sitting duck last time. At the time, I was run down from supporting Noah through the rapid-fire revelations we dropped on him. I was able to keep you relatively calm and help you adapt to the disclosures, but it drained me. In retrospect, I suppose I should have asked the council for help. I let Ulak surprise us. That will not happen again, I promise you that."

"You can count on me to be on the scene and ready to go. I promise you both, for sure," says Aditi with a serious tone.

"Before we return, you both should reach out and thank your trainers. They do not expect any kind of emotional farewell, but I know they will appreciate your gratitude. Also, drink plenty of water and have a very light meal before we go. You will make the dimensional jump while being awake this time. It can be a little disorienting. You may also feel a twinge of motion sickness. When back on Earth, you may experience 'jet lag' adjusting back to the day and night cycles. Any questions?"

Both Noah and Aditi smile and shake their heads. They are eager to return.

Chapter 40.

Best wishes, Master Noah

As the time to return to Earth nears, Noah feels a little sadness about leaving Pab and his Earth Council trainers. Events and disclosures have come at him so rapidly that he has had little time to look back and contemplate the enormity of his transformations and the new reality thrust upon him. Maybe that is how it should be. With all these changes and looming conflicts, there is little benefit in sitting and pondering. It is time to move forward and take on the new challenges, no matter how frightening they seem. He has no desire to return to his vacuous prior life.

Noah has already thanked his trainers individually and received their final thoughts. Briel urged him to keep envisioning the grand prize of a Homo Galaxus planet; be a catalyst for the transformation and the birth of a new world in harmony with the universe. Gilmesh reminded him to keep up his guard and fight with the determination of an Arcturian warrior. Uhlt encouraged him to always do what is necessary to create an orderly society and not get distracted by undue emotions. It is all good advice for the rise of the Homo Galaxus society.

Noah wanted to do one last thing before leaving for Earth. He wanted to say goodbye to Zizzletik, the first extraterrestrial entity he met. Noah experienced a wide range of emotions with his encounters with Zizzletik. At first, there was shock and fear, but now he feels fondness and something of a kindred spirit with him.

Noah reaches out and can see Zizzletik in the control room. There is time, so Noah leaves his room and hustles down to the control room.

When Noah arrives in the control room, Zizzletik sits before the lustrous metal mushroom pedestal at its center. There is a three-dimensional projection of weird-looking lights surrounded by a black star field. Reticulan script is scrolling across the image.

Zizzletik looks up and responds, *"Noah, hello. May I do something for you?"*

"I wanted to stop by and see you before I left. I wanted to thank you for your hospitality. You were the first extraterrestrial that I ever encountered. I was a little shocked at first, but your kind nature really helped me adjust. I truly appreciate it."

"You are welcome. I have enjoyed our encounters also. It is my duty to serve, and your kindness makes it a pleasure for me."

"May I shake your hand? I don't know if there is a reason or policy against it."

"*I am aware of the human gesture. The masters do not have such habits, but I can think of no reason not to. I would be honored to shake your hand.*"

Zizzletik stands and walks over to Noah, extending his slender arm and hand with long, thin fingers. Noah gently shakes his hand. Noah thinks Zizzletik's skin feels like fine leather.

Noah looks into the large black eyes that had frightened him at first. He only senses positive feelings. He says, "*Thanks again. I must now go back to meet up with Viera and head back to Earth. I hope to see you again sometime.*"

Zizzletik responds, "*Best wishes, Master Noah.*"

Chapter 41.

A final thrill before going home

Noah gets back to his room just in time to get a message from Viera. Pab is going to warp out of this hyper-dimension in about 10 minutes. Her advice is simple: "*Pull out a high-backed lounge chair. Recline back and relax. You will not hear anything or feel movement, but you will become disoriented; that is normal. We want you to feel an interdimensional transition as another lesson.*"

Noah immediately requests his chair and sits down. He takes a deep breath and reclines the chair slightly. Next, he reaches out for Aditi.

"*Well, here we go. This should be interesting.*"

Aditi replies quickly, "*Yes, should be. I'm not sure what to expect. I hope I don't puke. That would be embarrassing. Nevertheless, I'll take a little discomfort to get back to Earth.*"

"*You will be fine. I am the one more likely to embarrass myself. I'm going to stay connected to you, so don't laugh if I make a fool of myself.*"

"*Earth, here we come,*" replies Aditi excitedly.

They both sit quietly, anxiously awaiting the effects of a dimensional jump. Time seems to move slowly to further inflame their nerves. Suddenly, they are struck by a strong wave of dizziness. They feel as if the room is starting to collapse upon them. Their breathing grows difficult, and they grip the armrests to keep from collapsing. As they begin to wonder if they will pass out, they are slung backwards into their chairs by a surge of energy, not force. It's like a punch in the gut but without the pain. After regaining most of their wits, they can sense an enormous mass of familiar energy. They feel the Earth and the typical background of their own universe.

Viera contacts them both, "*We have returned to our home dimension. We will be in a high Earth orbit very shortly. How did you hold up?*"

Aditi cheerily responds, "*That wasn't that bad. It was truly a unique experience.*"

"*It reminds me of the night I had three beers,*" says Noah with a touch of humor.

Viera replies, "*I am glad to hear you are doing well after that. Change into your Earth clothes, put the jumpsuit in your gadget case, and meet in the hallway in 20 minutes. It's time to go. The ship transfer will be more exciting for you. It will also test your courage.*"

Aditi and Noah arrive in the hallway early; their eagerness to return to Earth has made them anxious and impatient. The effects of the interdimensional jump have almost completely abated, but the warning about the ship transfer is starting to trigger unease.

"Noah, is that what you are wearing? We must get you some new clothes that will allow you to represent us better. Do you work on the side at a carnival or something like that?"

Noah is a little defensive, "Don't you remember graduate school? I am blending in; everyone is a slob. I changed my hair. Doesn't that help?"

"Yes, your hair looks very good, but now your clothes seem out of place with your new, stylish hair. I hope we have time to go shopping when we get back."

Noah smiles and gives her a nod of approval. Their smiles quickly fade as they begin to wonder how they are going to transfer to Viera's vessel. They begin to speculate if there is a docking bay or perhaps a shuttle?

Viera's door hisses open with a mechanical foreboding due to their anxiety. She emerges, thoroughly poised, and dressed in a long, midnight-blue skirt that shimmers subtly under the corridor lights, her matching blazer tailored to perfection. A small designer purse dangles from one hand, while her space jumpsuit, folded neatly, rests over her arm.

Her voice rings out, crisp and commanding, "I am pleased to see you both so eager and speaking out loud again as Earthlings do. You are both about to make your first conscious inter-ship transfer. Now that you have your full telepathic capabilities unblocked and have undergone an interdimensional jump, it is time for another experience.

Viera pauses to draw attention to her next words, "This next experience will be extraordinary. And possibly terrifying. Do you have all your equipment? Your jumpsuits?"

Both Aditi and Noah nod affirmatively as their anxiety spikes and their throats tighten.

"Excellent," Viera said, turning sharply. "Follow me."

They move down the corridor that now seems to pulse with excitement and dread. They finally reach the control room, their breathing growing shallow with nervousness. Zizzletik sits before the sleek, mushroom-like metal console at the center of the room. Above the odd console, a three-dimensional projection hovers in vivid colors. It shows a large cylindrical vessel next to a much smaller vessel suspended in space, surrounded by a lovely matrix of stars.

Zizzletik looks up, *"Greetings, all. I am prepared to initiate the transfer. A portal will appear to open on the wall facing me. Signal me when ready."*

Viera glances at Noah and Aditi, reading the tension etched across their faces.

"Let's go now, before their nerves unravel."

Noah and Aditi look at each other wide-eyed, their apprehension clearly visible.

Zizzletik looks at the projection, and an eerie humming fills the air. The projection pulses and flickers. A radiant beam of light erupts between the vessels, forming a translucent tunnel that shimmers like liquid starlight. A circular aperture opens quickly on the wall, revealing a glowing brilliance beyond. Viera steps towards the portal, her silhouette framed by a halo of soft golden light. *"Come. Follow me. Experience the miracle of advanced multi-dimensional electromagnetics. You two may walk side by side through the beam. Gather your courage and step out into space. The beam will protect you and carry you safely through the void to the other ship."* Viera walks right up to the portal, waiting for them to move closer.

Noah and Aditi approach slowly, fingers entwined, hearts hammering. They summon their telepathic attachment to steady their nerves. From their new vantage, they see the other vessel; its entrance sits across open space. A faint beam of golden light connects the two vessels like a tunnel. Outside the beam, the void stretches endlessly like a bottomless pit that they now must cross.

Viera steps into the beam. Her body is lifted, and she glides weightlessly through the tunnel like a celestial figure, vanishing into the other vessel. *"Noah and Aditi, it is your turn. Step forward and join me here,"* commands Viera with a strong telepathic projection.

They grip their hands tighter and stare out from the edge of the opening. They hesitate at the edge, staring into the abyss of open space. Below them, the star field is amazingly beautiful. The beam is barely visible from within; it seems like they must step out into nothingness.

Aditi squeezes Noah's hand. "OK, spaceman, let's do this," says Aditi as she lifts her foot to take a step out into the void.

Noah instinctively follows her lead. The beam grabs them and pulls them into the tunnel of light.

Above them, Earth hangs in space, a luminous blue orb swirled with white, and is impossibly serene. Aditi gazes at it, her eyes wide with wonder. Noah looks back down at the stars, and something ancient stirs within him, a feeling he cannot appropriately describe. Awe. Humility. Perhaps it is a sense of being utterly small and impossibly insignificant while surrounded by unlimited wonder. Aditi and Noah drift through the faint tunnel of light, then step into the other vessel. The wall silently and swiftly closes behind them.

Aditi excitedly blurts out, "Wow, that was crazy. I want to do that again."

"That was incredible. I don't know what to say. I am still freaking out a bit," admits Noah.

"Noah, we are safe now, you can let go of my hand," says Aditi with a playful laugh.

Viera walks toward the center of the oblong room with glistening metallic walls. It is much like Pab's control room, but smaller, with only four chairs surrounding a much smaller metal mushroom console at the center. She sits in one of the chairs and motions Aditi and Noah to join her. They drop their gadget cases and sit with Viera.

"This is my ship. Her name is Lala. She is not as large or as fancy as Pab, but she has served me well. She is very bright and has the latest in cloaking technology, as well as several strong defensive and offensive capabilities. We are in high Earth orbit, and we should discuss our immediate plans over dinner up here. We left Earth on Friday afternoon. I will have us back at my office on Saturday night. I have a new credit card for each of you, and $ 5,000 in cash. Money should never limit our missions.

Relative to the Earth, you have only been away for a day. That will give you time to recover and adjust back to Earth time. Monday morning, Noah will face Ulak again. Aditi, you and I will be directly connected with him."

Chapter 42.

I am so glad to see you. I am grateful you cannot read minds.

Viera drops Noah outside the graduate student dormitory using her automobile, not Lala. It's about 8 o'clock PM on Saturday and few of the dorm room lights are on. Most grad students are nerds but they still practice the long-held culture of working hard, then playing hard. They walk down to their favorite bars as a group after work on Friday, then back home late at night after many adult beverages. The good graduate students will still make it to work early on Saturday morning. Noah never really took part in the weekly ritual but observed it with curiosity. Now that he is a beer drinker, he might have to give it a try unless it interferes with his mission.   Nevertheless, the sight of his old dorm gives him comfort.

Noah makes his way up to his room; he finds it just as he left it. It seems like it has been a very long time since he was last here, but in Earth time, it has only been a day. He stows his gadget case in the back of his closet.

He grabs a bottle of water from his refrigerator and sits at his small table. After taking a long drink of water, he wishes it were nectar from Pab. Collecting his thoughts and trying to adjust to his old life is feeling more difficult than he expected. Graduate school and everyday life on Earth seem so primitive after all the amazing things he has now experienced. He has seen things that cannot be unseen. There is no way his life can go back to the way it was. The extreme consequences of failure are sobering and force him to focus on his mission. He suddenly wonders if he is just avoiding the other part of his mission, the intimate Ruth mission. This thought drives him to act; yet he still senses his connection to Aditi and feels guilty about it.

He grabs his phone and calls Ruth. She is in her room and very happy to hear his voice. Within a minute, she knocks on his door.

Noah opens the door, and Ruth leaps into his arms.

She holds him tight as she kicks the door shut with a back kick. She speaks without releasing her hug, "Noah, I am so glad to see you. I was so worried about you. Your therapist called me this morning to tell me that you were fine and would be back tonight. You look good and by the way, I really love your new hair."

Ruth reaches up with one hand and pulls Noah down by his neck to kiss him. Noah reciprocates, sending amorous feelings telepathically. Besides affirming this part of the mission for them both, it pleases him to increase her happiness. Noah discovers a complex tangle of thoughts for Ruth:

gratitude, guilt, respect, pity, warmth, and incongruity. He also discovers an inner drive he once lacked, one that asserts itself and provides clarity and purpose. He feels a growing confidence, a strength that now overshadows his bland past. It is the Homo Galaxus rising in him.

A short while later, they are in his bed, naked and recovering from energetic intercourse. Noah is lying on his back with Ruth's head on his shoulder and her arm slung over his body.

Ruth breaks the silence in a soft voice, "Noah, what did the doctors tell you was wrong with you yesterday? You seem stronger than ever and are certainly in great shape. I cannot imagine that it was much of anything."

Noah recalls the cover story Viera gave him, "I was told that I was dehydrated and my electrolytes were out of balance. They gave me an intravenous fluid treatment and kept me overnight at the hospital for observation to be safe. It was no big deal."

Ruth pulls away and props herself on one elbow, looking at him with eyes filled with bittersweet tears. Angrily, she says, "No big deal. I am so relieved to hear that, but I imagined that you had a brain tumor or a leaky heart valve. I was so worried after you passed out so suddenly like that. You have to promise you'll take better care of yourself. I was terribly frightened."

Noah soothes her telepathically and physically, "Yes, it scared me too. I can honestly say that I am better now, absolutely better than ever. I am going to start taking better care of myself."

He kisses her and pulls her over to be cradled on her back in his arms. "I wanted to thank you again for getting me to the medical center so quickly after my collapse. You saved me, and I do not think that I have thanked you appropriately. I am so happy to be back with you," says Noah, glad that she cannot read his mind, which keeps drifting back to Aditi.

Ruth rolls over and squeezes Noah with her arm that is wrapped around him and says, "You are welcome. You can thank me one or two more times tonight, like you just did. That would be a good start."

Noah is thoroughly conflicted by his desire to complete this part of his mission and his growing desire for Aditi. He does not wish to hurt Ruth, who has always treated him with compassion, even though it is mostly due to Viera's psychic conditioning. He hopes for a speedy completion of this objective so he can move forward as a true Homo Galaxus with another.

In the calm center of his mind, Noah knows he cannot be with Aditi until he can impregnate Ruth. Thinking only about the successful completion of his mission, he implants immediate sexual desire into Ruth again. She starts kissing his neck and caressing his chest. He hopes Aditi isn't paying attention.

Chapter 43.

Ulak and the looming confrontation

On Sunday morning, Noah implants a suggestion into Ruth that she should go without him to the physics building so she can catch up on her research. This gives him the chance to go over plans with Viera and Aditi. Viera will take Lala in stealth mode and hover above the physics building while Aditi sits in the vending machine lounge in the adjacent building. She didn't want to be distracted by starting with her new group yet.

Their telepathic meeting took very little time, but it gave Aditi the chance to convince Noah to go shopping with her. It would be good to try out the new credit cards that never need to be repaid. Ruth was back Sunday evening for dinner with him at the dorm cafeteria, then another night of lovemaking.

Monday morning arrives, and his showdown with Ulak is finally here. Noah feels confident yet nervous as he thinks back to the last time. He sent Ruth ahead alone, saying he would catch up with her at the physics building. He doesn't feel like eating or talking this morning. He focuses on everything he has been taught. He wants to make Gilmesh and the others proud of him. He also wants revenge. After selecting a pair of slim-fit blue slacks and a designer shirt picked out by Aditi, he walks to the physics building deep in thought.

Noah reaches the fishbowl. He does not yet sense PIF or Ulak in the building. He exhales in relief but keeps his guard fully engaged.

Jesse pops his head out of his office, "Hey, Noah. Glad you are back and looking good. I didn't know hospitals also gave fashion makeovers. You look like you are cruising chicks at a dance club or something. Seriously, I am sincerely happy to see you have fully recovered. What the hell happened to you Friday?"

Noah turns and smiles at the familiar sight of Jesse, "It turns out that I was dehydrated and let my electrolytes get out of whack. They pumped me full of fancy saline, now I am good to go. I really wanted to thank you again for getting me to the infirmary so quickly. We should go out for beers again; It will be my treat."

Jesse smiles and nods, "Hey, a buddy has got to help out a pal in trouble. Free beer sounds like a good plan. I can't wait to see if you can handle your beer better now that your electrolytes are fixed. I don't want you to pretend to get wasted so you don't have to pay."

"Did I miss anything around here this weekend?"

"Not a thing, it has been quiet as a morgue around here."

"So, you didn't even see PIF or Ulak in here this weekend?"

"Nope, I was here writing another article draft all weekend and hardly saw a soul."

"Well, it's good to be back so I can keep you company," says Noah with a chuckle.

Noah goes to his desk and sets up his computer. He downloads the latest physics journal publication, and, once again, pretends to read it. He can feel a strong connection with Viera and Aditi, so he knows they are in place as planned. He reaches out to scan for Ulak and Professor Freidman. He feels his nervousness rising as time slowly creeps by.

He senses Ruth's growing anger from her office next door. He figures he should end this potential untimely distraction. He gets up and walks over to Ruth's office.

Noah walks up behind Ruth, who is sitting at her computer. He wraps his arms around her and kisses her on the cheek.

"Good morning, Ruth. I hope I am not disturbing you. I know you have been wanting to catch up on your research project. You look especially pretty this morning."

"Good morning, Noah. I am glad you are not ignoring me again. I am beginning to wonder if you are avoiding me today. You should know that I am always glad to see you; never worry about interrupting me. We are a couple now."

"Yes, certainly," says Noah while really thinking of the day he can be free of her. He kisses her again and says, "I suppose I should get back to work now. I am very far behind in my readings and really need to have a discussion with PIF. Let's talk more over lunch."

Noah walks back to his desk and sits down at his computer, his senses fully engaged. He doesn't want to reach out too far to find the professor, in case it tips off Ulak that he is back. Surprise will be an ally.

After half an hour of tension, Noah can sense PIF and Ulak in the building. He can feel their approach. They may already be in the professor's office. Noah sits up in this chair, fully prepared. Ulak's office is in the fishbowl office area, and he must pass by to get to it.

Noah feels a dull psychic haze nearby and turns to look out of his office and at the door to the fishbowl. Ulak is in full camouflage mode, so he cannot sense Noah. Then he sees a hulking person walk in; it is Ulak, all six and a half feet of him.

Ulak takes a step into the fishbowl meeting area and turns to look directly at Noah; he is very surprised.

"Ugh, you came back," grunts Ulak.

Noah feels a telepathic attack but easily blocks it. He is pleasantly surprised that Ulak is not as powerful as he thought. He feels Ulak strain to attack Noah, but with no effect. Ulak walks up to the doorway of Noah's office. His physical presence is intimidating as his large frame fills the doorway.

Noah smirks and says, "Yes, I am back. Perhaps you should consider leaving. We know all about you. Your plan will fail."

"You are a puny little shit. I can crush you like humans do, with my bare hands."

Ulak steps forward menacingly and starts to reach out to grab Noah.

Noah projects a stinger into Ulak's arm. Ulak pulls it back with a confused look on his face. Noah hits him with another stinger right in his gut. Ulak takes several steps back. Noah then feels Aditi and Viera hit him with repeated stingers. Ulak contorts and writhes, then stumbles back. He turns and runs down the hallway to Professor Feingold's office. Noah jumps up and pursues him. Ulak bursts into the professor's office and locks the door behind him.

Ulak is in full panic mode. He pulls his phone from his pocket and speed dials a stored number.

"This is Ulak. That hybrid has returned and run me out of my office. I think he has help nearby. I locked myself in the professor's office; I put him to sleep. What do I do now? I can't go back out there."

A calm voice replies, "Just wait there. I will send campus police to collect you. Tell the campus police to take you and the professor to his house. Wait there for further orders."

Noah stands in the hallway, surprised by Ulak's retreat, but is enjoying the sweet feelings of successful revenge.

Noah messages Aditi and Viera, "*Well, that was interesting. He has locked himself in the professor's office. I don't think I should try to get in there. He was not nearly as strong as I expected. He was certainly surprised, and that may have helped.*"

Aditi replies, "*Yes, he went down quickly. I think that if we put more effort into an attack, we could take him down.*"

Viera comments, "*We could possibly do that; however, he is not as powerful as we thought. That suggests that there were others actively connected with him in the first encounter. I am scanning for any others who may drop their cloaking. We need to locate and identify them. Noah, keep an eye on Ulak. Let's see how he gets out of this.*"

Noah casually strolls back to the fishbowl and leans up against the wall in the hallway. He concentrates, using his newly acquired remote-viewing skills to peer into the locked office. He sees Professor Feingold slumped over at this desk and Ulak pacing back and forth in the office. Noah sees that the professor is breathing, so he is still alive. He wonders if he should use this opportunity to erase the professor's memory if Ulak is no longer protecting him, but knows it would be more important to capture Ulak.

"I see police cars and an ambulance racing toward the physics building. It looks like they are being used to remove Ulak from the building. I will follow them in Lala and update you later," reports Viera.

Noah waits calmly in the hallway. Soon, several campus police officers and two EMTs with a gurney arrive at Feingold's office. Ruth and Jesse finally hear all the commotion and join Noah in the hallway. The EMTs and the police enter the office and reappear quickly with the professor strapped down on the gurney. Ulak leaves, surrounded by campus police, carrying the professor's computer and briefcase. Ulak turns toward Noah, sneering as he walks out.

Jesse hears the commotion and joins Noah in the hallway. He sees the professor being carted off and says, "What the hell is going on? Did PIF die or something?"

"No, Ulak said he passed out and called 911," Noah cynically responds.

Ruth gasps and says, "You passed out last week, and now the professor has. Is this building toxic? Should we tell someone? I am a little nervous about all this."

Noah tries to calm Ruth, "No, I think it is just a coincidence. You have seen how hard PIF has been working himself. I was just irresponsible and not taking proper care of myself. This all just happened at about the same time. I wouldn't worry about it at all; I think we should just go back to work and not dwell on it. I'm sure we will get an update soon."

Ruth nods and slowly walks back to her office. Jesse stands unmoving and staring directly at Noah. His stare is piercing, sending a strong message: he isn't buying Noah's story and knows more about what is going on than meets the eye.

Noah likes Jesse and knows he's already onto his secrets. He has many connections to military-industrial organizations that have likely been corrupted by the Dracons. He knows he must do something.

Noah sighs and leans into Jesse to whisper, "OK, what do you think is going on?"

Jesse nods and says, "I have left myself a bunch of notes that tell me that you are an alien and that you keep wiping that from my memory. Your fainting spell on Friday was very odd, especially when it happened at the exact time that Ulak appears. Now the professor goes down, and the police escort them out of the building. That Ulak fellow is a weirdo who is now living with the professor. All these things are too odd to be ignored. You might as well let me in on the situation. I can take it."

"Very well. Let's go out tonight, and I will tell you as I buy you the beers I owe you for your help last Friday. How does that sound?"

"It sounds like a plan, good buddy. Let's leave here at five."

Noah and Jesse return to their offices. Noah closes the door, expecting to hear something from Viera. It doesn't take long.

"Noah, what do you plan to tell Jesse? This could be a major issue if not a step toward a triggering even on its own."

"Jesse has been my friend and knows certain forbidden things from his internships with the high-tech aerospace companies. I certainly want to warn him about Ulak. Also, if I tell him too much, we can wipe his memory if needed."

"That is acceptable. You should implant a large dose of doubt into Jesse, regardless. That will make it less risky. Can you do that?"

"Yes, I can and will do that," says Noah confidently.

Aditi joins in, *"What do you want me to do in the meantime?"*

"Aditi, you should walk around campus and scan for that dull, dark presence that Ulak gives off. We need to find the others if we want to successfully capture Ulak. If you get lucky and get close enough, you can detect other Dracon hybrids. I will pick you up when you contact me."

Noah rests behind his closed door, feeling pretty good about the morning. Last week, Ulak nearly killed him, now he chases Ulak away in an embarrassing retreat. He is troubled knowing that there is at least one more Dracon hybrid in the vicinity. He is confident that their team is up to the challenge. While pondering just what he will say to Jesse later, he senses Ruth getting impatient. He realizes that she will not be happy to hear that he is going out for beers with Jesse.

Aditi is still connected actively to Noah and suggests, *"Take her out to lunch and break the news to her in public. She won't have a tantrum in public and initially will be impressed that you are taking her out to lunch."*

"That's a great idea. Do you want to go too?"

"Noah, don't be a fool. You really do not have much experience with women. Our time will be here soon enough."

Ruth is thrilled by the lunch invitation from Noah. They leave the physics building to walk to a nice Chinese restaurant just off campus. They casually chat about physics and share concerns about their professor. After they are out of sight of the physics building, Aditi sends a suggestion to Noah to hold Ruth's hand. Noah takes Ruth's hand and can feel a surge of warm feelings from her. Soon they reach the restaurant and sit at a small table for two. They order jasmine tea, kung pao chicken, and fried rice.

After more light chitchat and after the food is half eaten, Noah breaks the news.

"Ruth, I need to take Jesse out for beers tonight. I promised to buy him some beers for helping get me to the infirmary. That's what he wanted."

Ruth makes a face and angrily responds, "Really? Don't you remember what happened to you last time? You were lucky you didn't hurt yourself worse than you did. Do you think that it is a good idea?"

Noah is a little shocked by the instant hostility he senses in Ruth. He sheepishly responds, "Yeah, I know. I didn't know what I was doing then. I know what I am getting into this time. Also, my electrolytes were all messed up then. I'll be fine."

"So, this lunch is some kind of distraction, so you can tell me that you are going out tonight. Do you think I am stupid?"

"No, no, not at all. I did miss you while I was in the hospital. I thought this lunch would be a nice outing for us. I need to keep my obligation to Jesse, and this lunch was to make up for tonight, I suppose." Noah feels the anger rise in Ruth.

"Oh, so you think you can do whatever you want and bribe me with food to make me happy with your poor treatment of me. I am not a water faucet that you can turn off and on when you feel like it. You are supposed to think about both of us when you make plans. You should have asked me before making plans. Maybe I should go with you and Jesse."

"No, that won't be good. I need to have a private talk with Jesse."

"Oh, I get it. You are now keeping secrets from me. You had better not talk about me while out swilling beers with the riffraff. You need to..."

Noah snaps and projects into Ruth's mind. He freezes her, then implants thoughts of approval for his night out. He wipes out her angry feelings and responses.

Ruth snaps out of it and says, "How late do you think you will be out tonight with Jesse? Come on over to my room when you get back."

Ruth once again starts chatting about physics.

"How about those Homo Sapiens' emotions? Just think if you were fully human, you would not be able to stop her outburst like you just did," projects Aditi with a hint of humor.

"I don't know how Homo Sapiens men do it. I don't think I want to know."

"That is another reason why they are doomed to fail. Without a real psychic connection and their immediate default to emotional responses, humans never truly connect and are never honest with one another. They live very lonely lives of conflict compared to us. You will see the difference soon enough with me."

Chapter 44.

Secrets and more secrets

The afternoon is quiet, but perhaps only superficially. Deep down, Ruth may be giving Noah the silent treatment. She sneaks out early and heads back to the dormitory, thinking Noah would not notice. Noah sensed her departure and the presence of her negative secondary emotions. He would need to remember to project positive emotions to her before seeing her again.

Noah detects Jesse shutting down his computer for the day. He quickly turns off his own computer and steps out of his office locking the door behind him. Noah feels no need to lug around his primitive computer any longer. He is actually looking forward to having a beer, since there is no extraterrestrial nectar available.

Jesse steps out of his office to find Noah patiently sitting at the conference room table.

Jesse smiles and cocks his head, "You're ready to go. Of course, you are. You know what all of us are thinking all of the time. You probably can order us around or make us think whatever you want us to. Am I getting close to the truth?"

"Jesse, let's not talk here. I want you to hear things that are actually forbidden for me to tell you. There are too many keen ears around here. Let's get going and get to Buck's Bar and Grill for some ice-cold beers."

"OK, let's get out of here. Many of the best discussions happen when drinking beer."

Noah and Jesse leave the physics building silently. Noah can sense Jesse's excitement and anticipation to learn his secrets. After about 100 yards out, Noah starts talking.

"Jesse, I want you to know that I am your friend and a true friend of the world. You have correctly deduced that I am not a human, but I am not an ET either. I am a hybrid created to live on the Earth and save it from destruction. I didn't know this myself until a short while ago."

"No shit. How is it even possible that you didn't know?"

"I lived such a sheltered life and was pushed up grades in school, so I was surrounded by kids who were about ten years older than me. I was always an alien to my classmates. I had it all explained to me all at once because there is a major conflict nearing a significant point that could lead to the destruction of Earth if we lose. My mission here is to stop Ulak and prevent him from using Professor Feingold to expose advanced physics to humans. That forbidden knowledge would trigger an extinction event for the human population of Earth. I am here to stop it."

Jesse is stunned and stops walking. "Son of a bitch. Why the hell would they want to destroy us? And who the hell are 'they' that are behind it?"

Noah turns to Jesse and projects a little bit of emotional relief for his spike of stress.

"I will give you the short version of the situation. There are many advanced civilizations in the galaxy. They have formed an alliance to preserve the peace and help primitive societies develop appropriately. The Earth is quarantined and may not leave the planet. Humans are not allowed to know of extraterrestrials' existence, nor to develop technology that would give them access to space and other dimensions. If humans gain any of this knowledge, it triggers a catastrophic extinction event. The planetary reset button gets pushed."

"That seems like an awfully extreme response. Humans are not that terrible."

Humans have always been extremely violent and corrupt. Think about all the never-ending wars, the violent crimes, and the corrupt, oppressive governments. Now all these humans have access to nuclear weapons. I have seen what a truly advanced society looks like. It is amazing and has little in common with Earthly societies. More advanced technology must be accompanied by cultural norms that are strictly enforced. Otherwise, this high technology can destroy entire planets. These societies do not want violent, barbaric humans zipping around the galaxy with nuclear weapons. It is really that simple. Humans are not yet worthy to join with advanced societies."

Jesse starts walking again, "Well, that is a kick in the nuts. It hurts a lot to know that we are still just crude, ignorant savages. I suppose we look like stupid monkeys to them. I guess it makes sense. I would not want monkeys with machine guns running around town. OK, I get it, but what's the deal with that creep, Ulak?"

"As you might imagine, the situation is more complicated. There are remnants of a race that survived the last intergalactic war. They destroyed their opponents completely, but at great cost. They are the Dracons and their home planet is barely habitable. There are very few of them left scattered around in small enclaves. They are on Earth, too. They are supposed to keep hidden and not interfere with human society, but we believe that they are violating the galactic code. The Dracons have an ancient claim on the Earth that they wish to enforce. They do have allies in the galactic organization. Ulak is a hybrid they created to help start a triggering event that would wipe out humanity, allowing them to claim the Earth as their new home planet. Others and I are working to stop them."

"Why don't you guys just go to the President and tell him to get his act together. With this horrible consequence held over our heads, he could work to prevent us from doing these things that would bring on a planetary catastrophe. I would think any leader would go for it."

"That offer was made decades ago, and a treaty was put in place. There are groups within the government collaborating with us. However, others have made deals with the Dracons for advanced technology and weaponry. They don't know they are making deals with those who would destroy them. I imagine that some of the companies you have worked with are actually aligned with the Dracons."

That stops Jesse in his tracks again. "So, you are telling me that people I may know are really working with creatures who want to destroy us?"

"Yes, I am telling you that. I would like to believe that you would work with me to prevent a human catastrophe. You could be a double agent for the good guys."

Jesse just nods and continues walking in silence. Soon they reach Buck's Bar.

Jesse opens the door for Noah and says, "I really need a beer now."

Jesse and Noah head down to the far side of the bar near where they sat the last time they were here. The bartender, now familiar with them both, automatically brings over two beers.

Noah breaks their silence, "Jesse, do you think you could keep all of this a secret and work with us? I think we could be very effective together."

Jesse takes a long drink of his beer from the brown long-neck bottle. Noah does the same. Jesse looks at Noah with a funny expression on his face.

"Well, there's a problem. I already told them about you. Man, I am sorry. I didn't know the whole story. I hope you can forgive me."

Before Noah can say or do anything, his vision starts to blur, and his thoughts begin to swirl uncontrollably. He begins to lose his balance. Suddenly, two men from a back table rush forward and grab Noah by his arms. They drag him out of the bar with Jesse following. As soon as they get out the door, a large black panel van screeches to a stop. The driver opens the side door, and the two men with Noah lift him inside.

Jesse steps in after them, and one of the men slams the side door shut. After all that stuff that Noah told him, he feels terrible. He wishes he could do something about it now, but these three men look really serious and dangerous. They lay Noah down on one of the bench seats in the van. Jesse is paralyzed by his remorse. Then he sees the driver slump down over the steering wheel. Next, the two sitting beside him collapse forward onto the van floor.

Jesse jumps as the side door slides open. He sees a beautiful caramel-skinned woman with long, shiny black hair standing there. She steps in and closes the door behind her.

She says to Jesse, "I am Aditi, a friend of Noah. Help me get the driver out of the seat. I don't have time to explain. Hurry before others arrive."

Aditi grabs the nearest arm of the driver, and Jesse reaches up over the seat to help drag the driver out from behind the wheel. They pile him up on top of the others, and Aditi jumps into the driver's seat and accelerates into traffic.

"Look, Aditi, I didn't mean to do this to Noah. I didn't know about their scheme. I only told them that I thought Noah was a hybrid alien. You don't need to kill me too. I won't tell anyone anything else," says Jesse as he sits down on the bench seat with his feet on the pile of men.

"Relax, Jesse, I did not kill these men, and I know you did not intend to hurt Noah. I am not going to hurt you; stop worrying about that. I appreciate your help moving the driver. You and your tricky friends here may have helped us figure out a way to take down Ulak. However, I cannot let you see where I am taking this van."

Jesse passes out and falls across the bench seat.

"Viera, I have Noah and four men in their black panel van. What now?"

"Continue down the street you are on. Turn right when you get to a McDonald's restaurant. A few blocks further, you will see a Walmart. Drive behind it and park the van, and I will collect all of you. Give me at least twenty feet of space on three sides of the van."

Ten minutes later, Aditi parks the van behind the Walmart. A golden cylinder of light appears, and instantly, Aditi finds herself in the control room of Lala. There is a pile of four unconscious men next to an unconscious Noah on the floor. Viera is waiting with five levitating stretchers. They maneuver the stretchers one by one and place the men on them using a levitating device that looks like a large block of metal with a handle on top. Viera places immobilization sheets over the four humans. Viera orders Lala to move these humans to another room, and they float away to disappear behind a door.

Next they get Noah onto a stretcher. Viera signals Lala to send her the medical unit. A black object shaped like a large parenthesis floats over to her. She places the device over Noah's torso. A band pops out from the unit that Viera wraps around his forearm.

"Don't worry about Noah. The medical unit will have him back to normal shortly. They only gave him a quick-acting tranquilizer. He will be fine," says Viera.

"Did you see how those men escaped detection?" asks Aditi.

"Yes, that was interesting. They were all watching videos on their phone. Apparently, the connection of the human mind to video programs is extremely strong. It obscures most other thoughts. It is essentially a cloaking device for humans against telepathic scanning. This could be useful for us if we need human aid to take out Ulak."

Aditi continues, "Yes, agreed. Did you notice how the bartender doped Noah's beer without any of us detecting him? I thought I felt something that made me think he had been hypnotized. He did not know he was spiking Noah's beer. There was some kind of trigger, or maybe just seeing Noah with Jesse was the trigger. Whatever it was, it was very effective."

Viera nods and says, "Yes, we may have just learned some new tools to better fight Ulak." Humans may become much more useful to us."

Noah begins to stir on his floating stretcher. He opens his eyes and is surprised to see that he is back with Viera and Aditi on the sentient vessel named Lala.

Viera sees Noah waking up, "Just lie there and relax. I will not remove the medical unit until it completes the detoxification cycle. The allies of your pal, Jesse, tried to drug and abduct you. They wanted to get your genetics analyzed and study your brain, as if their crude knowledge and methods would tell them anything useful. Aditi stopped a three-man team that tried to take you. She followed you to the bar and acted quickly when they grabbed you. We have them, along with Jesse, on board with us now."

"Aditi, thank you. I have fallen victim to my inexperience once again, but you were smart enough to sense their plan."

Aditi smiles, "You are welcome. Don't be so hard on yourself. I was following you out of curiosity and wanted to know what you were going to say to Jesse. Also, I wanted to see if you made a face when you drink beer. These agents were very clever and have found ways to prevent us from easily detecting them and their foul plans. It is pretty ingenious. I wonder if the Dracons taught them. Anyway, this plot has given us a couple of new tactics for taking out Ulak."

A green light begins flashing on the medical unit. Viera walks over to Noah, removes the armband, and sends the medical unit away. Noah sits up on the levitating stretcher.

"How do you feel?" asks Viera.

Noah shrugs his shoulders, "I feel fine. No issues at all. What do we do now?"

Viera responds quickly, "We need to get you back to your dormitory. Ruth is there, and she is very anxious to see you. You still have that mission to complete. After that, Aditi and I need to put these agents through a full abolition. I propose that we drop them into different large cities with a burning desire to preach the gospel to the homeless and downtrodden. We will tell them that their names are the same, John

Nocard. That is Dracon spelled backwards, just in case they are ever found. It is a good warning."

Noah jumps to his feet, "We can't do that to Jesse. I think he could be a valuable asset to us in the future. It would not be right, he didn't know what they were going to do."

"I am only talking about the agents. It would look suspicious if Jesse disappeared and would draw too much attention that we do not need. The question is just how much of his memory we allow him to keep."

Noah suggests, "I think we should let him keep all of his memories of tonight's events, including the things I told him. However, he can be put into a state of hypnosis and ordered to keep my disclosures secret and add a large dose of doubt to it just in case. Also, he would pay less attention to me if a burning desire to write up his thesis and graduate is placed in his mind."

Viera crosses her arms and paces back and forth. She stops and turns to Noah, "Very well, I think there are long-term advantages in that plan for Jesse. However, I will ask Uhlt to come and do the hypnosis; he is extremely skilled at it."

Noah smiles, "Thank you. I think it will work out well for us going forward."

"Noah, tomorrow you need to contact your friendly government agents who are following you. Tell them about Ulak and ask them to follow him and the professor. Let's see how Ulak responds tomorrow, then we can make   our   next   plans."

Chapter 45.

Some humans are still useful

Noah leaves Ruth's dorm room early in the morning after a long night of make-up sex. Human women run so hot and cold. I suppose she was happy to see him so early in the evening and stone-cold sober. This supposed relationship certainly feels like a one-way street, except for the sex. Noah is struggling to find the deeper understanding of human society that the Earth Council wants him to see. Maybe not? Perhaps there are aspects of life that cannot be easily explained; they must be experienced.

Noah told her that he would not be going to the physics building until much later today. He told her he had to have his electrolytes checked again, then had a therapist appointment afterward. Noah heads back to his room and takes a shower, then picks out a couple of items from his new wardrobe to wear.

Noah sits at his small desk in his dorm room and reaches out for Aditi.

"Good morning, Aditi. Where are you today?"

"I stayed on Viera's ship. I'll move to my apartment today, then start with my research group tomorrow. We went back to the Earth Councilors' vessel to have Uhlt work on Jesse. He also helped with one of the abolitions and really liked how we planned to return them to the streets. The agents were dropped off separately in New York, Chicago, and San Francisco. Just a short while ago, Jesse was left at the physics building. He will be a little confused today. Viera wants you to contact the friendly agents as soon as possible. She says you should assume you are being watched, so be a little tricky about how you meet up with them. Tell them that there is at least one other hybrid in the area besides Ulak. Also, inform them that there are opposing government agents in the area and that they have tried to abduct you. See if they know anything about them that may help us. Tell the friendly agents to surveil the professor; Ulak should be with him. Also, ask them whether they will work with us to get Ulak, and tell them we may need to implant thoughts and modify their memory. Once you've done that, come to Viera's office. Do you have all that?"

"I do and should get to her office late this morning."

Noah says goodbye to Aditi and begins reaching out to Curt, the lead agent on their side. After a few minutes, he finds the familiar essence he seeks.

"This is Noah. I need to speak with you. There are possible other agents in the area. In half an hour, keep circling the University Library. When I sense you, I will come out of the east-side entrance for a quick pick up."

Noah senses affirmation from Curt and heads out to the library, where you need a student ID to enter. There are multiple ways in and out of the building. Non-students cannot follow him, and it will take four people to watch all the doors.

Noah heads out to the library. It is a longer walk to it than the physics building. There is not much sidewalk traffic because it is off-semester. Noah tries to nonchalantly look over his shoulder to see if anyone is following. He senses no ill intent, but remains cautious. He doesn't want to be abducted again or worse.

Noah reaches the library and shows his school ID to enter easily. He recalls coming here to track down very old journal articles that had not been digitized for a class assignment. That seems like such a long time ago. He loiters in the central area of the library, where all the mainframe terminals are found when one needs to search for books. He sits at an open terminal and pretends to search. He scans the area for Curt. Soon, he detects him approaching the area and messages him to stop at the east door. Noah hustles to that exit and waits inside the door. He sees a white van pull up and knows with certainty that this is the one. He quickly walks out and gets into the van. It is just like last time. Curt sits on a stool in front of his monitor and equipment, and Noah sits on the stool beside him. The van quickly accelerates into traffic and heads away from the campus.

Curt shakes Noah's hand and says, "I am very glad to see you again. We were watching our cameras when you collapsed as your professor brought in Ulak to your meeting. I thought he might have severely injured you or maybe killed you. Our mission to eliminate that creature seemed impossible at that point. Then we see you return and chase him off. That was spectacular. I am glad you reached out. What do you need from us?"

"It is good to be back. I am much stronger now than before I went away. The situation is more complex now. There is at least one other hybrid in the area. We need to find them before we can take down Ulak because they can combine forces and watch each other's backs. You could help us with simultaneous activities. Would you be willing to collaborate with me directly?"

"Yes, of course. We want Ulak gone as much as you do."

Noah smiles, "Very good. Would you be willing to let me implant thoughts and impressions into you both? It can disguise your intentions if you are detected. It will be less risk for yourselves and offer greater chances for success."

Curt purses his lips in obvious self-deliberations, "If it means that we can help you eliminate Ulak, we will do whatever you think is necessary. We have no idea what to do at this time. Anyway, if you are what I think you are, you could do that to us without our approval. I appreciate you asking."

"I am working with others. We should be able to find the other hybrids, then we can move forward. In the meantime, would you be willing to surveil the professor and Ulak?"

"That is what we were doing when you contacted us. We will reacquire and continue. I have two burner phones. Would you like one? The other's number has been set up in speed dial and is also in the recent call log. This way, you can find us more quickly, and we can contact you directly. Feel free to smash it if you think it is a problem."

"Sure, why not, since we will be working together. There is one other thing you may not know. An opposition team of agents tried to abduct me yesterday. I was drugged and hauled off to a van. They didn't know my partner was following me. They were quickly subdued, then eliminated. They are from the other part of your government and industrial complex that has sold out to the Dracons. Do you know anything about them being in the area?"

"I'm sorry. Those guys are super spooks operating out of the darkest, most secretive places. Even the President cannot find out anything about them. We'll keep a lookout, but I am not confident that it will do any good."

"Very well. At least you know about them and their recent activities here. They taught us something I will share with you, since we are on the same side. It's a way for humans to hide their thoughts from telepathic scans. If humans are watching videos, that dominates their thoughts. It is camouflage from simple telepathic scans. I recommend you watch videos while surveilling hybrids."

"Thanks, that trick could be very valuable. We feel like sitting ducks around Ulak."

"I will contact you after we find the other Dracon hybrids, then we will include you in our plans to take them down."

"Good luck, my friend. We'll be waiting. Here is your burner phone. Call me when needed, and I will do the same."

"Thanks. Can you drop me off near the physics building? I have to get back to work."

Chapter 46.

The calm before the storm

Noah is dropped off at a major street that bisects the campus, only a few blocks from the physics building. This gives him time to update Viera. He knows Aditi is still tightly connected to him and likely heard the entire conversation with Curt.

"Viera, are you there? I have an update."

After a few moments, Noah gets a response.

"Yes, I am listening. I am still with Aditi. We are getting her set up in her apartment. She did hear most of your conversation with the friendly agents. I understand that they are on board and ready to assist us."

"That is correct. I have a burner phone that I can use to contact them more readily."

"A burner phone? Well, that is acceptable now, but I want you to destroy it after this mission is completed. They can track you with it, or if his organization is compromised, other adversaries can follow you too."

"OK, I will do that. Right now, I am heading to the physics building to see what is going on there. I could hear something about Professor Feingold."

"That is a good idea. Also, see if you can get into the professor's office. We see the professor recovering at home, with Ulak by his side. Tonight, at midnight, we will try to smoke out the other hybrids in the area who are supporting Ulak. I want you in your room, alone, by then. I will drop Aditi off then. Do you understand?"

"Yes, will do."

Noah arrives at the fishbowl to find the conference room empty. He walks over to Ruth's office to find her in deep concentration while making notes from a journal article that she is reading on her computer. She hears Noah and stands up with a lovely smile on her face. She steps toward him, and he gives her a big hug.

"Did your doctor's appointment and therapy session go well?"

"Yes, all good. What is going on around here?"

"Well, if you open your email, you will see that we were told that PIF will be working from home for a while as they try to figure out what caused his medical episode. Also, Jesse is in bad shape. He must have had way too much to drink after you left him at the bar. He really seems out of it, but he said that he has started writing his thesis. He won't get much writing done today, judging by his appearance. He looks terrible."

"Maybe I should talk to him. Perhaps I can get him to go home and sleep it off."

"That would be a good idea. We can have lunch after that."

Noah nods and smiles. He then turns around and heads next door to Jesse's office. He finds Jesse sitting in his chair in front of his computer. A new blank text file is open, but nothing has been typed out. Jesse stares motionless at the screen.

"Jesse, hey, how are you doing today?"

Jesse slowly turns to Noah, and he looks like he is in a deep daze. "Hey, Noah. Yeah, I am feeling exhausted right now. I must have really drunk way too much. I sort of recall some really freaky things you told me, or did I imagine it? I don't know."

"Jesse, I told you not to start doing those shots of vodka. Even I know that sort of thing can sneak up on you and mess you up."

"Man, oh man, I don't remember any of that."

"Jesse, you need to go home and sleep this off."

"No, I have to start my thesis. I need to graduate and get out of here. I need to get to work and write it up."

"You are in no shape to do that in your current condition. You can do that tomorrow after you rest. You are just wasting your time right now."

Noah projects a powerful message to Jesse to make him go home and sleep.

"You know, you are right. I am going home now."

With that, Jesse stands up and walks out, leaving his computer running. Noah turns off his computer and walks back to the fishbowl.

Ruth is standing there, "Good, you talked Jesse into going home. Boy, he must have really tied one on last night. Good thing you came home early to me. Are you ready for lunch?"

"Oh, I forgot to pick up lunch from the cafeteria. Let me dash down to the vending machines and pick up something. I'll be back in ten minutes."

This gives Noah a chance to check out the professor's office. He stops in the hallway outside Ms. Bouche's office, which is the outer office leading to the unlocked door of Professor Feingold's office. He projects a craving for a chicken sandwich and waffle fries to her. He hears her shut down her computer and grab her purse. She is soon out the door, on her way to pick up her favorite fast food.

Noah waits until he hears Ms. Bouche get on the elevator, then he walks into Professor Feingold's office. There is no laptop computer, and the desk has only a few scribbles on a notepad, but no hard copy of a presentation or article. The printer has nothing on it as well. The large whiteboard does have several troubling equations. Noah can recognize field equations that are clearly forbidden. If the physics community gets these, it could rapidly become a triggering event. Noah erases the whiteboard and leaves the office to grab a few snacks from the vending machine for lunch with Ruth.

Chapter 47.

Let's rattle the cage

Noah is back in Ruth's bed, wide awake and thinking about the day. He is starting to wonder if doing one's duty should be its own reward. He had lunch with Ruth at the physics building and used the afternoon to discuss tonight's plan with Viera and Aditi. He walked back to the dorm with Ruth for dinner. They managed to have mildly interesting discussions about physics. Almost automatically, they were back in her room having sex as dusk fell. Later, she initiated another round of intimacy. It all feels so clinical now.

His psychic connection with Aditi is much more fulfilling than all the sex he has had with Ruth. He senses a few aberrant feelings in Ruth's mind now that he has time to analyze their situation. He senses she is starting to see him as a fancy accessory, like a designer purse. Their initial burning desire was filled with excitement, and the relationship was sealed with loving phrases and hot-blooded intercourse. He wonders how much of that was instigated by Viera and the Earth Council. After they mutually acknowledged their relationship, thoughts from Ruth's inner psyche started appearing that were loaded with selfish motives. At this point, it has become increasingly apparent that humans are always isolated individuals, no matter how much or how little physical interaction or sweet-sounding dialogue there is; this isolation all too often leads to selfish thoughts and actions. A telepathic society has open connections with individuals, which automatically generates completely honest relationships and civic responsibility with true concern for others. When human selfishness is coupled with the powerful emotional responses that generally dictate human actions, it is amazing that there is any order to their society. This observation must be part of the understanding that Viera and Briel want him to gain from this relationship. Noah craves to see Aditi in person again. He anxiously awaits her arrival tonight.

It is now eleven o'clock, and Noah is getting anxious. He wants to go back to his room and take a shower before Aditi arrives, however Ruth's naked body is halfway wrapped around him. There is no way to escape without waking her. He can wait no longer and starts to slide away from Ruth and out of bed.

Ruth stirs and says in a sleepy voice, "Hey, where are you going?"

Noah says nothing but projects a command, "*Go back to sleep, wake up at six AM.*"

Noah hustles back to his room and gets cleaned up. He wants to put on his space jumpsuit for tonight's mission, but knows that he cannot. He puts on his levitating belt and stuffs his stun cylinder and a couple of flares in his pockets. He sits and anxiously awaits Aditi.

At exactly midnight, Aditi contacts him.

"Noah, I am on the roof of your dorm. I will be down to your room in a sec."

"Do you know my room number?"

"Don't be silly, I know most everything about you. I hope you have some testosterone left for this mission tonight. Just kidding, don't worry."

Noah is once again embarrassed by Aditi, but she does it in such a fun way that he doesn't care. He feels her good intentions and never needs to guess or worry about hidden meanings.

Noah feels Aditi's presence and then hears a faint knock on the door. He rushes over and opens it, letting Aditi inside. Aditi is wearing black yoga pants and a loose-fitting long-sleeved dark gray shirt. Her hair is pulled back into a ponytail. She has a shoulder bag over one shoulder, presumably weighed down with gadgets . Noah does see that she is wearing her levitating belt fanny pack.

"How did you get off the roof? There were at least two locked doors you would need to open. That was part of the orientation for new students to discourage depressed students from jumping off the roof," asks Noah.

"I could have used the levitating belt, but Viera gave me another device. It can open any tumbler-based lock or disable any magnetic locking mechanism. It's pretty cool." She reaches into her shoulder bag and pulls out a small metallic cube.

"That's impressive. I want one. I guess we should go now. We need to walk to my car, then drive to the professor's house. That will take a while."

Aditi grabs his arm. "Wait a minute, you look ridiculous with all that stuffed into your pockets. I expected you would do something nerdy like that. I brought you a small, manly backpack for your gadgets. Sling it over a shoulder like a bad hombre would."

She reaches into her shoulder bag and pulls out a black backpack. Noah takes it and pulls the gadgets from his pockets.

Noah stops his car several blocks from the professor's house. It's nearly 1:00 AM.

"I have to check in with our friendly human agents."

Noah pulls out a small flip phone from this new backpack and makes a call. Curt and T.J. are at the house and tell him that all is quiet. Noah warns him that they are nearby and will be testing Ulak's defenses.

Noah parks the car in front of the house. He concentrates, searching the house for Ulak. Without the line of sight, it will take a little extra effort. Eventually, he finds him in a room asleep.

"I got him. Let's rattle the cage."

Noah sends a stinger into Ulak, who jumps out of bed. Noah then uses his combined force with Aditi to push into Ulak's psyche. He can feel Ulak weakening. He projects a message, "*Give up Ulak. Leave now while you can.*"

Ulak grabs his phone and dials a familiar number and says, "It is Ulak. I am under attack. I need help."

Suddenly, Noah feels Ulak's strength rapidly increase. He is much stronger now and can push back effectively. It seems like a standoff to Noah. Ulak is now matching their combined energy. Noah and Aditi continue to push back, but no advantage can be gained.

Ulak replies, "*Ha, you need to give up. You cannot defeat me. The professor has finished his calculations and written his paper. It will soon be presented, and you will have lost. You should go away and save yourself.*"

Noah continues to push against Ulak until he receives a message from Viera. She has been hovering in Lala above the area.

"*I have the location. I know where the other one is and who they are now. Go back home now. We can talk about it tomorrow. Come to my office tomorrow at 10 AM,*" messages Viera.

Noah breaks contact and speeds away in his car. Aditi directs him to her new apartment complex. It is a nice place, not too far from campus. She has Noah pull into a small circle drive in front of the main entrance to her building.

Aditi turns to Noah and says with a comical tone, "That was fun. Thanks for the lift. We need to do this again sometime. It sounds like we were successful in getting the other hybrid to show themselves."

"Yes, but did you hear him say that the professor has completed his mathematical proofs and is ready to present them. That's a triggering event."

"Don't worry. It just means we need to take them out now. I think we can figure that out tomorrow."

Aditi then grabs Noah and pulls him in for a kiss. It is a long, passionate kiss with a full telepathic connection. He has never felt anything like it; it is truly sublime.

Aditi pulls back and smiles, "We need to talk privately tomorrow. Get some sleep; I have several things to run by you after we are rested and refreshed. Please pick me up at 9:30 tomorrow morning and drive me to the meeting with Viera."

Aditi quickly exits the car and heads into the building.

Noah sits there for a moment to try to figure out what she needs to run by him. He realizes he has no clue and stops wondering about it before driving off. He is only thinking about that kiss now.

Chapter 48.

How do we know what we know?

Noah drives back to his dormitory after dropping off Aditi. He is too tired to speculate about what in the world Aditi is thinking and what she needs to tell him. He can only lament about why females always act so mysteriously, even Homo Galaxus females. That triggers concern about his other female, Ruth. She will be angry again when she wakes up, and he is not there. He hopes to get a few hours of sleep in his own bed before Ruth wakes up. She will wonder what happened to him last night. He feels he has enough energy to implant a false memory for her. She will readily believe that he woke up, felt unwell, and went to his room for his electrolyte supplements. Also, he will implant the memory that he told her to meet him for breakfast at 7 AM. At breakfast, he can tell her that he is going to see the doctor again; that should be a good cover story for the meeting with Viera. He is grateful that Ruth is not telepathic.

Noah manages to get a full four-hour sleep cycle and feels well-rested when he meets Ruth for breakfast. The implanted memories worked perfectly, and she is very sympathetic and concerned when he tells her he is going to the doctor today. So far so good. Ruth heads to the physics building, and Noah goes back to his room, where he can focus on his real problems.

Back in his room, Noah thinks about Ulak's claim that the professor's paper is written and his presentation is ready to go for the national physics conference. The Earth Council and the Galactic Confederation could easily consider it a triggering event. Viera is going to expect good ideas from him to help devise a plan. He needs to think uninterrupted, free from frivolous issues with Ruth and her flaring emotions.

Noah arrives at Aditi's apartment building a little early and parks his car in the circle drive where he dropped her off last night. She senses his arrival and tells him she will be down shortly.

Aditi arrives at the atrium of the apartment with an obvious spring in her step. She rushes out the door and into Noah's car. She puts a hand behind his neck and pulls him into a kiss.

"Good morning, Noah. I hope you are ready to put together a battle plan. I am ready to take that ugly sucker down for good. Viera did find his accomplice, so we should be able to make this happen. I am feeling really good about it now. How are you today?"

"I am doing well. I did get a little sleep, which really helped. However, I am very worried about the idea that the professor has finished his mathematical proofs and is ready to present them to the physics world. That could be game over for the Earth. That really has me on edge."

"Nothing is going to happen until the conference. All we have to do is take out these Dracon attack dogs now, and it's game over for them. I know we can do it."

"I like your confidence. I suppose I am the designated worrier for this team. I also have been thinking about what you were talking about last night. What do we need to discuss?"

"We can have that talk after our planning meeting. Focus on that first, then we can come back here and talk. Is that OK?"

"Certainly. Let's get to Viera's office now."

As they are near Viera's office building, Noah gets a message.

"Drive to the top floor of the parking garage. We need to meet in Lala. Step out of the car, and I will pick you up."

Noah follows orders and drives to the top of the parking garage. He and Aditi step out of the car and look around, finding themselves alone. They are surrounded by a golden glow of light and are quickly transported into Lala. They see Viera sitting in one of the chairs at the center of the control room and join her there.

Viera starts the conversation, "Thank you for getting here on time. I have just directed Lala to start her built-in flare system. She is projecting telepathic interference outside of the vessel. I do not want any Dracon or Dracon hybrid detecting any of our discussion. The downside is that we cannot access anything outside of the vessel. It's a fair trade-off. Last night's operation went well, but we need to act quickly. I heard Noah's concern about the state of Professor Feingold's work. It should be considered vitally important that he and Ulak be stopped. Everything is on the table. Do you understand what that means? If we need to blow up the entire physics building to stop him, we will."

Noah interrupts, "I don't think we need anything drastic like that. Last night, we were about to take down Ulak until he got help. All we need to do is separate him from his ally."

Aditi adds on, "Yes, I was ready to slap a restraining collar on him."

"Our operation did not allow us to snare Ulak, but I did detect where his partner is living, and this morning, I discovered his name. This will surprise you. He is John Carpenter, the assistant Dean of Sciences for the university. He lives in a fancy townhouse in a high-end neighborhood outside campus, between the football field and the cyclotron facility. He has been here at the university for many years. He has been attached to the sciences, directing funding and projects to physics, genetics, and other worrisome areas," says Viera.

Noah interrupts, "We need to take him out also. If we take out one, the other will go down more easily. We just need to isolate them."

"Yes, that is correct. Gilmesh followed our operation last night and then gave me a battle plan. I think it will work. Noah, you will need to use your friendly government agents. They will need to unwittingly help us. You will need to implant false ideas and hypnotize them in case they are detected. You should have them watch videos as extra telepathic camouflage. We will also need all our devices. We must act tonight before any reinforcements arrive. So here is the plan…"

Viera and Lala drop off Aditi and Noah at their car. Aditi is very excited and confident after hearing the plan. Noah feels good about it, but as usual, he is a bit worried and nervous.

Once back in the car, Aditi says, "It's time for us to have a private conversation. Park in my apartment complex's garage. The security code for the gate is 1-3-3-1, and my parking spot is 221, so park there. Let's not talk until we get there."

Noah drives Aditi to her apartment in silence. Noah cannot imagine what she needs to discuss. Another mystery from her seems to draw him closer, like a moth to a flame, perhaps. Maybe that is part of women's power: they keep men curious and interested. Noah gets through the gate and parks his car at her assigned spot. Aditi takes his hand and leads him to her apartment.

Once inside the apartment, Aditi raises her index finger to her lips to signal Noah to stay silent. She goes to a closet just inside the door and retrieves her gadget case. She sets it on the dinette table and opens it, pulling out a telepathic flare. She pushes the button to activate the device. Noah feels an internal screeching in his mind, something like the sound of a buzzer combined with fingernails dragging across an old-fashioned chalkboard. All telepathic abilities are now obscured.

Aditi speaks first, "Now we can talk without being monitored by Viera or the Earth Council. I have been aware of my hybrid status, extraterrestrials, and the galactic secrets much longer than you. This extra time has brought on some nagging questions about it all. Now that I have watched your rapid transformation, I really need to talk about it. Think before you answer; do not reply immediately. Do you think we are puppets that are being directed to do the bidding of the Earth Council, or are we really being trained to take the Earth to the next level of civilization?"

"I think it is obvious that they are training us to help create an acceptable civilization on Earth. I think it is training, not manipulation.

All teachings are essentially manipulation at their core," says Noah confidently.

"Noah, think about the incredible transformation you have made in a very short period of time. You went from a naïve physics boy genius to an alien hybrid who is now about to battle with an opposing alien hybrid. The knowledge of more advanced extraterrestrial existence was dumped on you instantly. Also, they told you that you were not human; well, at least not a Sapiens human. Then you are whisked away and dumped on an alien vessel to get lessons from a variety of extraterrestrials. Nobody could go through such a shock unless they are managing their thoughts and controlling their mind. You should have been driven to insanity or at least suffer from post-traumatic stress syndrome. It is just not possible for it to have happened naturally so easily."

"That makes sense, but mind control could have been necessary due to the fact that there was no time. Viera was quite open and honest about stabilizing my mental state. There is a situation at hand that could be a triggering event; that takes precedent. I was treated that way because it had to be done that way. There was no time to slowly train me. I believe in their sincerity and good intentions. They taught us how to detect lies, and I have never sensed anything but the truth from them."

"Sure, but how do you know that we have the ability to detect their lies. Maybe their lies are not detectable by us lowly hybrids. They are so much more advanced and mentally superior. If we are unable to detect falsehoods from our extraterrestrial sponsors, we exist at their mercy. We would then have no hope of knowing anything about what is real and what is a deception. Humans live in a world of undetectable lying, and it is one reason they are doomed to failure. When human liars tell others that they can be trusted, it never goes well for the naïve trusting people, now does it? We can implant thoughts into humans or wipe out their entire life of memories. These extraterrestrials can certainly do all that to us. How do we know what is real or what is implanted? We could be experiencing a total fantasy. Maybe we are really strapped down to one of those tables on their vessel and are in a simulation right now. We do not know what we do not know. What if the Dracons are the good guys, and we are really working for the bad guys? How do we know?"

Noah pauses, trying to answer. "I suppose we cannot really know for sure. Although they did give us full access to the collective, all their amassed galactic information. I have spent considerable time searching for it and never saw anything that would make me suspicious of them."

"Again, they told us that it was all information and that we had full access. We don't know what we don't know. They could still block certain things from us, or, worse yet, the collective access we're given could be a fake one. We know they can wipe from our memory anything we see that contradicts their narrative. There is no way for us to confirm anything with certainty. We could be merely pawns, directed by our extraterrestrial overlords and used to eradicate their enemies' pawns. They could flush us when we completely eliminate the opposing forces who might be trying to do things that are actually better for us."

"Aditi, let's not get hysterical. Let's think logically. I am sure you had the talk about information, knowledge, and wisdom. It is all about verification. Ulak's attack on me seemed like a frightening verification. Also, why would they go to all this trouble to develop Homo Galaxus and put us through all that training if our only duty was to destroy Dracon hybrids?"

"If this is a proxy war and the enemy is using telepathic troops, our side would need to do the same. There is certainly significant intrigue that prevents them from fighting directly so they create us to keep up with all the Ulaks and the like. Remember, Viera said that the hybrid assistant dean has been here a long time. Our side is simply playing catch-up in the arms race, and we are the new weapons. We could just be disposable soldiers who will be terminated after the war is over. With all the psychic powers flying around, I just wonder what is real and what is implanted." Aditi is now fully flustered and agitated, having overrun her logical self.

"You sound like those humans who have lost their minds because they believe that they are living in a simulation of some kind. It is impossible to disprove such a claim. The story our extraterrestrial sponsors have given us has self-consistent logic. The Dracons are real; we have seen one, and I have felt the pain delivered by one of their hybrids. I know Viera is real, and I am happy to know you are real, too. I think you are worried about the true motivation and intentions of our extraterrestrial sponsors. If for no other reason, my time with Briel gives me great faith in their good intentions. I cannot imagine anything more pure and noble than his psyche. The feeling I have when in his presence is uplifting and wonderful. I will not believe that he would or could be part of any despicable secret plan. You must have had similar feelings around him."

That gets Aditi thinking, "You make a very good point with Briel. I agree that he is a special being, and if you cannot trust him, there is no trust to be had in the galaxy. What could we do anyway? We can't run; we can't hide. They would find us and punish us; there would be nothing we could do to fight them. I suppose I need to focus on Briel when my faith wanes. Your calm logic helps me with these nagging questions. Thank you for that."

Noah turns to Aditi, grabs her by the shoulders, and hugs her gently. He pulls back and says with a very serious look on his face, "I am going to do what I think is the proper thing to do, no matter if I am being influenced, directed, or controlled. I will continue to analyze and verify the situation. That is all any of us can do. I have faith in our trainers and believe they want us to build a better civilization on Earth. Everything we have been through lately seems very logical to me. We had Briel teach us about the true purpose of life and the true nature of our reality. He preaches that our purpose is to seek the objective truth and align ourselves with the frequency of the Universe. Next, Gilmesh showed us that we need to be strong to protect an advanced society. Unless we have the power to protect and defend ourselves, society will eventually be conquered. Then, Uhlt showed us that a society needs connection and agreement to set the standards for right and wrong. Deviant beings cannot be ignored in a proper society because antisocial behavior must be eliminated. You see, they are teaching us what we need to know to build the proper foundations of a new, advanced society. All that information is not necessary for a foot soldier. I am satisfied and truly believe that we are the first wave of a new species of human that needs to step up and civilize the Earth."

Aditi smiles, "I am happy to see that you have not lost your rationality. You do have the steady mind of a deep thinker. I suppose I have driven myself into a Sapien-like hysterical state. I do love the thought of us helping to create a new, better society. We can make this happen in our lifetime. That is a dream worth fighting for and should be real motivation for me when I get apprehensive or paranoid. So, what about you and me? I have strong feelings for you and truly like you. We have been intentionally put together. This could essentially be an arranged marriage based upon implanted feelings. At this moment, I don't care whether they put these thoughts into my head or not. I want to be with you. Are you committed to being my life partner?"

Noah doesn't hesitate. He smiles and says with an unflinching tone, "I am. I want to be with you as a fully committed Homo Galaxus couple. I felt a great attraction to you the moment we met. I do not care if these feelings were enhanced or implanted. My affection is strong and feels as real as anything else. I want to be with you and work with you to create our new world."

Noah and Aditi lock eyes and then embrace.

Noah holds her tightly and asks, "What do we do now?"

"My original plan was to have sex with you while the flare was on. That would explain why it was on and provide cover for our discussion of my skeptical, paranoid ideas. Our handlers will turn away from watching us during private emotional actions like sexual activity. I had no idea our talk would end with vows of commitment exchanged. Right now, I say we turn off the flare and have truly intimate relations, physical and psychic intimacy. I want to have Homo Galaxus sex with you right now."

Noah leans in and kisses her passionately, then says, "I agree wholeheartedly. Let us seal our vows."

Aditi breaks the embrace and turns off the flare. She takes Noah's hand and leads him to her bedroom.

Chapter 49.

Putting the pawns in place

Noah sits in his car in the parking garage of Aditi's apartment complex. He is still feeling the glow from the most amazing experience he just had. Sexual relations with Aditi involved levels of connection that no human could ever provide. Their psyches were coupled in addition to their physical intercourse. Homo Galaxus couples will be strongly motivated to marry within their species and avoid mating with Homo Sapiens females.

He would have stayed with Aditi all day, but he has much to do before tonight's assault on Ulak. Aditi helped remind him of his duties and sent him out with two of her flares. She told him to come back after dark to pick her up; they can celebrate after their victory tonight.

Noah pulls Curt's flip phone and calls him to set up an immediate meeting. Curt suggests a shopping center parking lot that is not too far away.

Noah arrives at the parking lot and finds no trace of Curt nearby. There is no sign of a white panel van either. In a few minutes, the van arrives and parks at the far corner of the lot. Noah knows that both Curt and J.T. are on board and cannot detect any belligerent thoughts from either of them. He drives over and parks next to the van.

The van door slides open, and Noah quickly steps inside and closes it behind him. As before, he sits on a stool next to Curt.

Curt talks first, "What is going on, Noah? Why did we need to leave our surveillance of Ulak?"

"We discovered the other Dracon hybrid. With your help, we want to take out Ulak tonight and maybe this other hybrid."

"Absolutely. We will do whatever you need. Who is this other hybrid?"

"This will freak you out. It is John Carpenter, the assistant dean of sciences at the university. Apparently, he has been here for some time. I can only imagine what he has been promoting while in that position. No matter, tonight we take them out and should get them off the planet. I need you to move your surveillance to his residence. I will call you when I need you to act. In order to avoid detection, you need to constantly watch movie videos or play video games to camouflage your thoughts while staking out John Carpenter. Also, I would like to now hypnotize you for another layer of protection. Is that acceptable?"

"Noah, you do what you need to do. We are on board after watching what you did to Ulak the last time at the university. What do we need to do?"

"Just sit and relax your mind, I will do the rest."

Noah puts them into a sleep state and begins to implant thoughts. He gives them two flares and tells them that they are locator beacons. He will call them and tell them when to press the button, then drop them off at John Carpenter's townhouse. He then orders them to follow John Carpenter if he leaves his house and to activate the second flare while following him. He directs them to stay as close as they can, no matter if he leaves on foot or in a vehicle. Noah reinforces that their job is just to observe, not to take any action at this stakeout. Noah wakes them up and shows them the button on the "locator beacons" that they will need to push to activate them.

Noah leaves the van, and Curt and J.T. head off towards their new surveillance site.

Noah heads back to his dorm room to get any rest he can manage before tonight's action. He makes it back to his room and lies down. He knows he won't sleep, but he can rest his body and get his head together. He is confident, but he knows unexpected events could make it very dangerous very quickly. He can feel fear and anxiety encircling him, and he begins to rationally keep those negative emotions at bay. To act bravely is not about eliminating fear; it is about overcoming fear to be able to do what is necessary. He is gathering all the bravado he can. However, he still has nagging thoughts in the back of his mind, thanks to Aditi. How did I get to this point? I am about to lead an assault on a Dracon hybrid; this action could involve violence, injury, and potentially death. Is this the new me or am I being controlled to act this way? There's no going back either way. He finds that the more he thinks about Aditi, his courage surges.

Noah's phone rings; it's Ruth.

"Noah, are you alright? You never came in to work or called me."

Noah snaps himself out of preparation for tonight and must think quickly, "Ah, yeah. I am resting in my dorm room. The doctor switched me to a different electrolyte supplement and told me to rest tonight. I suppose I dozed off and lost track of time."

"I am glad to hear it. I will stop by, and you can walk me to dinner. I will make sure you eat something healthy."

"OK, see you then," says Noah, making a face. This is the last thing he needs right now. He has already moved past Ruth in his heart and mind. He cannot wait to end it with her. She is nothing compared to Aditi. He needs to just have a quick meal with Ruth, then get rid of her for the rest of the evening.

Within a few short minutes, Ruth and Noah are in line at the cafeteria. Ruth is behind him in line, telling him what he needs to eat. He ends up with a salad with vinaigrette dressing on the side, grilled chicken, mashed potatoes without gravy, and a double batch of broccoli. She vetoed soup, pizza, hamburgers, French fries, and apple cobbler. That did not help Noah's mood.

As they sit down to eat, Ruth starts asking questions, "Noah, what is going on with you? You seem so distracted and uninterested in your work. First, you show up one day all weirded out and depressed, you go out and get drunk with Jesse, and then you pass out at a group meeting. I feel something is wrong with you."

"No, I assure you that I am fine. You should be worried about Professor Feingold. He is the one acting strangely. You know if he goes away, we need to find a new research advisor and maybe a new school. Perhaps that is stressing me out. Doesn't it worry you at all?"

"Well, you have a point there. I have not considered the disarray for us if PIF retires. I have been thinking about you and all your odd behavior. You have been changing a lot. You suddenly seem so strong and mature. Also, I approve of your new hairstyle and clothes, but I wonder what prompted these changes in you. It was a nice surprise, but it has me wondering. Anyway, it seems like you have been avoiding me yesterday and today."

"No, I haven't been avoiding you. I have been a little under the weather and had many things to do, like doctor appointments and pharmacies."

Ruth smiles and puts a hand on Noah's shoulder, "Well, tonight I will pamper you and make sure you get some rest."

Noah panics, "No, I need to just go back to my room and have a quiet night's rest."

"Noah, that's what I mean. Stop being a dick. What are you doing? Are you trying to get rid of me?"

Noah needs to lie again, but decides to act differently. He doesn't have time to fight with Ruth.

Noah freezes Ruth and projects an agreeable response into her, "*Stop. You feel sorry for me. You want me to go straight up to my room and get a full night's sleep. I will see you tomorrow.*"

Ruth's tone and message change at once, "Noah, you are right. You should go straight to your room and get a good night's sleep. I will see you tomorrow for breakfast."

Noah adds another series of commands, "*Stop talking and finish your meal. Kiss me goodnight on the cheek, then go back to your room. Meet me for breakfast at 7 AM tomorrow.*"

Ruth quickly finishes dinner, kisses Noah on the cheek, then excuses herself and heads off to her room. Noah sighs in relief.

Chapter 50.

Conflict reveals one's true self

Noah and Aditi sit in his car, parked near Professor Feingold's house. They are carrying every device Uhlt has given them. They are quietly waiting for 11 PM, the designated start time for the operation. They both sit and concentrate on the house. They see the professor and wife in bed and sleeping. With the greatest of focus, they can detect a hint of the dark fog from Ulak cloaking himself. As expected, he hides rather than show himself telepathically. Viera confirms their observations as she hovers above in Lala who is in high stealth mode.

Aditi looks at her watch, "Noah, it is time. Are you sure you don't want me to do it?"

"No, thank you. I have spent a semester in his group, so I should do this. You do his wife."

Noah directs his telepathic focus toward Professor Feingold; he feels a twinge of guilt and remorse, but he must do what he must do. He reaches past his conscious area to reach deeper. He senses his beating heart and begins to apply gentle pressure on it. He squeezes with light pressure, slowly increasing the force. He only wants to trigger chest pains, not a full heart attack. Then he hits the point where the professor starts squirming and grasping his chest. Aditi then wakes his wife and implants a high level of anxiety and two words, heart attack.

Ms. Feingold wakes up to see that her husband is in severe distress. She turns on the light on her nightstand and looks closer at her husband.

"Isaac, Isaac. Are you having a heart attack?"

The poor professor cannot speak and can only stare at her with a look of pain and desperation.

She grabs her phone from the nightstand and calls 911.

Noah then forces the professor to pass out and stops squeezing his heart.

Soon, Noah and Aditi hear sirens in the distance. It doesn't take long before there are several vehicles with flashing lights in front of the professor's house. There are two police cars, an EMT truck, and a large firetruck.

Noah and Aditi sense that Ulak drops his cloaking for a quick scan. He must have heard the commotion and is checking out what is going on without leaving his room. He quickly goes back into his cloaking mode.

Before long, the professor is wheeled out on a stretcher. The EMTs load him into their ambulance and speed away, siren blaring. The fire truck leaves next, slowly and without its sirens. Ms. Feingold drives off in a rush, with one of the police cars escorting her. The other police officer drives off shortly thereafter, and the street is once again quiet and dark.

Noah waits for a few minutes to make sure all stays quiet, then looks at Aditi and nods. Noah grabs his flip phone and calls Curt and J.T., who are at John Carpenter's townhouse.
"Activate the locater beacon and place it at the front door."
"I will have it at the front door in ten seconds," says Curt before hanging up.
Without saying a word, they exit his car. They both feel the disturbing mixture of anxiety and anticipation shrouded in a thick haze of fear. Noah and Aditi approach the front door and launch their telepathic assault on Ulak. Aditi activates her levitation belt and floats to the back door. They feel Ulak weakening, his ability to push them back fading. Then, a screeching, buzzing psychic blast hit them. Ulak has activated his own flare, ending their telepathic attack.
Before Noah can consider his next move, he hears a crashing sound and a scream from Aditi. Noah's emotions surge with worry and dread. He immediately activates his levitation belt and rapidly floats around the house.
Ulak has crashed through the back door like a linebacker. He is making a run for it and apparently rammed into Aditi to send her flying through the air and crashing into a tree.   Aditi must be dazed or unconscious, because she has dropped to the ground to lie in a motionless heap.
Noah gets to the back yard in time to see that Ulak has stopped running away. He sees Aditi on the ground and is walking toward her. With the flare still active, Aditi cannot protect herself with her telepathy. Ulak can use his immense size and strength to easily kill Aditi with his bare hands. Noah leaps into action upon seeing Aditi in danger.
Noah grabs his stun gun from his pocket and flies straight at Ulak. He starts firing his stun gun. With his and Ulak's movements, he misses with his first two shots. Noah panics as he races toward the still-conscious Ulak, who now sees him. Ulak turns toward Noah with a vicious expression on his face. Noah ignores a wave of fear and continues to accelerate toward Ulak.
The third shot hits Ulak and stops his movement, wiping the menacing glare from his face. The fourth blast drops him to the ground.
Noah rushes over to Aditi. He is relieved to see her eyes open and her breathing heavy.
"Are you hurt?"
"I am bruised and sore, but OK. He ran into me while I was levitating by the door and sent me flying into this stupid tree. I had my breath

knocked out of me. I am fine." She reaches into her shoulder bag and pulls out a restraining collar. "Go put this collar on Ulak before he wakes up. Then find his flare and turn it off."

Noah does as he is told. He feels great relief when he clicks the collar around Ulak's neck, and it activates itself. He finds a flare in one of Ulak's pockets and turns it off.

Immediately, he gets a message from Viera, *"I'm overhead and saw it all. Good job. Now, stand back, and I will take Ulak and lock him down."*

Noah moves back to Aditi, who is now sitting up and looking much better. A cylinder of light appears, and Ulak is then gone. Noah reaches for Aditi and pulls her into a big hug.

"We did it. The big, bad Ulak is gone," says a jubilant Noah.

Aditi kisses Noah, then says, "You also saved me. Ulak would have broken my neck if you had not acted so quickly. Thank you."

Noah looks relieved, yet still deeply disturbed. He pulls her into another hug and whispers in her ear, "When I heard you scream, my heart nearly exploded. I was afraid, thinking the worst, as I came around the house. I saw Ulak moving toward you and felt intense fear. Then something from deep down rose up inside me, and I was no longer afraid of Ulak. I realized in that instant that I cared more about you than myself. I knew then that I loved you with my entire essence. I was prepared to give my life to save you. I think my childhood ended completely at that moment. Until you care about someone more than yourself, you are still a child. Aditi, I love you."

"When I opened my eyes and saw you, I knew I felt the same about you. I feel it in my every thought and feeling. If the roles were reversed, I would have torn Ulak to pieces to save you. I cannot imagine love greater than what I feel for you."

Noah pulls back, sighs deeply, and says, "A brush with death and accepting responsibility for each other ahead of ourselves is quite the bonding moment. What a crazy engagement party."

"Well said. I think this has also prompted your sense of humor also. Hey, we are a team now. No one threatens one of us without the other stepping in."

Aditi kisses him again and replies, "...and it feels so good."

Viera interrupts the moment, *"Go inside and find their computers, storage devices, and any writings. Then, get out of there before anyone shows up. Hurry."*

They ransack the professor's office and Ulak's room. They take everything that could possibly contain any forbidden physics and get back to Noah's car with their arms full. They dump the stuff in the trunk and get in the car and drive off towards Aditi's apartment.

Before they reach Aditi's apartment, the flip phone from Curt rings. Noah fumbles trying to pull the phone from his pocket while driving. Aditi grabs the steering wheel to help.

"Hello Curt, what's up?"

"This guy is making a run for it and seems to be in a hurry. He just sped away in his car, and we are following him right now. We have the second locator beacon with us and turned on. Did you get Ulak yet?"

"Yes, we got him. Your assistance helped us tremendously. Stay with him and keep me posted."

"Rodger that."

Noah hangs up and turns, "Aditi, the other hybrid, John Carpenter, may be trying to escape. Our friendly agents are following him."

"*Viera, did you catch that?*" projects Noah.

"*Yes, I did. Keep me updated. We would like to know what the other hybrid is planning.*"

"*We have more restraining collars. Do you want us to capture him also?*"

"*We do not know what this one is planning, and we have no idea of his resources. Normally, we would have detected a vessel or advanced weapons if they were sitting out in public. Maybe you should join your friendly agents in pursuit, but be careful. Do not engage before checking back. I will check with the Council and get back to you. I will provide cover from the air again as soon as possible.*"

Noah turns to Aditi, "Our evening is not finished yet."

Aditi pats Noah on his thigh, "Good, two for one works for me."

Chapter 51.

Collision at the cyclotron

Noah's flip phone rings again.

"He has been driving like a maniac and went to the university cyclotron collider. We are parked outside the main entrance. He incapacitated the guard at the desk, do not know if it was a termination. We will wait here for you."

"Good idea. We are not very far away," replies Noah as he steps on the accelerator.

Aditi heard Curt's report, "The cyclotron? Why would he flee there? It is just a large circular basement loaded with magnets and electronics. Does he want to collide some protons together or what? This collider is not powerful enough to open a portal."

Curiosity and apprehension begin to build in both of them. The capture of Ulak has given them confidence, but the mysterious nature of this new hybrid enemy also brings new fears.

"Good question, but it seems he has a very important reason to be there. Tell Viera while I focus on driving there as fast as possible."

Noah reaches the cyclotron's main gate and quickly parks behind the van. Curt and J.T. get out of the van when they see Noah. They all gather behind the van to block any potential views from the building. From the van, there is an entranceway to the cyclotron about fifty yards away. The driveway curves up to the front of the cyclotron building with decorative hedges and plants lining it the entire way. The entrance features a long glass wall, with a grand atrium behind it. There is a guard desk on one side. Noah can see the unlucky night watchman slumped over the guard desk.

Noah has visited the cyclotron only once and is familiar with its layout. The above-ground part of the complex is essentially two stories of offices and conference rooms. In the center of the building, a large room has stairways that lead down to the cyclotron collider control room. There are multiple doors that serve as access points to the large circular cyclotron tunnel system.

Curt speaks up first, "There has been no change. We guess there are only a couple of people inside besides the guard, based only upon the number of cars in the lot." He looks at Aditi, then back at Noah.

"This is my partner, Aditi. She is also a hybrid like me and tough as nails. Aditi, this is Curt and J.T.; they planted the flare for us. Ulak has been taken off the planet, so the original mission objective has been achieved. That problem has been resolved, now we need to get this guy."

Curt responds, "This person is in an agitated state and likely desperate. He drove recklessly, and a responsible high-ranking administrator at the university would not take such a risk, fearing an embarrassing accident or arrest. He doesn't seem to care, so that makes him dangerous. We need to proceed with great care."

"Please turn off that beacon we gave you. We might be able to sense where he is and what he is doing."

Curt goes back to the van's front seat and returns with the flare. It is deactivated, yet Noah senses a flare in the distance, deep within the cyclotron.

"Bad news, Mr. Carpenter has set off his own flare. That means he doesn't want us to gang up on him and take him down telepathically. That is just what Ulak did. The good news is that he has no other backup, or he wouldn't need to use the flare. We need to go in and get him without using telepathy. If he has a firearm, it could be very dangerous to get him with just our stun cylinders that have a limited range," says Noah in a somber tone.

Curt steps forward and says, "Let us help, this is our kind of work. You just need to follow us in case the conflict turns back into a psychic battle."

Curt opens the van's back door, revealing a metal lockbox bolted to the floor. He unlocks the box and opens the lid. There are two large assault rifles and a container with grenades and smoke bombs. There are two bulletproof vests also. Curt grabs the vests and hands one to J.T. They put on the vests and fill pockets with ammo magazines, smoke bombs, and grenades.

Curt pulls out his phone and makes a call, "Black wolf, this is Big Dog. We have a hostile trapped in the university cyclotron. Get here and be prepared for a full operation."

Curt hangs up and turns back to Noah, "I just called in our reinforcements, but it will take them a good while to arrive. Here is the plan. J.T. will take the point. I will provide cover. You two need to stay closely behind me. Let's be as stealthy as possible. We will move from cover to cover out here and in the building. Are you with me and ready to go?"

Aditi boldly says, "Let's do this."

Noah nods in agreement.

Curt and J.T. pull in together and whisper back and forth, discussing their plan of action. Curt turns back to Noah and gives him a thumbs-up. Noah nods and returns the gesture. J.T. creeps to the edge of the van and peeks around it. He then dashes to one of the gate supports at the entrance while Curt points his gun toward the building. Then Curt quickly follows with Noah and Aditi right behind him. They use the same tactic to move to the hedge row. Once there, they crouch down and creep all the way to the entrance way.

J.T. runs into the entrance atrium. He checks the area and motions for the others to follow. A large double door beside the guard desk is the only access point into the building. J.T. peeks into the small windows on the door and gives a thumbs-up. He pushes on the door, but it is held shut by a large magnetic locking device. Aditi steps forward with a small metal cube in her hand; she touches it to the door and the door opens. She holds the door open for them to enter with J.T. in the lead. J.T. peaks around the corner.

"We have hallways to the left and straight ahead. Which way?" says J.T.

Noah speaks up, "I have been here before. If you go left, you reach more offices, then a hallway on the other side that parallels the one straight ahead of us. We should take the one straight ahead because it will directly lead to the control room and access to the underground tunnel."

Curt nods, "That sounds like a good plan. Let's go."

J.T. heads down the hallway with his rifle pointed forward. Curt follows about ten yards behind, ready to supply cover. Noah and Aditi stay a few feet behind Curt. Both hold their stun guns. J.T. stops at the point where the hallway reaches the large open room with the stairways down to the control room.

J.T. steps out to dash over to an open stairway that goes up to the second floor of the offices. As soon as he steps out of cover, there is a shrill electronic squeak, then J.T. explodes. What is left of his torso and head flies backwards and bounces off the far wall.

Curt instinctively drops to the ground, and Aditi shrieks.

A voice shouts out, "You should not have followed me. You forced me to retrieve one of my weapons. You are greatly outgunned. You can retreat now, or I can kill you, too. All I want is to get to my vessel that I have stashed in the woods behind this building."

Curt angrily yells back, "You can go to hell. How about that?"

There is an electronic squeak, followed by another loud explosion. An office along the perimeter of the large control room is completely destroyed, a cloud of dust and debris billowing in all directions.

The voice from the control room shouts again, "Are you still there waiting to die, or have you now come to your senses and retreated?"

Noah shouts out, "We know all about you, Carpenter. The Earth Council wants to take you off this planet and interrogate you. You don't have a chance. Turn off that jamming flare, and we will end this now."

"Ah, the new hybrids. It will be a pleasure killing you, too. You are all fools."

Another blast takes out another office.

Curt yells, "Run." He fires several rounds down the hallway toward the control room and sets off a smoke canister before he runs.

The three sprint back down the hallway and head for the door that leads back to the atrium. Curt stops before going through the doors of the atrium and throws a grenade down the hallway into the smoke screen.

As they seek cover in the atrium, the heavy double doors explode.

Curt fires his gun into one of the large panes of glass of the atrium to create a quick escape route. Aditi and Noah run out as fast as they can. They hear Curt firing more shots and look back to see him running towards them now. He dives behind one of the hedge rows halfway up the driveway.

Noah and Aditi reach their car and crouch down behind it. They look through the car windows toward the cyclotron building while trying to catch their breath. They have lost track of Curt but know he is somewhere along the driveway in the bushes. They see John Carpenter peek around the corner of what is left of the doorway at the atrium.

Curt opens fire at him, emptying an entire magazine into the area. As soon as he runs out of bullets in his magazine, a large shiny gun appears around the corner by the guard desk. It begins blasting indiscriminately up and down the driveway. Dirt, bushes, and cement are flying everywhere. Noah sees many craters that have been blasted into existence, with smoke hovering around the whole area.

Noah looks again after the blasting stops. He sees a person step into the open, then jump back behind cover in the atrium. There are no further shots coming from Curt. Noah's heart sinks thinking that Curt has been killed, too. Then the fear hits him like a slap in the face. They are now alone. Noah peeks over his car again and sees a menacing silhouette with a large weapon in front of the wrecked atrium. The figure creeps down the driveway with his large frightening weapon while keeping a careful eye on the hedge row where Curt was last seen. John Carpenter is slowly making his way to the end of the driveway.

A cold chill runs down Noah's spine. Noah turns to Aditi, "Oh shit. He is coming for us now."

As soon as those words leave Noah's mouth, the van explodes into pieces, and the wreckage flips over upside down into the middle of the road.

Noah dives on top of Aditi as the van explodes. "Are you alright?"

"Yes, but what do we do now?" says Aditi, very frightened and flustered.

Noah holds up his stun gun, "You run, and I will try to take him out with this."

"No way, that's suicide. I am staying with you. Let's make a run for it together."

Noah and Aditi stare at one another with fear and desperation in their eyes. Thoughts of death flash through their minds.

Suddenly, there is a flash of light and a third person appears next to them. It's Gilmesh. He wears an impressive silver jumpsuit and a matching helmet. He has a large shiny shield in one hand and a large gun strapped to his other forearm. He makes quite an imposing sight, and they are delighted to see him. He has a look of intense determination about him; they know he is here to save them.

"I will take charge now. He violated several Galactic Codes and triggered my wrath," says Gilmesh with a deep, strong voice.

Gilmesh activates his shield, which crackles with electrical energy. The shield shimmers with light and projects a powerful-looking halo. He jumps up and runs past the car into the open. He holds his shield in front of him as he lopes toward the driveway.

John Carpenter fires a blast at Gilmesh, but either misses or the shot is deflected by his shield. A smoldering crater blasts into existence beside Gilmesh, who quickly points his weapon and fires. John Carpenter is blown into pieces, and his horrible weapon drops to the ground. Noah feels his telepathic powers come back; the flare must have been destroyed with him.

Gilmesh lowers his shield and walks back to Noah and Aditi. A person with his hands up limps from the ditch alongside the driveway. It is Curt. Gilmesh turns abruptly and raises his weapon, but Noah sends him a quick message: he is a friend, helping us.

Everyone regroups next to Noah's car.

"Gilmesh, thank you for saving us. I was out of good ideas," say Noah.

"You are very welcome. When that disgusting hybrid began to use forbidden weaponry on Earth, I had the authority to act. It was clever of him to hide his forbidden weapons here because the radiation from this collider would prevent the detection of his illegal weapons. As you know, I cannot allow such egregious code violations to go unpunished. I was aboard Viera's ship to accept the prisoner you captured earlier, but I was also prepared to deliver swift justice if needed. This is the Arcturian way. That is why we place a great priority on battle fitness and training. I am glad you and Aditi are safe. You did very well tonight. You were never expected to need battle training."

Curt interrupts, "Sir, it is an honor to be in your presence again. You are an amazing warrior. However, it might be wise for you to go back to your ship before any other humans arrive. I have a specialized team on the way. They will be able to cover up all the alien evidence and produce a valid cover story. However, it would be difficult to explain you to normal humans who may be here very soon."

Gilmesh turns to Curt, "Sir, you have a valid point. Thank you for being part of the government that abides by the treaties. You have two talented hybrids here who can skillfully assist you. I will go now. Be well."

Gilmesh walks out to the middle of the road and disappears in a flash of light.

Noah turns to Curt, "Again? You have met Gilmesh before?"

Curt smiles proudly, "Yes, there was messy business in Alaska years ago. Gilmesh took out a renegade ship of ETs who were poaching humans to harvest them for unique biological extracts. He is one hell of a fighter pilot, also. Gilmesh is a true warrior who acts to stop evil and preserve justice. He is the best kind of ally to have."

Aditi takes a close look at Curt and sees that he has a large wound on his leg and several more bloody spots on his body. "Curt, you are wounded."

"Yes, no big deal. This can easily be patched up. I am sorry I could not return fire after one of those explosions threw me for a loop," says Curt in an odd matter-of-fact way.

"So, what happens now? This place is a disaster. There are dead bodies in that building and all that hard-to-explain destruction," asks Aditi.

"I have a clean-up team that should arrive shortly. Could you stay here with me for a while? It would be quite helpful if you put a proper cover story into the minds of the emergency response people who should show up soon. Also, you should retrieve that space gun over there and get it off the planet."

"We would be happy to help you," replies Noah with pride and a sense of relief.

Aditi walks over to Curt, "I am sorry about your partner. It is so sad."

Aditi hugs Curt.

"Thank you for that. I have lost many friends and colleagues in battle. It is never easy. Sometimes I think it is more painful to be the survivor, not the casualty."

Aditi runs to Noah and grabs him tightly as her tears pour out, as the images of J.T. being blown up into pieces linger in her mind. Noah's eyes start welling up with tears, but then a flood of bright, glowing energy strikes them both. He can feel Viera, Briel, Gilmesh, Uhlt, and others he doesn't know. The horror of the incident begins to abate. Noah and Aditi's feelings reverse from negative to positive with full emotional repair.

Briel sends a message to them both, "*You are part of us, and we are part of you. There will always be terrible events, so know that you will always have our support. Never will you be allowed to suffer alone. Our connections are our strengths. You both showed great courage and performed amazingly well. Thank you.*"

Noah and Aditi release their embrace and look at each other. They can tell that each other is re-energized and emotionally uplifted. Noah gives Aditi an "I told you so" look.

Chapter 52.

One battle does not end this conflict

After three hours of helping Curt and his team, Noah drives Aditi back to her apartment. They are in good spirits but thoroughly exhausted mentally and physically. They both feel a profound confidence and a legitimate sense of accomplishment. Success in their first deadly combat has forged an iron will that has changed them.

As they approach Aditi's apartment complex, Noah asks, "Can I take a nap at your place? I am tired as hell. That was quite an evening."

"Hey, wake up. You forgot that you promised Ruth that you would meet her for breakfast, all rested and recovered. Suck it up, buttercup. You need to go back to your dorm and get cleaned up. You'd better start chugging coffee so you can look a little perky at the very least."

Noah shakes his head, "Oh no, I did forget with all this excitement. When can I get away from her? This needs to end."

Aditi puts her hand on his shoulder and says, "You know what you need to do to end that part of your mission. Once you get her impregnated, your mission with Ruth is complete. You just took out two vicious Dracon hybrids; you should be able to put up with Ruth a little longer. I had to do the same thing a year ago. Hang on, partner, you can do it. It won't be much longer, then we can formally pair."

"Yes, Yes. Wish me luck, I am going to need it. It is going to be a long day."

"Well, good luck then. I will check in with you later. I am supposed to start my postdoc today."

Noah pulls into the circle drive of the apartment complex to drop off Aditi. She kisses him, then goes in and heads straight to her apartment. No words are necessary now that their psyches are tightly bonded.

Noah enters the cafeteria promptly at 7 AM. He is wearing a new designer shirt and slim-fitting slacks; his hair is perfect also. He sees Ruth wave to him from a table, so he quickly grabs some food and joins her.

"Good morning, Noah. How do you feel today? You look strong and confident today, and it is a sexy look for sure," says Ruth in her bright and energetic voice.

Noah is happy to hear that she thinks he feels better. He wonders what she is seeing; perhaps last night did fundamentally transform him. He must be doing something different because he feels totally exhausted and sleep-deprived. Noah continues the deception, "Thank you. I do feel much better today."

"Did you hear all those sirens in the middle of the night?"

"Yes, I think I heard something like that," says Noah with a straight face.

"I checked the news this morning, and they said that there was some sort of disaster at the cyclotron."

"Well, let's hurry and eat and get to the physics building. I bet somebody there will have more information about the event. I am curious to hear what happened officially."

Ruth looks at Noah lovingly and puts a hand on his forearm, "OK, we will get there soon enough. But first, I want to talk with you. I did a great deal of thinking last night and want to run something by you. I think after the next semester ends and our dorm contract is up for renewal, we should get an off-campus apartment together, just the two of us. What do you think?"

Noah is shocked and does not know what to say. Finally, he says, "Wow, that is a big step. I had not considered that. What will my mother say?"

"It will be all right. I know this is a shock for you. I get it, it is a big step for me too. You will have the entire next semester to slowly break it to your mother. I should probably meet your mother soon anyway. I am sure she will like me."

Noah panics, then hears Viera contact him.

"Noah, do not worry. I will take care of Ruth for you. You need to get to the physics building and act as if nothing has happened. Agree with her and tell her that you will start working on her plan."

At the physics building, police cars are parked at the front entrance. Noah and Ruth hustle to the elevator, racing to their offices. A police officer with a clipboard stands by the elevator as Ruth and Noah arrive on their floor. He asks to see their identification and records it on his clipboard.

Ruth asks, "What is going on here?"

The officer looks up stoically, "Several events took place last night. I see that you two are in Professor Isaac Feingold's group. His wife wants his group to know that he had a heart attack or stroke last night. The postdoctoral fellow in your group who was staying at his house is suspected of stealing the professor's computer and research documentation. Also, this foreign postdoc is the prime suspect in the terrorist attack that took place at the cyclotron collider last night. Four people were murdered, including an assistant dean. This Ulak person is a fugitive and is considered to be extremely dangerous. There is a detective on this floor who will be interviewing everyone. Please go to your offices and wait for him. There are also grief counselors available if needed. Thank you for your cooperation."

Ruth is shocked, and Noah can sense the fear, shock, and sadness overtaking her. He liked the cover story Curt's team produced. Noah projects comforting feelings to her as they walk down the hallway to the fishbowl.

As they enter the fishbowl, Noah is surprised to see a familiar figure. It is Viera dressed in a stylish, yet somber, dark gray skirt and matching blazer. She stands as they enter.

"Viera, what are you doing here?" asks Noah.

"Good morning, Noah. Good morning Ruth, I am sorry to meet you again under troubling circumstances. I am here because I volunteered to assist the grief counselors."

The two women exchange greetings. Noah can feel that Ruth is a little intimidated by Viera once again.

Viera informs them that Professor Feingold is in the hospital but is doing well. Ulak is a fugitive and suspected of having stolen research documents and participating in a terrorist attack at the cyclotron."

Viera turns to Ruth, "Ruth, you look distressed by these events today. I would like to talk with you in your office. I think I can help you work through everything you are feeling. I just finished a long session with Jesse. He is back working on his thesis and doing much better. Noah, I will stop by and talk with you after Ruth and I have finished."

Ruth and Viera close the door behind them for a private discussion in Ruth's office. Noah goes to his office and turns on his computer. He wants to go online and see what other news is out there concerning the events at the cyclotron.

After about thirty minutes, Viera walks into Noah's office and shuts the door.

"It looks like our government friends created a very plausible cover story for the cyclotron and for Ulak's disappearance. That was quite genius; they certainly know what they need to do to cover up forbidden extraterrestrial events."

Viera nods, "Yes, they are exceptionally good at creating false knowledge for the masses. Their organization has been doing that for a long time. The Earth Council is very pleased that you two captured Ulak. He is being transferred to the Galactic Supreme Council. The Dracons could be in significant trouble."

"That's fine by me. Both Ulak and that John Carpenter guy were vicious characters. Something needs to be done to find all the Dracon hybrids."

"Yes, indeed. You and Aditi will certainly be involved in many more missions. By the way, I have some good news for you. During my meeting with Ruth, I sensed that she was pregnant. I definitely detected another life force in her. She does not know yet. This means you have completed the other part of this mission."

"Oh no. What do I have to do now?"

"Do not worry, Noah. I will take it from here. I have just put a block in place for her; she will never ever know that she is pregnant. She will start therapy with me next week, and I will begin to restore her mental state to what it was before you and she met. I will slowly guide her into losing interest in you. It may be a painful experience for you for a while because she has a great deal of anger towards men that I blocked before she ever saw you. At the proper time, we will abduct her and take the fetus. Your job is over; just let the situation play out. I will be available to help you if things get too confusing or complicated."

"When do I get to be with Aditi?"

"Very soon. Be patient for a little while. You may start secretly meeting up with her now if you do not let Ruth or anyone else know."

"Thanks, I can live with that."

Viera picks up her briefcase, sets it on her lap, opens it, and hands Noah a hard drive and a stack of papers in a manila folder. "Noah, these are research documents that have been created for you. It opens a new area in String Theory that will create another diversion for the humans, keeping them away from any forbidden physics. This is essentially your thesis material. We will ensure you earn your doctorate within two years. That is, unless another critical mission pops up and we need you elsewhere. It is quite possible, because the Dracons never surrender."

Noah squints his eyes to produce a profoundly serious expression on his face. "The Dracons better plan to leave the Earth. Homo Sapiens are a stubborn breed, and even though I am only half, I carry their blood too. If the other Homo Galaxus are anything like Aditi and me, we bring our advanced abilities backed up by the resilience of our ancestors. I know the combination is quite formidable. We will defeat the Dracons one way or another. The Earth will be a Homo Galaxus planet. We will have victory, no matter the cost, the challenge, or the risk. After last night, a burning fire has flared up inside me. I feel it. I am now a warrior with a planet to win."

THE END

About the Author

Joe Pelati is a retired research chemist with many patents and novel technical implementations. He has hiked nearly every trail in the Grand Canyon, studied traditional kung fu/tai chi, and played high-level soccer. He has a Ph.D. in chemistry from Indiana University and currently resides in Texas. For more information, visit joepelatimedia.com

www.ingramcontent.com/pod-product-compliance
Lightning Source LLC
Chambersburg PA
CBHW070459260626
47161CB00004B/1369